Dance the River Whale

In fond memory
of my grandmothers,
Nellie Young Parent
Alida Braconnier LeBlanc

Dance the River Whale

A NOVEL BY RON MERCIER

DEERBRIDGE
·BOOKS·

Excerpt on pages 5, 6 from *Grandmothers of the Light*
by Paula Gunn Allen. © 1991 by Paula Gunn Allen.
Reprinted by permission of Beacon Press, Boston.
Poem on page 253 from *Earth Medicine: Ancestors'
Ways of Harmony for Many Moons* by Jamie Sams.
© 1994 by Jamie Sams. Reprinted by permission
of Harper Collins Publishers, New York.

Designed/produced by Margaret Dodd,
Studio K Communication Arts
Title page illustration by Nyease Somersett
Printed by Gilliland Printing

Published by Deerbridge Books
PO Box 2266
Pittsfield, Massachusetts 01202

Library of Congress Catalog Card Number 98-94935

ISBN 0-9668527-0-2

In medicine stories as in medicine life, it is always difficult to discern where the mundane merges with the arcane. Their boundaries are not sharp and distinct but barely discernible and, for long stretches, invisible, like faint trails in the grass and forests left by small creatures. So in all stories from the oral tradition, some of the details are from the world we know while other details refer to the supernatural or nonphysical universe. Many times the stories weave back and forth between the everyday and the supernatural without explanation, confusing the logical mind and compelling linear thought processes to chase their own tails, which of course is a major spiritual purpose behind the tradition's narrative form.

For those raised in the rationalist world where the linear mind reigns supreme, distinctions are mighty. In it there is no possibility—other than the imaginary or "psychological"—of being seated amidst the rainbow. To rationalists, giants, like the "little people" (and like their contemporary counterparts, the extraterrestrials), are clearly figments of overactive imaginations and "mass hysteria." Yet traditional people insist that conversations with animals and supernaturals—little people, giants, immortals or holy people—are actual. They tell many stories about women or men being changed into bears, about Antelope Spirit girls playing with a human girl, about Ogre Women—huge and terrifying—abducting children, about meetings with Thunderbirds, Dlanua, katsinas, goddesses, and gods....

Are those who make such assertions pulling our collective leg? Are they caught in the sort of projective neurosis that some psychologists claim for writers and investigators of contemporary paranormal experiences with strange beings who do not obey this reality's physical laws? If so, there still remains the peculiar fact that their accounts often predate those of modern white Americans and are to be found in oral accounts deeply embedded in the community's ritual tradition.

Presumably, shamans are describing what they have seen, what they have experienced, or what they know to be the case even if they themselves have not experienced it, much as a San Franciscan who has never been to London speaks of it as though it really exists. True shamans live in a world that is alive with what is to rationalist sight unseen, a world pulsing with intelligence. To them...[this] is the ordinary, the real world.

Interchanges with the supernaturals are the bedrock of native spirituality. What are called "myths" in the white world, and thought of as primitive spiritual stories that articulate psychological realities, are in the native world the accounts of actual interchanges.

from *Grandmothers of the Light:*
A Medicine Woman's Sourcebook
by Paula Gunn Allen

Contents

1

Sign of the Whale

That Wednesday, I walked the railroad tracks to Cannery Bridge, drunk again. It was familiar, a ritual begun two years before when the drinking took a turn for the worse. My feet fell easily into the rut I'd made along the track and down the grassy incline to the underpass. In the early days I'd sleep it off on the embankment, but these last weeks I woke mornings with my face stuck in gravel or pressed against pavement. I prayed for the banality to end, but when the damp coolness of stone under the bridge revived me, I got up to face yet another day.

Taxi driver Lenny had long been picking me up and driving me home. At Ingram High, he'd been a friend, the closest I came to having one until I met Anna Ruggieri. I felt closer to her than anyone, even my grandmother Têtreault who'd raised me since I was a month old. Anna was the one I told about my drinking.

Each step I took that afternoon was a premeditated step down the ladder to hell, consumed by hatred for my grandfather and the despair of never seeing Anna again. Every step was filled with the memory of her love for me, my grandfather's spite, and the struggle of those emotions for my soul. Anna and my grandfather intertwined in my last thoughts in a way I could never have predicted.

She knew about the strife with my Pépère Têtreault. Anna knew I stayed away from home, spending more and more time on the banks of Stocking River, siphoning my grandfather's liquor supply into the emptiness I felt as my grandfather's anger seethed. When I didn't show up for dates, she looked for me at my favorite haunts on the river, shared only with her. Not even my grandfather, who'd taught me to fish the river, knew these places. She'd look for me in one after another of them until she found me slumped against a tree or draped across a rock, always drunk.

Long after Anna graduated, I obsessed about her. While she was away studying to be a nurse, she wrote letters that I never answered, but every time I heard from her, I set off on another binge. My grandfather and I were not fighting anymore, not because we'd made up, but only because we rarely saw each other and I'd made his habit of angry silences my own. I stopped confiding in Mémère altogether. I didn't like myself much when I graduated. I found work at Tilson's Cannery, hosing and scrubbing down the troughs the lobsters were funneled into from trucks. Not only had I become a loner, I'd made no attempt to reconcile with my grandfather. The more my grandmother pleaded with me to do so, the more I withdrew until finally I didn't visit either of them anymore.

When I learned that Anna had returned from out of state to work at St. Philomena's Hospital, I went out of my way to avoid her and drank more heavily. As before, I ignored her phone calls and she stopped calling. Toward the end of April Lenny, fearful for my life, contacted Anna in the hope that she could convince me to get help. Without success, they spent numerous night hours searching those old haunts Anna thought I might be in along the river or on the beach at Horseshoe Bay. I'd been able to keep the ritual at Cannery Bridge secret.

Today the too-blue sky seared my eyes. So I concentrated on the monotony of the grooves of the path until urged by a sudden premonition to look again at the sky, where the burning of blue had been replaced by a sea of iron gray. My entire body was drawn by my gaze into the sea, which revealed itself a liquid tapestry of finely woven hills, valleys, woodlands and fields, the Ingram of my childhood that wrought in me a strange tenderness. The scene unfolded gently, bearing my childhood up to interrupt the ritual that could only end in death.

Even when my attention returned to my steps along the track, I observed the tapestry flowing toward me and beginning to unravel so that its strands of iron gray disappeared, leaving in their wake only the luminous threads of whitest cloud. The radiance became a vast funnel, narrow at its source and expanding northward. I stood in awe of a drama I vaguely recognized as my own, which stirred in me the ancient longing of childhood. Like a great eel, the funnel moved noiselessly and sinuously through the grayness above the hills, valleys, and woodlands of present-day Ingram on a course parallel to the seacoast and in the direction of Riverton.

My feet were lifted and catapulted forward by the rhythm of that large organic motion in the sky. My body flew over swells of hill and into soundings of valley toward Lindsey, a smaller fishing community south of Ingram. I was riding the sea again, a sensation I knew well as a boy for having fished with my grandfather on the river and in the bay. It occurred to me that the luminous organism in the sky, reviewing the life I'd decided to end, was none other than the whale. My grandfather and I had met him once before when our boat drifted across that invisible line that divides a bay from the main. Then, I'd been so preoccupied with hanging onto a cod my grandfather had hooked and keeping my balance in the boat that I didn't notice our disappearance into one of those deeper valleys of the sea.

Having re-emerged from the valley not only with our lives but with our catch secured to the gunwale, I was amazed by the stillness that followed swiftly after the turbulence. The sea was glass. But only when the stillness had converted my heartbeat to its slow sturdy rhythm did the whale surface a hundred yards away. His appearance, swift and noiseless, left me wondering if I'd seen him at all. Today, by the track, the same stillness returned, omen, I thought by strange reasoning, of the whale's reappearance.

No sooner had I named the creature than it revealed itself. I saw its light filter through the grayness of the sea till it displayed the source of its power in the symmetry of its skeletal structure. The celluloid of an enormous X-ray etched on my eyeballs with the articulation of each part of the skeleton so clear that I could never doubt the presence of the whale in the sky that evening. I scanned its length from the smallest of its caudal vertebrae to its massive jawbones. The light emanating from the bones blinded me momentarily, forcing me to lower my gaze to the ground, where cornflowers blossomed from crusts of soot. I could not remember the last time I'd looked at flowers. It felt more as though they were looking at me, the brilliance of their blueness piercing my darkness by the impress of whalebone light.

When I looked again at the skeleton, its light, no less intense than before, seemed gentler. I noticed disturbances in the vicinity of the great mammal's tail. Gradually shapes emerged, indefinite at first, but becoming more distinct as they moved along the shining arc of the backbone. A procession was in the making as cowled wraiths floated one after the other on either side of the skeleton. Each detached a knobby vertebra from the backbone and reverentially held its radiance up to the surrounding darkness.

I knew the whale to be alive and whole, though it offered me only its skeleton as proof of its existence. I knew too that the monks, who accompanied it on what I sensed would be a long pilgrimage, had been conjured up from the dark nave of my childhood. As an altar boy, I'd been taught by Father Etienne of St. Anne's to walk slowly and respectfully toward the altar bearing the candlelight symbolic of the mystery of Christ's death and resurrection. The monks, too many to number, carried the light of each vertebra with a respect engendered not only by years of prayer and service, but by an untold suffering. It was impressed on me by an unseen power that their suffering was as intrinsic to the light they held in their hands as was Christ's to holy Mass. They bore the light of the whale as I'd carried that of the altar, without the least diminishment of its source. While the monks plucked every vertebra from the whale's back, the animal lost none of its radiance, propelling itself forward to set the sanctuary of the southern sky aglow.

With a last slap of its great flukes, it disappeared amid a turbulent spume of cloud. With that, my feet moved freely again through the long grasses and cornflowers to my planned death. But just as I welcomed the freedom to execute my plan, I was stayed by the singular determination of the unseen power to teach me the identity of each of the light-bearing monks. As soon as the whale sounded the southern sky beyond my ordinary sight, the cowls of the monks were pulled back one by one to reveal a single identity. Beneath each robe strode the hulk of the same body; seared into each thick neck, the singular rope burn. I was appalled to learn that each of the acolyte monks was a replica of the man who had not only failed at life but failed even his attempt at death—my Grandfather Tétreault. I was appalled that his cowardly form should accompany the noble creature on its pilgrimage of light.

Forced by the unseen power to replay my grandfather's attempted suicide, I saw myself returning home from Stocking River. As I neared the crest of the wooded embankment that dropped precipitously from our backyard down to the river, I caught sight of my grandfather perched on a ladder he'd propped against the giant oak tree I used to swing from as a boy.

"Pépère," I screamed. Instead of answering me, he cocked his arm and hurled a writhing snake into the last light of day. I charged from the woods, my eyes burrowing twilight for the quickness that twirled itself around the largest bough of the tree. Lunging at the ladder as it began to sway, I rammed my chest into it, trying to pin it against the bough. With a thud, the ladder dropped into the crotch between bough and trunk—my grandfather was saved.

"Don't move, Pépère!" I shouted as I climbed up the ladder and thrust my knees into his legs to immobilize him. The tension of his body pushed hard against mine in a last effort to execute the deed.

"Pépère!" At my command, his body relented and his resolve left him as soon as the last glimmer of day slid behind hills the other side of the river. He let me lean across his back to loosen the rope and pull it free. I never forgot the sound it made when it gave way and retreated, hissing, into the high grass.

I didn't realize until this moment, as I surveyed the approach to Cannery Bridge and gauged the distance between myself and the underpass below, how shamed my grandfather must have been that day. He was seventy then; I, sixteen. I, "le petit morveux," the "little snotnose," in the habit of either ignoring or defying him, had witnessed his failure to kill himself. I felt no compassion for him now as I resolved to succeed where he had failed. I was determined not to go on living a life as futile as mine had become. As I stumbled down the embankment, my eyes filled with the sparkle of cornflowers, I fell by the side of the road in a swath of burnt grass to wait for dark. Then, I'd show him how it was done.

While I lay in the stubble, yearning for the peace that surrender to one's destiny ought to bring, I found not peace but only the hot dither of a brain that confused past with present, and muddled dreams.

"Lenny, why did you have to let Anna see what I've become? Remember the day at Trovert Lake? After you and Gin went home, I sat with Anna on the beach and we watched the sun turn red, slip into the water and shimmer slowly toward us. She shed her clothes and swam to meet the sun halfway, caught it between her outstretched hands and, diving, dragged it down with her. As she walked back naked toward me, she held me fast to her beauty while she whispered how much she loved me. Lenny, why?"

My brain manufactured a rapid succession of images fraught with a tenderness that would not relent but sharpened into persistent heartache: Mémère pouring me the hottest coffee I could stand against the shiver of shoveling snow; the diamond edge of a boat cutting into the glass of a calm sea; the press of Anna's skin against mine long after we'd kissed goodnight.

I had sense enough to hide from passersby. There was reasoning enough left to position myself under the bridge to escape the probe of headlights. I knew enough to wait until after the workers drove to Tilson's before the late night shift. Meanwhile, I lay out of sight, listening to my inaudible moans and whines, to different parts of my consciousness engaging in spurious dialogue about what I could have done to avoid this end, and to an unfamiliar part of my brain trying to break through the confusion. Finally, it wasn't the desperation of words that moved me grudgingly to tears but the light from Anna's eyes, distillation of the summer's blue cornflowers, piercing my heart with the same urgency I felt the day we met in the cafeteria.

"Anna," I cried out as the sun gleamed fiercely before its fall.

What makes you think she is looking for you? asked a voice unlike any I'd heard from the conjurings of delirium.

"She came with Lenny the last time," I answered meekly.

Did you not make it painfully clear that she was not to come again, that she was, in your own words, to 'leave you alone'?

"Yes."

Then, why do you pursue her with whimperings of a false hope? The voice was a woman's; it cut through my self-pity with imperial directness.

"I don't know."

You must know. She spoke with the authority of the unseen power that had insinuated itself into the earlier events of the day.

When night came, I raised my head to search the embankment for the light of Anna's eyes. *In vain*, the woman's voice insisted. Seeing nothing but the random illuminations of a single firefly, I laid my head down and fell asleep.

When I awoke, I spied a distant needle of light, brighter than any images of day, spear the darkness. Despite efforts to shield my eyes from its brilliance, it struck through my forehead to a view of the river of my earlier childhood where my grandfather cast his line like a liquid needle to the mystery of fish rising ever gladly to his mortal stabs.

"I loved him for teaching me to cast the way he could," I said aloud.

I know, the woman affirmed.

"My Mémère called me his 'little shadow' because I followed him everywhere."

I know, she acquiesced.

"I'd walk with him to the bus stop on his way to work."

You would wait for him at the bus stop when he came home.

"He never minded me pestering him."

He let you work side by side with him in his beloved garden.

"That's right. Even though he'd have to straighten out my messes."

Do you remember him asking, always with a pat on the shoulder, how you managed to get so dirty?

"Every time he asked me that, I'd shrug my shoulders and he'd laugh."

Then, the two of you would laugh together.

"What happened to us that it got so bad we couldn't talk to each other anymore? That he got so dark and quiet I wanted to cry? I loved him."

You loved him.

In the time it took the needle to splinter into blinding shards of light, I struggled to my feet, staggered to the bridge and crouched in shadow for the opportune moment.

"Anna, he loved me."

It was impossible to determine how long it took for my first awareness of the cold hard dampness under my head. Shortly after, light raged in my eyes. The wrenching of a voice came last.

"Tom, it's Anna. Can you hear me?"

"Yes."

"Can you sit up?"

"I don't know."

"Try to sit up." When I tried to raise my head, I felt a pair of strong hands secure me under the arms and hoist me to a sitting position against a clammy wall. Lenny, I thought. To my rescue again.

"Please get that light out of my eyes," I pleaded, trying to turn my head away. Lenny extinguished the headlights of his car, keeping the parking lights on to warn approaching traffic.

"What time is it?" I asked irritably.

"Almost eleven," Anna answered. "We've got to get you out of here before the three-to-eleven starts coming out."

"Am I bleeding?"

"I don't see any blood." Anna leaned over me, checking my body from head to toe. "No, no blood," she repeated. "Did you fall, Tom?"

"But the impact? What about the car that hit me?"

"You didn't get hit by a car," Lenny assured me. "You probably passed out, but you're lucky you didn't get hit. Damned lucky. Can you stand up?"

"But I did get hit," I insisted. "I went flying."

Convinced I was hallucinating, Lenny shrugged and glanced at Anna.

You were hit all right, but not by a car, the woman interjected.

"What hit me?"

"Rotgut," Lenny gibed. "You reek." Keenly aware that the others couldn't hear the woman speak, I listened intently to her version.

In the instant it took you to realize that you love your grandfather as much as he has always loved you, the Whale of your vision circled back the length of an ocean from his luminous sounding in the southern sky to slap you with his tail out of harm's way. Simple as that. When Anna took hold of my hands to pull me up, we were both surprised by the strength and push of my legs.

The next morning, I couldn't lift my head from the pillow, no matter how hard I tried. I fancied my head one of the large stones at Cannery Bridge. With time I was even able to discern the features of my new head of stone, which bore an uncanny resemblance to my grandfather when he was my companion and best friend.

You are very much like him, the woman said. I watched my detached head float high over what seemed to me the grandest river in the world.

"The Stocking?" I asked.

No, she denied, with a tone that implied I should've known better. *That is the River of the Fourth. Watch.* I watched in disbelief as my head, the stone, floated high above the river and grew in density and weight as it ascended. I was further amazed that, at the apex of its climb, the head transformed from reluctant shadow beneath the cowl to forthright brilliance of Whale's bone.

You are very much like him, she said. *In his strengths and his weaknesses. You must come down, my godson, before it is too late. You must come down to the reality of the bond that exists between you and your grandfather.*

"How?"

Simply give him your hand. Come walk with him on the river. As soon as I willed my hand into my grandfather's, my head of stone eased itself in lightness and light toward the river; and without losing any of my grandfather's lineaments, including the thick ropeburned neck, the more my own it seemed. *Have no fear of the River of the Fourth,* she reassured, *for its waters will transform your being into a living bridge.*

"What do I do?"

Take your grandfather's hand as soon as it emerges from the river and dare become more bridge than blockhead. She laughed. *But mind you, godson, blockheads often do make wonderful bridges. Capable of sustaining not only the full weight of Whale, but the brunt of a pilgrim's journey.*

2

Whale Words

W hen Lenny and Anna urged me to go to the hospital, I insisted I detoxify back at my apartment. For three days Anna hardly left my side, managing me without Lenny's help except for the second night with the DT's at their worst, when his pressure to subdue my flailing felt like the weight of Whale. Saturday I lay in bed, weary with fighting, trying to reorient myself to time, and desperately to remember last night's dreaming. Through the cacophony of my waking hours came the single refrain the woman hooted at me in every dream since that fateful night at the bridge.

"My blockhead, my blockhead, prepare for Whale to knock some sense into that block of a head. Tête de pioche. Tête de pioche. My blockhead, my blockhead…" Over and over again she scolded in a maddening singsong. Aching ribs suggested I'd been tossed about in a darkness larger and a time longer than any I could imagine. My mouth was as dry from thirst as my body was wet with fever. Earlier desperate efforts at rolling out of bed in pursuit of alcohol had been thwarted by the inertia of my own "blockhead." I thought I heard the woman laugh through her rantings, and the splashings of the whale.

When Anna turned the key in the door, I looked away, regretting promises I might have made and wasn't ready to keep. But as she pushed the door open, I was turned around by an inevitability moving me toward the woman who kept opening doors I thought I'd forever shut.

"Hi," Anna whispered as she caught me looking at her. "I thought you'd be sleeping."

"Oh, I just woke up," I lied, not wanting her to know how long I'd been trying to get up for just that one drink.

"How are you doing?" she asked. I tried to raise my head.

"Hey, hey," she cautioned. "Not so fast. Let me help you." Placing one hand under my head and the other behind my back, she eased me into a sitting position. As soon as my head left the pillow, it began to throb with pain.

"Now I know why my head didn't want to move," I whined.

"What?"

"Nothing, Anna." How could I begin to explain the strange imaginings of my fevered brain?

"The fever's gone," she declared after a casual check of my forehead. "Marvelous recuperative powers, I'd say," she added while she took my pulse. "You're going to have to eat more solids now and get your weight up. You're just bones."

Though she hadn't made much of the malnourishment and dehydration she'd been treating with a punishing diet of liquids and supplements, I knew she'd been concerned about the depletion of my body's scant reserve. "The DT's are one thing, Tom," she lashed out, "but pneumonia, that's another. I don't know if your body could handle that." Despite the cautioning, her voice betrayed its natural buoyancy now that I was out of danger.

"Now sit there. Don't try to move till I get over the other side. It won't take a second," she said calmly, letting go my hand. Daylight slipped through tears in the shade of the room's only window. "There, that's better. Now I can see what I'm doing. Let's try standing you up. Come on now. Up. Up. Ready?"

"Sure." I struggled to straighten up.

"You don't sound sure to me, but let's give it a try anyway," she groaned as she swung my legs around. Steadying me, she watched me bring my feet to the floor.

"I can't believe this, Anna," I panted, stopping to catch my breath.

"You'd better get used to it, my dear. You've been in bed almost a week, you know. The only thing that surprises me is how much, not how little, you're doing. Just take it slow." As I tried to find her face behind the laserlike flashes emanating from the torn shade, I yearned for the woman I'd nearly lost. "Come on, Tom," she encouraged. "Hold my hands and let me feel that amazing push your legs gave the other night. I know you can do it again." While she tugged, I tried to push. "A little wobbly but not bad," Anna joked approvingly as I got to my feet. "You want to walk a little?"

"Yeah."

"The quicker the better…as long as you don't try to do too much too soon." Turning sideways by the bed, I put my arm around Anna's waist. "Remember the last time you did that?" she asked, smiling.

"No," I answered, disappointed in myself.

"At my senior prom…the first time you'd ever danced. I was amazed at how quickly you learned. Remember?"

"Yeah," I answered, recalling for the first time how beautifully dark she'd looked in her white gown and how her blue sapphire eyes discovered in me the longing that I could not bear her to see. Soon after the prom, I fled, avoiding her at every turn and drinking more heavily. "But drunks don't dance." I didn't dare look at her, certain that my eyes would meet with a calm but stern rebuke.

"Don't you think it might be different this time, Tom? I heard a difference in your voice the other night. Didn't you?" Her arm tightened about my waist.

"Yeah," I hesitated, spying from the dark of my uncertainty the monk with the deep rope burn in his neck attempt an awkward waltz across the sheen of a vast ballroom floor. He failed like the one-year-old who leaps into the daunting space of life's first dance and finds no one there to catch his dreams. "I can't make it, Anna."

"Only one time up and back," she encouraged. "Just once."

"I can't dance," I answered in a voice full of the longing of my own first dream. I craved a drink.

"Come on, Tom. Up once and back." After Anna helped me walk up and back the length of the cramped gloomy room, I plummeted to my bed, exhausted. One thought tormented my inertia until I fell asleep: get to that rubbing alcohol staring at me from the night stand before she remembers to take it away.

I awoke to the percolation of coffee like the stammering of a jackhammer in my ears, with the sting of a blinding sun in my eyes. Anna saw me turn from the light.

"Sorry, but I had to raise the shade to get some air in here."

"That's okay."

"I forgot the fan again."

"You really don't need to bring it. I'm used to the heat up here." Though Anna had lifted the shade more than halfway, there was little air sifting through the window screen because the squat apartment building across the alley blocked most breezes from the harbor. For the first time I cringed to think that I'd never bought a fan because I spent most of the money I made at Tilson's on liquor. The realization that I'd been a charity case at the Cannery irked me. I sickened at the thought that my boss suffered my absenteeism because his son and I played baseball together in high school. While I kept my eyes closed against these intolerable reminders, I was aware that everything in the room had its proper place. The path by the bed that Anna had cleared of months of clutter and dust made everything in the room seem ordered and ordained. By what power, I wondered.

It is the Whale Way, the unmistakable voice of the woman proclaimed. *The Pilgrim's Corridor. The first step of a belated first dance.* She laughed uproariously.

"Ordained," I declared, unable to explain the word.

A Whale word, the woman said. *Who can explain?*

"What did you say?" Anna asked.

"Nothing," I muttered. "Just thinking out loud."

"Coffee's almost ready," she said as she washed down the oilcloth on the table.

"When are you going to get some sleep?"

"I got a little while you were sleeping."

"In the chair?"

"Of course. I'm used to that." She moved swiftly back to the set tub where the percolating coffee continued to stammer its thunder. Though the smell of coffee nauseated me, I welcomed it as an essential part of the ritual that was to have climaxed in my death under Cannery Bridge. I welcomed it by force of habit as the prelude to another mindless unfeeling day of drinking. I welcomed its short-lived settling of stomach and nerves in the service of ritual.

Ordained, the woman said.

"Coffee's ready," Anna announced as soon as the thunderous staccato stopped. I winced, knowing that, as an element of ritual, it held a far different meaning for me. For Anna, I thought it could only mean the healing inherent in its aroma and the pleasurable bite of its deepest darkness; she had an uncanny way of finding the hidden good and joy in things. While Anna poured the coffee, I managed for the first time in my recuperation to sit up in bed by myself.

Ordained, the woman said. *To enter the Way of the Whale, your Pilgrim's Corridor.* I leaned against the headboard to where I'd watched the stars each night before the poison got the better of me. It was the only place in the room where a tiny corner of the sky was visible. When I first moved into the room, a time of heavy drinking, I used to look for the few stars in that dark corner to show me the way back to my first dream. When they appeared, the gleam was magic enough to grant me sleep.

"Well done," Anna shouted when she spotted me sitting up. "I told you you were a quick learner," she added as she placed two steaming mugs of coffee on the table. "Do you think you can make it over here? Maybe we can scare up a breeze by the window."

"Sure. Why not?" I waited for Anna to slide the two chairs out from under the table before I began moving toward her.

"Here, let me help..."

"No, I'm all right. Let me try. I think I can make it alone." But as soon as I stood up, my knees gave way and my body shook uncontrollably. Without a word, Anna reached out and helped me into the chair by the window. When she was satisfied that I was safely settled, she sat across from me. "I thought I could do it alone," I said meekly. "I thought..."

You have never been hit by a whale before.

"What? What did you say, Anna?"

"Nothing, Tom." The inimitable laughter rode through the window on an inaugural breeze. I studied Anna's face to see whether or not she'd heard the woman. I saw nothing in Anna's expression to indicate she had. Nothing. Her unresponsiveness was troubling; it confirmed my suspicion that there was as much wrong with my brain as with the rest of my body.

"Feel that breeze, Anna?" I asked, trying not too cleverly to hide my distress.

"No, not yet." I heard the laughter again and felt the sea breeze wrap itself around my neck. "Felt it that time," Anna cried jubilantly. "Just what the doctor ordered. I almost forgot; I brought a couple of ham-and-egg sandwiches from the hospital. Let me get them," she said, jumping from her chair. "Hungry?"

"A little."

"Good. You really have to start eating more." She slid a sandwich across the table to me. As the breezes multiplied, bringing a tincture of the sea into the room, I asked myself how I could have suffered to be apart from this beautiful woman who'd told me so many times that she loved me. How could I have been stupid enough to prefer loneliness and boredom to her? The woman's laughter clanged in my head like a bell on a storm-driven buoy.

"Tom, I meant to ask you something," Anna said, leaning across the table, her slender fingers cupping her chin, her face almost touching mine. I drew back because her natural warmth, which I both passionately feared and yearned for, terrified me. When I pulled back, Anna did not. Her blue sapphire eyes sought mine. "Do you remember the first thing you said to us when we found you under the bridge?" I tried hard to remember.

"No."

"I remember it clearly because it seemed so strange at the time." My curiosity was piqued.

"What?"

"The flowers. Remember?"

"No."

"'But it's not time for them to bloom,'" you said. "'The cornflowers, what are they doing here? They're not supposed to come till late July. It's only June. What are they doing here?' You were frantic. I told you I didn't know why, and that made you more frantic. You swung your arms around, repeating, 'What are those flowers doing here? They're not supposed to be here.' Then you passed out."

"I don't remember that," I admitted somewhat peevishly, trying in vain to recall the moment.

"You're sure?"

"Yes."

"You said it so clearly." As Anna spoke, a faint glimmer of feeling but not of words surfaced. It was as though I'd been transported into the presence of a beauty too exquisite for my senses to contain or my mind to comprehend.

"I'm not so sure now, Anna. I seem to remember something but...no cornflowers."

"Thought it might be important, Tom." I swilled the coffee, wolfed down half the sandwich, and felt like puking but didn't.

"You okay? I didn't mean to upset you, Tom." Anna was prepared to abandon the topic, but I felt compelled to hang onto it.

"I wish I could tell you more, Anna." From then on, I sensed an invisible conspiracy to reconnect me with what made my life worthwhile. It began unobtrusively, like this morning's initial breeze, by evoking the image of Anna naked at Trovert Lake and transforming slowly, languidly, into a white rosebud opening to the light of truth as I'd never known it before. The fullness of the woman's laughter was borne by the sudden ripeness of sea and summer breezes.

I clearly heard the rhythmic sound of Anna's breathing. How could anyone's breathing become so much a part of another's being? Hers rushed like great sea winds through the caverns of my hearing. Her every move dissolved in my senses. Her silhouette fell into the arc of my seeing with the compelling eternity of a waterfall. Her stillness gathered the slightest movement in the room to a heightened vibrancy the moment it came in contact with my skin. At the heart of the conspiracy, she became the object of my acute mistrust. Her presence was so tactile and oppressive that I wished myself dead. The scent of her perfume, now detected, annihilated my sense of smell.

But through my sense of hearing she antagonized me the most, through those ordinary words that, once fallen on deaf ears, began to be heard. The words rankled my apathy. Now, when she called my name across the table, I heard it—guileless words spoken by a heart empty of judgment and blame.

'Ordained,' speaks the Whale from the wisdom of Her who knows your family's pain. The woman did not laugh.

"Anna, I'm tired. I'd like to go back to bed."

"Okay. But first, walk just one more time. Up to it?"

"I don't know."

The Whale Way back to your first dream is no easy matter, but you must try. The woman's exhortation was kindly but emphatic.

"I'll try," I said.

"Good," Anna replied. I let her help me to my feet and we slowly walked the short length of the room and back. When I lay down, my body sank into the mattress with that heaviness that earlier had been the unique property of my head. My whole body is a "blockhead," I thought, laughing loudly enough for Anna to hear.

"What are you laughing at?" Anna asked.

"Nothing."

"Nothing is good," she said, smiling. "It's so good to hear you laugh again."

You are starting to get it, chimed in the woman's voice from somewhere so deep I could barely hear her. *The heavier the stone, the stronger the bridge*, she added, her more spontaneous laughter rising to the surface, where it shattered my eardrums with its din and made a place for the silence that followed. With the silence came the darkness and through the eternal pair descended a sea of light, a fierce gossamer, to enfold me while I slept.

When I woke, it was to mist and whistle. "Tom." I barely heard Anna call. Instead, I heard with startling clarity the sounds of my Grandmother Têtreault's silver tea kettle. Rumbling, hissing and spitting against the cold of winter mornings and nights, it was the bright symbol of the joy I experienced growing up with my grandparents. Without their love in my earliest years, the absence of my father, their son, and of my mother, "la putain," would have been unbearable.

My Mémère's kettle always seemed to be at a boil. Its mist, a constant presence, wrapped itself around every piece of furniture in the house. There was comfort for a little boy in those invisible layers of steam that sometimes seemed all that held me to the world when I began to miss my parents. They wrapped and buffered me against the insults my grandfather leveled at my mother. I understood most of the names he called her. "Putain" was the one I didn't understand. When provoked one day by my grandfather's repeated disdainful use of the word, I learned from him to my twelve-year-old horror that it meant "whore." It was then that my hatred for my grandfather began.

In the fitful penumbra of my waking from dream, I heard Anna's breathing commingle with the "shhh" of steam as it poured from the kettle. Anna had become associated at a deep level with my Mémère.

Ordained, the woman solemnly swore.

"But why did he have to be such a son-of-a-bitch?" I cried, lurching forward in bed. Anna held me till I sobbed myself to sleep.

A week later I was walking about the room without assistance, but it had taken me that long to gain the strength and confidence. I hadn't consumed a drop of alcohol, but that had proven no easy trick. At my suggestion, Anna emptied the apartment of a few nip bottles and half a quart of gin I'd wrapped in a towel and shoved under the tub in the bathroom. Despite my good intentions and as soon as I was able, I rummaged everywhere in Anna's absence but no luck; she'd been thorough. Today would be different, I promised myself. Today I would not search. Today I would not crave a drink. From a distance the woman's derisive laughter cautioned me not to underestimate the difficulty of the path the Whale of my dreaming had set me on. Remembering how near death I'd been, I prayed for the craving to stop.

"Good morning," Anna greeted cheerfully as she threw open the door.

"Hi," I answered sheepishly. "I didn't hear you coming." She knew nothing of my desperate searches.

"Bad night?"

"No. Distracted, that's all."

"Room looks good," she remarked, surveying the tidiness and discovering the window's square of sun mirrored brilliantly in the middle of a well-made bed.

"Thanks. I don't ever want it to go back to the way it was."

"Ready?"

"For what?"

"You're kidding, right? We're going for a walk. Right?"

"I forgot."

"Well, you look ready to me." I hadn't forgotten but was afraid that leaving the room meant I'd soon be going out alone and putting my fragile sobriety to the test.

"You've been cooped up long enough. We're walking on the beach just like we planned. Like before. Remember?" I'd been trying not to remember, because reliving memories of our ramblings along the beach or river bank had only invited the thirst and the certainty that I'd be drunk before the day was through.

"Yes, I remember." The simple way Anna dressed accentuated her beauty. Loosely fitting, her lavender blouse and off-white skirt disclosed the ample grace of her body. Her directness and emphasis on action enhanced her physical attributes, every movement telling—none wasted. When she reached for my hand, the beauty of woman was revealed as dance, choreographed before time, executed in that one moment in time for which it was conceived. This was too much tenderness. How could I not remember?

"Come on, let's go!" She tugged me gently out the door and led me down the dingy stairway to the sun-drenched street. It was nearing ten o'clock. The rattle and clank of trucks on Kettle Street celebrated the catch of the day on its way to local markets. I'd been confined to my room little more than two weeks, but walking outdoors seemed strange. My steps were tentative; my eyes, unused to the inflexible brilliance of the sun. The cobbled street presented a challenge not to fall flat on my face.

It was hearing more than the other senses that captured this primordial day most acutely: the churn and squeal of sand against the roundness of stone; the slap of wind at sails a mile away; the shrieks of gulls fighting for scraps. There was comfort in these sounds I'd known since childhood. As Anna and I neared the beach, I marveled at the wholly original sounds underfoot squishing on the dune. I reveled in the hiss of sedge against my jeans, Anna's laughter adrift on the bay, breaking silences too long kept.

I grew up three miles northwest of Horseshoe Bay, and I came here when I was troubled. There was constancy, whatever the weather or season, in the cobble, the gulls, the sand, the sea and sky. I never knew what to expect at home from my grandfather. I'd sit up on the dune or walk to the water's edge, like Anna and I were now, to watch the fishing boats come in. Dots in the dawn at first, they transformed imperceptibly into recognizable shapes. I learned to identify each dot, not by its shape but by its sound. There was no logic to it—only the magic of a willing ear put to the emergence of a blip on the gray horizon. "That's Jim Pearson's boat," I'd yell at a dot in salutation. "Hey, *Flycatcher!* And there you are, your lordship, *Pembroke II*. I'd know you anywhere." *Billy Boy* veered in mostly broadside with a gurgle and a mountain of foam. "There you are, *Billy!*" *Cup a Soup* eased in on the sea's silences...sweet and sure. "I know you, *Cup*."

I learned the individual sounds of the songs the women sang as they waited on stormy days for their fishermen to return. Songs from their hearts broadcast to the elements, to Jesus, to Mary ever Virgin—as greeting, as prayer, as angered pleading or mindful surrender. I was there when songs were swallowed whole by the unhearing mystery of the sea. I was there when *Cup*, of sleek strength and unusual skill, didn't make it home. There too when songs of supplication failed and women, unable to leave or weep, remained on the beach only feet away from where Anna was standing. With the suddenness of my grandfather's lure striking its target, I realized that sound had been a source of fact and satisfaction since my earliest childhood, and that in one of my first dreams I'd been initiated to the haunting song of the Whale. *The words will come*, I heard the woman say. *The words will find you*. Again she wasn't laughing.

As I watched Anna, I observed how sturdily she stood. Supple and tough, she was like those yellow birches on the hill behind my grandparents' house. When a blast of wind blindsided her, she bent her knees, arched her back a little and gave no ground. I rejoiced at her unintended victory as a gust tugged at her hair, billowed her blouse and wrapped her skirt around her thighs. Like the fishermen's lovers and wives, Anna had been patiently waiting for me to come home. She'd been singing her prayer into the wind, trusting powers stronger than my death wish to secure my return. As I sat in the sand, I mourned our loss of time together walking the beach and seeing the sea through each other's eyes.

My mourning reinforced my solitude and our mutual need for distance before we could come together in love again. The tears, begun more than two weeks ago under Cannery Bridge, continued to flow. I was glad Anna couldn't see me cry as she was still turned seaward. I tried to follow her to the water's edge, but couldn't. It seemed that Whale, who'd called to me in my boyhood dream and swum into June's evening sky, was blaring nonsense into my head to confuse me.

Humble pie is a seeing eye, the woman chortled.

She and Whale, I presumed, were implicated in my solitude. I approached Anna. At zenith, the sun shone brightly on our separateness.

"Let's take our shoes off!" she shouted with a sudden enthusiasm that suggested a magical spell had been broken. She kicked her sneakers off while I sat in the sand to remove mine.

"We'd better put our sneakers higher up the beach," I called. "Look how fast the tide is rising." Where the water had begun lapping at Anna's toes a minute ago, it now swirled around her ankles. She scooped up her sneakers and mine, flung them far inland, and ran at the rising tide.

"Come on, Tom. The water's not cold." How could I not believe her when she cavorted in it with a colt's abandon, spraying rainbows through the sunlight with great swipes of her arms. She snatched my hands and dragged me into the waves.

"That's freezing," I protested, pulling back.

"You big baby," she chided, yanking me all the harder. "You're not getting off that easy!" She led me further into the bay until we were waist deep in water. Freeing one of my hands, she turned toward the horizon so that we waded side by side.

"Watch out, Anna," I shouted, pulling her toward me as the bow of a dory, which the tide had just lifted, swung around only inches from her head.

"We'd better get out of here," I warned. "The boats are coming up fast and some of them have pretty long lines."

"Not so fast, sailor." Anna encircled me with her arms and held tight. Her sturdiness anchored us in the shifting sand.

"At this stage of my recuperation," I conceded, "I'm no match for you." Whereupon, she pulled me underwater.

"Come on, Anna," I burbled when she let me up, "what do you want?" I nervously eyed the freewheeling boats. The lines secured to the moorings began to pop as they tightened against the swell. Pop! Pop! Ropes, rubbing aft, keel and bow, stretched with a long whine and held. Pop! I watched a bobbing armada build behind us. "Anna!"

"One kiss," she teased.

"Okay."

"That was too easy." Pop! Bright turquoise crests leaped at us and incandescent foam swirled about our necks. Pop! "You remember, Tom, when we used to wrestle in the surf. You never gave in that easy." Without warning she locked her fingers behind my neck, fell backward and pulled me down again. We kissed underwater till, gasping for air, we rose together to the surface. Anna laughed with an explosion of salt water, spittle and air. I was laughing too.

Noted, the woman proclaimed with a piercing cackle. With no effort on our part, Anna and I found ourselves ankle deep again at a safe distance from the boats.

With Anna still clinging to me, I was filled with the joy I remembered when we'd once been as close and carefree as this.

But my solitude returned. She responded to it with a tender kiss.

"See, wasn't that fun?" she yelled back at me as she ran out of the water.

"Yeah," I spluttered sarcastically, blowing water from my nose and breathless with the exertion. When I caught up with her on the dune, I collapsed in the sand. "Enough," I gasped.

"It's a good beginning, Tom." No sooner had she sat beside me than jets of sand flew into our faces. Anna leaned against me and thrust her arm up to protect her face.

"Kelly!" a woman's voice scolded just as we dared open our eyes and glimpsed a St. Bernard bound toward water's edge. The dog stopped short of the dock and waited for a man to emerge from a thicket of stubby piers. As soon as he came into view, she vaulted the distance between them, leaped up and planted her huge paws in his chest; more than her match, he pushed her backward with the thick barrel of his chest. As they made their way toward us, the dog lunged at his legs in a futile attempt to knock him off balance.

"What a big old weakling you are, Kelly. Can't even knock an old guy like me down."

"Warren, have Kelly apologize to those good folks," the woman above the dune called out. "She threw a good ton of sand on them."

"You did, did you?" the old fisherman chided. "Apologize, Kelly." Upon command, the dog stretched out on the sand, laying her massive head between her great paws. "Good apology, Kelly."

"She's wonderful," Anna said, scratching the dog under the muzzle.

"She gets carried away once in a while."

"No problem," I said.

As the pair climbed the beach, the dog kept trying, again to no avail, to bring her companion down. We watched them join the woman on Pearl Street, and the little black pickup bounce over the cobbles of Kettle until it disappeared.

"That old guy reminded me of my grandfather...the way he used to be. We used to play around like that when I was a kid. Wherever he went, I tagged along." I followed the tracks of the man and his dog in the sand from the foot of the wood stairs to the water line where they seemed to fall off the face of the earth. My grandfather's and my friendship came to a similar end many years ago. "Oh my God, Anna!"

"What?"

"I forgot the letter."

"What letter?"

"My grandmother's letter. It's in my pocket. It must be soaked." I stuck my hand in the back pocket of my jeans and retrieved it. "Look, it's mush," I exaggerated, handing the envelope to Anna.

"It is not," she insisted more emphatically than I expected. "The envelope's intact and the writing's not even smudged... perfectly legible. She removed the letter from the envelope. "It's wet but nothing a little drying out can't cure." She handed the envelope and its contents back to me. The blue sapphires gleamed. "What are you up to, Tom?"

"I didn't know how to bring it up."

"Just bring it up. That's how." Clearly Anna was running out of patience with me. "There was a time when you were able to tell me anything." She placed her hand on my leg. "Just tell me."

"She wants me to go see my grandfather in the nursing home. She never asks me for anything and I don't want to let her down. But I tell you, I'm not up to it now. Here, read it." I handed her the letter, while I retraced the trail of the man and his dog and watched the boats ride the tide and settle into a predictable rhythm.

"She's begging you to go, Tom," she said, folding the letter carefully, then giving it back to me. When I stuck it in my pocket, she pushed me backward in the hot sand, sat on my stomach and leaned forward till our noses nearly touched. "But it's your decision. You have to make up your own mind." She gave me a quick kiss, jumped back up and pulled me to my feet. "Let's go," she said. As we walked up Kettle Street back to my room, I thought I heard a whisper about the likelihood of Whale speaking its most luminous words when we least expected them.

3

The Dark Woman

It was July. I was stronger and Anna wasn't coming mornings anymore. I'd been walking to the river or to Horseshoe Bay almost every day. This morning I planned to walk the bay shore all the way from the north breakwater to the dock, sure I could manage that without any difficulty. When I jerked the window shade up, I knew by the haze and the reflection of white sun in the windows across the alley that the day would be scorching. It was early. Anna was probably on her way to her apartment after her night shift. To escape the heat of noon, I was about to leave when the door rattled with a knock.

"Anna?" I was hoping I wouldn't see her today because I didn't want to discuss my grandmother's letter.

"It's only me," she answered much too cheerfully as she entered. "We've got to talk."

"What about?"

"You know perfectly well what, Tom."

"You think you'd get tired of bugging me," I answered peevishly. I sat on the bed, too embarrassed by my thoughtless words to look at her. She sat by me.

"This is the first time I've mentioned it since you showed it to me on the beach." She spoke softly.

"I know." The gulls' cries, eerily amplified by the labyrinth of steep narrow alleys between buildings in the block, jangled in my ears.

"What's the matter?"

"I thought I was coming to terms with my anger but...I still can't think of him without wanting to strangle him."

"Your grandfather?"

"Who else?"

"I thought we'd come to an understanding...that we'd talk about things." Anna struggled to maintain her composure. I'd seen her lose her temper before, but not without provocation—her Italian heritage filled her with just enough fervor and sarcasm to win an argument without looking out of control.

"I know." The sweetness of our time together on the beach two weeks ago brought with it an intolerable feeling of vulnerability, deeply associated with my resentment of my grandfather. Wanting Anna to see me as reliable and strong, I'd avoided talking and, for that matter, even thinking about him.

"I've got to get some sleep, Tom. I'm sorry I brought it up; it could've waited." She started up from the bed but I took her hand and she sat back down.

"I've wanted to talk to you about it, Anna, but it's like it's always been. When I even think about him, all I want to do is drink...and believe it or not, I'm fed up with what the drinking's done to me."

"I know, Tom. But he's dying. He wants to see you." Her voice remained soft and soothing in contrast to the frenzied cries of the gulls feeding on the bay. I was moved by Anna's softness in the stiff white uniform that seemed too harsh for her lithe beauty.

"What do you think I should do?" It was a rhetorical question; I knew what she'd say. I walked to the window where the screen, threadbare as it was, thwarted any offshore breeze.

"Go see him, Tom." Her look was as unflinching as her answer had been direct. Though I thought seeing my grandfather was a fate worse than the death I'd narrowly escaped at Cannery Bridge, Anna's stand provoked reminiscences of a contradictory and more disturbing nature. I imagined myself, a four-year-old boy, holding my grandfather by the pant leg on the bank of Stocking River, wishing I could be with him and fish with him forever.

"I don't know if I can face him without saying or doing something I'll be sorry for."

"You know, don't you, that your grandmother would never have written if your seeing him didn't mean the world to her? She knows how hard this will be for you." Anna joined me at the window. After she'd brushed the sweat from my forehead with the back of her hand, she wrapped her arms around me.

"How did she stand him all those years?" I was fighting Anna's calm intuition with all the desperate logic I could summon.

"She's never asked for anything before." Anna tightened her grip.

"I know."

"You know which nursing home he's in?"

"The only one he'd ever agree to. It's owned by a Frenchman."

"Where is it?"

"Not far from Mémère's, on Trovert Lake Road."

"It's been a while since she wrote you."

"I know."

"I'm going home, Tom." She kissed me slowly on the mouth. "I'm not working this weekend. Want to go out for supper tonight?"

"Okay." She left. The gulls' cries stopped and in that silence, I heard my grandfather cry out to me in anguish.

The sense of order that had entered my life in the last couple of weeks dissolved faster than I could bear. My perennial dryness of mouth intensified. Any alcohol would do…beer, cheap wine, anything to quench the thirst. Even though I knew Anna had rid my room of alcohol, I searched every inch of the place to find something—anything—to drink. The sweat that poured from me smelled excruciatingly like gin, and the swelling fury of its entice-ment drove me to the futile search. I thought of every bar on Kettle Street and in the neighborhood, stewing to think that none of them opened till ten. The drug store opened at nine. My only hope was to scavenge the beach for what a fisherman or some partying kids might have left behind.

As I fled down the street from old demons, I welcomed their pursuit, dubious of having surrendered the comfort of ritual too soon. The white sun, beginning its westward arc over the bay, scoured Pearl Street, the dune, the wood stairs and the beach. Whatever secrets it pried loose from grasses and rocky crevices, from fishermen's tracks and the most minute depressions in the sand I scrutinized, there was no alcohol to be found. The fever in me raged and its demons demanded satisfaction. Tethers at moor-ings stretched and screamed. Loosed boats slammed deliberately and furiously into one another. Phantoms flew from airborne nets, whirling packing cases and splintering barrels. The sea blazed. Masts succumbed to its flames, wavered and crashed ashore.

White fire crackled everywhere. Waves leaped like flames of white fire. With what poison was the sea retching fire? It seemed not unlike that which convulsed my body. With the sea's convulsions of white fire, each drop of its poison was mirrored dripping from the melted sun. Each drop, from sea and sky, declared itself a revelation. Each, a candle flame. Each, a blue sapphire. Each, a cornflower ground up to replicate the prim-ordial poison.

You have no clue, my beloved blockhead, the woman said, *what agony there is in living a life truly. Do you?* The sea and the sun contin-ued to heave blossoms of white fire. *Do you want a stomach ache? I will show you a stomach ache. Drink this,* she commanded as fiery blos-soms, the final distillation of the universe's original poison, lapped at my lips. *Drink and die, my pup. Drink and live, godson. For these are*

not the weak intoxicants that induce the abstractions of death and the paro-
dies of life. Drink, beyond the silliness of your attempts at life and death, from
the blossoms of your People's dreaming. For your People. Then, a final revelation—two eyes of the whitest fire peering at me from the
stillness of a purple field. Drawn, against my will, to dream those
fearless eyes, I learned that one eye was the reflection of a moon
in the river of the other. A full moon deep in a faraway river. The
field on the river bank was the body of a red woman stained
purple by twilight. She rose from her sleep to show me the youth
and nakedness of her mystery. Serene face. Full breasts, small
waist, swollen hips, muscular legs, and hardened, heavily veined
feet. She leaned forward and offered me her hand.

As I took it, thunder broke the silence with a fierce insistence. My arm recoiled to a stab of lightning.

"Son," a small voice called through the thunder. "You'd
better get out of here while you still can," the thin warning came.

"Pépère, I can't make it! I can't make it," I screamed as run-
away logs, broken loose from a barge on the river, reared up and
threatened to knock me from the boulder I'd been fishing from.

"Give me your hand, Thomas. Give me your hand," the
small voice called through the thunder. I wondered and worried
why my grandfather's voice had become so small...so uncharac-
teristically frail. I let go my fish rod, squatted down on the boulder, grabbed one of its many jagged horns with both hands, and
braced myself.

"Thomas," my grandfather called out weakly, pronouncing
my name in French. "Thomas, tête dure, donne-moi ta main...
give me your hand! Now! You won't be able to hang on. There are
too many logs. Hurry!"

"Are you my Pépère?" I cried out as logs lurched menacingly toward my rock.

"Oui, Thomas, I am your Pépère. Vite! Hurry! Stand up and
reach out to me," he tried to shout in an ever-weakening voice
through the thunder, gripping a birch sapling for anchor with his
right hand and stretching his left down to me from the high bank.

"Why is your voice so small?" I asked, hunched over the boulder and throttling the jagged horn. Before he could answer, darkness overcame me and I rocked in its soothing to the sound of a distant sea. Sound of surf washed over and over me, through and through every gaping pore of my fevered skin, washed the thunder out of my ears and eased the peace of the white-fire-eyes-in-the-purple-field into the final spasm of the deeper poisoning.

Long, long and long the surf eased the peace through darkness till she finally spoke. *It is time for your decision, godson. The gift of the ancient poisoning is not to be taken lightly. Refuse this time and in all likelihood the power of its healing for dreaming and for vision will not be offered again. Let not the rending of your soul be for naught. The peace of the final spasm, remember, is not received until you choose. And in the sphere of the deeper power, there can be no peace without forgiveness. You are forewarned; I can do no more. But choose quickly, my dear, before the fever in your body consumes the power of choice.* The voice of the woman was familiar but her words and tone were not. She spoke more gravely and formally than before and with an eerie calmness that paradoxically and eloquently conveyed the urgency of the moment.

"Pépère," I cried across a vast distance. "I'm afraid. I don't know what to do." I squeezed the jagged horn till my hands bled, while the water's roar and the riot of logs smashing against one another deafened me.

"You have to trust me, mon Thomas," he called through the thunder as forcefully and as calmly as I'd ever heard him speak. "Debout, mon garçon, debout. Stand up."

"I can't. I can't let go."

"Ferme tes yeux, Thomas." I never remembered his voice being this calm and clear except when he was teaching me to cast with the measured instructions that eventually elicited the perfect throw. "You must trust me," he implored. I did. I closed my eyes. "Bon," he continued with the serenity I experienced as the essence of the purple field beyond our most intractable differences and resentments.

"But…"

"Shhh, Thomas. Ecoute. Listen to me. Slowly now, slowly. Let go of the rock. Slowly. Good," he said, when I'd loosed my grip and retracted my fingers one by one. I felt a forgotten warmth issue from his words much as I did when I was a boy following his infallible cues to the letter. The rush of water and the rumble of logs receded.

"Okay, Pépère, what do I do next?" Again our minds melded as they had long ago when, without a word from him, my hook, like his, slipped with deadly accuracy into the stillness of the darkest pool.

"Thomas, lift your right arm…slowly. That's it. Bon, comme ça. Straight out. Aim for the sound of my voice. Do you hear me?"

"Yes, Pépère."

"Oh, that's good. Right there; keep it there. Now don't move it until I tell you to. Okay?"

"Okay." I was standing.

"When I say go, take my hand. Comprends-tu? Understand?"

"Yes, Pépère, I do."

"Are you ready?" There was no need for me to answer; no need for him to say, "Go!" On silent cue, learned a long time ago before dear friends became sworn enemies, I let go. My hand writhed at the clasp of a hellish fire.

"Son," the small voice called through claps of thunder. "Let me give you a lift to your feet. You've got to get out of here and tend to that burn. Come on now, Kelly, back off and give the man some room." After I was helped to a sitting position, I recognized, through the acid white cinders floating around me, the old fisherman and the St. Bernard. The earlier volleys of thunder I heard must have been Kelly's effort to bring her master to my rescue; for as soon as the man turned to the dog and said, "Stop," the thunder ceased. "Up you come and on your feet," he urged as he tightened his fiery grip on my hand and hoisted me up.

"Thanks," I said feebly, watching the last of the white fire vanish into the haze that blurred the horizon. The St. Bernard had dug a moat around me in her attempt to wake me. "Thank you, sir, and thank you, Kelly." When I tried to bend down to pet the dog, I nearly collapsed, more from dizziness than from the wobble in my legs. The man took hold of my arm to steady me.

"Can we give you a ride?" he asked, furrowing his brow. "Lobster red, you are, son. You ought to get checked out at the hospital with that burn. How about we give you a ride?"

"No, thanks. I don't live far from here. I'm sure I'll be fine once I get out of the sun." I didn't want to be treated at St. Philomena's where I was sure to cause Anna embarrassment. Kelly's carryings-on brought the man's wife down to the beach.

"What's going on, Warren?" she demanded. As she got a good look at me, she let out a little yelp. "Oh, my Lord," she said. "You've got yourself quite a burn there, young fella."

"He ought to get checked out at the hospital, but he's of no mind to do that."

"Well, the two of you ought not be standin' and jawin' out here where he's bound to cook up some more," she shot back at her husband. "You ought to know better, Warren." The pale blue skirt and frilly white blouse failed to soften the grit of a plump, startlingly white-haired older woman. "That burn needs tending." She stepped backwards and suddenly fell into Kelly's trench, shrinking her scarcely four feet into three. I couldn't refrain from a laughter that promptly set my face on fire. Her husband laughed too.

"Warren, will you get me out of here," she ordered, the crow's-feet about her eyes and mouth twitching with amusement.

"Celia, didn't I tell you you were shrinking a little every day? Didn't I? Up you come," he added with unabashed affection as his hands swallowed hers and effortlessly pulled her out of Kelly's moat.

"It's a darn good thing most of you was covered up," she scolded. "But your arms, face and neck are near blistering and will if you don't hose down and cool off. Come on, Warren, we're giving the boy a ride whether he likes it or not." She smiled warmly at me. I liked her. I liked them both. "You can hang on to me if you like," she offered.

"No hospital," I insisted.

"That's fine," she answered, "as long as we get you out of the sun."

"Where do you live?" the man asked.

"The corner of Friend and Kettle." Since I couldn't actually feel the heat, I didn't share the couple's concern. But when I started toward the dune, my head began spinning again and my knees buckled.

"Hang on, Warren," his wife urged, "till I get a hold of him." When she'd clamped an arm around my waist, she called out, "Okay, let's go." Kelly jumped up and padded through the soft sand toward the dune. That was the last thing I remembered till I found myself sitting beside the fisherman and his wife in their little black pickup, sipping iced water from a thermos she held to my mouth.

"Easy does it," she cautioned. "That's awful cold. I always pack a lot of ice in the bottle because Warren enjoys it so in the summer." I couldn't tell whether the water was hot or cold…only that it switched my senses back onto a jarring awareness of everything around me. Even with the windows open and a new wind gusting through the cab, the smell of fish on the man's clothes nauseated me. That was strange because I'd grown up with the smell of the river and the sea deep in my nostrils. Catching and cleaning fish was second nature to me. Why should this fishiness then, the essence of home and sometimes the only compass I could depend on, so unnerve me? The dog's tail banged against the wooden side rails till the entire truck shook.

"That means get going," the woman chuckled. When we arrived at my apartment building, I insisted on making my way up the stairs by myself. Though the couple made no attempt to dissuade me, I saw the old woman looking back as the truck bounced away over the cobbles. The last I saw of Kelly was her broad muzzle thrust beyond the lip of the raised tailgate. I thought I glimpsed the white circle in her brown forehead gleam with the brilliance of guiding star.

I brought the smell of fish and its attendant nausea with me into the room. Though I'd meant to sponge down with cold water, I fell asleep as soon as I lay on the bed. A dog barked endlessly while I slept. It wasn't Kelly. It was, I was told by the unfamiliar voice of a woman, the herald of the essential fire at the heart of all the poisons in the world. The woman's voice reminded me of Celia, the fisherman's wife. It sounded simultaneously that of a girl and of a very old woman. There was no separating young from old, for both aspects of the one voice and of the one woman had celebrated with song the initial and initiatory extraction of every poison from the mystery of earth. Celebrated the quintessential fire at the heart of every poison in the world. Celebrated the healing inherent in each poison when it looms its deadliest.

It is, the Dark Woman announced, *the barking of the first fire before it came to be known by any living creature on this planet. Before it was known as 'poison,' as 'death' and as 'healing,' it was barely a sound, a shiver only of the call to life. Before the Whale crawled the earth and long before it took to sea, the sound became a barking.* Baffled by the Dark Woman's declaration, I watched Whale, luminous with the fire of initiation, crawl out of the mud of the night of my near death and begin to walk.

"Oh you beauty," I cried. "You're walking. I never knew you could. How pleased I am to know you can." No sooner had I said the words than I began to doubt what I saw and what I knew.

Do not doubt your vision, my godson. Take to heart what you have been given to see. Know that Whale presently walks the earth to make those impressions wherein you will walk and by which you will find your way. Whale is ever for you and your mother's People the bearer of the first fire; by that light will he walk you and your People into beauty. Do you know who brought you the white fire while you lay helpless at the brink?

"Was it you?"

Yes, the Dark Woman said, more gently than I could bear. The white fire, which had been feeding on my flesh since the beginning, leaped into my heart and barked continuously until I woke.

"Tom." When I opened my eyes, I found Anna leaning over me, calling my name. "God, what happened to you?" she asked, shaking her head in disbelief. Her blue eyes blazed with the fire that burned in me. "Where have you been?"

"The Horseshoe," I answered. She ran from the room and quickly reappeared, one arm draped with towels and the other cradling a porcelain basin filled with water. But before the cold compresses touched my skin, I knew that the healing had already begun—that Anna's treatment had been meant only to complete the cure, for she had not insisted I go to the hospital as I'd expected her to.

"You'll be okay," Anna said softly. She took my hand.

"Yeah," I concurred weakly, finding it more difficult to believe in the inner healing implied by the Dark Woman than in the physical healing.

Anna sat by me on the bed. What was it, I asked as I was drawn into sudden involuntary reverie, that made my skin pucker to the coolness of oceans where Whale invisibly swam? What was easing me back to the freedom I'd experienced when my rod yielded to the visionary power of the river? Was it the river that long ago captured my heart, and not my heart the river? Was it Anna's unseen power or the fall of the late afternoon sun that caused my eyes to close? I could feel the sun drift into shadow and understand how shadow ripens with sun till one becomes the other not only to perception but in reality. Was it the cold compress that induced my dreaming? Was it Anna? Something that shines through the medium of woman or balm? Something that loves whatever it passes through and puts it completely at ease? I drifted into a profound sleep.

"What time is it?" I asked Anna when I woke. In the darkness, I couldn't see her, but I knew she would be there.

"It's almost twenty of nine. You slept well, Tom." She was sitting at the table by the window.

"Why don't you go home, Anna? You must be tired." That's not what I wanted to say. I wanted to tell her to stay...and how much I loved her, but I could not. "I'll be okay."

"I know."

When Anna left around ten, I lay quiet and content, remembering the details of my vision of the Dark Woman. The room filled with the fragrance of lavender. "Anna?"

No, the Dark Woman replied.

"You?"

Yes.

"But I can't see you."

As it must be. Listen carefully, godson. When you walk in the mud prints of Whale, however vast they appear, you are never lost. The reassurance in the Woman's voice made me search the corner of the window for my cluster of stars. *Beautiful, are they not?*

"But why do I always feel so lost?" I asked. "Always looking for a drink? Didn't I already decide once and for all to straighten myself out?" The Dark Woman laughed with delightful abandon.

There are many thresholds of decision, she began. *Do not despair when you find yourself making the same decision over again. You must believe, my godson, that however similar the thresholds of decision appear, each is quite different. Each, necessary. You will want for direction. You will thirst. You will hate your grandfather. You will doubt not only your decision but your very existence. But be assured that, whenever you seem to be starting over, you are deepening your life and apprenticing yourself to the Whale Way. Do you understand?* She laughed before I could say no. Her laughter, buoyed by the exuberance of an ancient song, shook my stars into the luminous nebulae that clouded the windowpane. *How is the burn?*

"Much better," I answered, only mildly surprised that the effectiveness of Anna's care—or something more—enabled me to move my head and arms without discomfort or constraint.

See what a little of the old poison can do. The Dark Woman remained silent for a while. When she resumed, her voice seemed nearer and more familiar. *Godson, you are healed. I must go.* Just as I'd not wanted Anna to leave, so I clung to the Dark Woman's invisible presence and to the dread of losing whatever self-assurance I'd been given. *Not so,* she protested. *You lose nothing you have earned by accepting the challenge of another threshold; this, you have done.*

"But..."

Not so, not so, she insisted, accurately reading my skepticism. *But why did you not tell Anna that you had decided to visit your grandfather tomorrow?*

"I did tell her, didn't I?"

How dare you pretend with me? Her tone of amusement was as barefaced as my lie. *You must give a voice to your experience. Begin by telling those who love and believe in you.*

"But Anna already knew, didn't she?"

Yes, she knew; but in the future, she will need to hear your voice, as will your People. Do you hear me?

"Yes."

Trust your voice, she whispered emphatically.

"I'll try," I muttered.

The Dark Woman laughed her sympathetic laughter. *As you seek your voice remember that, to the eyes of your mother's People, each threshold appears as a distinct and distinctive wave on their river...your river. For now, that is all you need to know.*

With her departure, the nebulae began to glow with the light of that white fire that my grandfather's lure slipped into the night where the great ones hide. As I drifted into sleep, reciting the rosary for the first time since I left home, I thought I glimpsed Whale rising to the light.

4

Anna's Fire

Before dawn, I sought out last night's stars before they disappeared. Thinking I'd never seen the stars so bright, I beheld them until the last possible moment when the increase of earth's star eased them into the sky of another's contemplation. Even more eventful than the remarkable healing of my body was the release of my mind from its preoccupation with painful memories.

It was as though, for the very first time, I was hearing the Dark Woman say: "...to the eyes of your mother's People, each threshold appears as a distinct and distinctive wave on their river...". The words, "your mother," produced a sadness in me that I'd not felt since the day I learned that the French word "putain" meant "whore." There was no rush to sadness at the moment I heard the word "mother," but a gradual welling of loneliness in my heart reminiscent of the time a crimson sunset slowly filled the river and my young eyes with an ineffable yearning for God. I could now hear the waves on her river; each wave, distinctly. Wave upon wave. Threshold upon threshold.

With my head still turned to the window, brimming with the light of a new day, I resisted the urge to ask the Dark Woman to clarify recent events. If an explanation were warranted, she would've given it. I stayed in bed until Anna came in around eight o'clock.

"Hi," she said.

"Hi, yourself."

"And to what do we owe this disgustingly cheerful disposition?" she asked with feigned disapproval.

"I had a good night, Anna."

"Good, let's have a look," she bubbled as she tore the sheet away and slid into bed beside me. "Oh, that is good," she said, rolling over on her stomach and closely inspecting my face, neck, shoulders and arms. "There's not a trace of redness left. Those were second degree burns, you know."

"You sure?"

"I'm sure," she answered smugly. "They're all healed up."

"You don't seem surprised."

"I'm not." She laughed, jumping back on her feet, twirling, leaning over and kissing me on the forehead in one silky motion. "But what were you thinking yesterday?" she asked, the expression on her face changing suddenly from mischief to concern.

"The truth?"

"Of course."

"I wanted a drink pretty bad. I checked out the bars and package stores, even though I knew they were closed."

"Desperate, huh?"

"Then, I scavenged the beach."

"Find any?"

"No," I answered, squirming. "I'm famished, Anna. How about we get something to eat?" When I attempted to get out of bed, she dug her fist hard into my sternum.

"No, you don't. Stay right where you are," she ordered, as she applied more pressure.

"Nothing. I found nothing…but would've drunk anything I could get my hands on. That's the truth." She relaxed the pressure.

"You promised to tell me when you were hurting."

"I know." I didn't remember promising Anna a thing.

"Tom, when are you going to start confiding in me?" Her eyes betrayed a disappointment in me that I found intolerable.

"I'm sorry…"

"I care about what happens to you." Her voice was barely audible.

"I was pissed at myself not so much because I couldn't find a damned drink but because I craved it so badly. So, I lay on the beach and fell asleep feeling sorry for myself. And that is the truth." When I offered my hand diffidently to Anna, she took it and sat down beside me. We didn't speak. The silence proved as effective in drawing out long unspoken feelings as had that intangible "something" in extracting the excruciating pain of the sun's burning. I divulged thoughts that were as foreign and unthinkable to me as once had been the existence of the Dark Woman. I spoke in a whisper.

"He was such a tall man then…my grandfather. Giant to me. Always a giant until the day I left home after I graduated from **Ingram**. He walked like one. Thud, thud, thud! The whole house shook every time he walked up or down the stairs. I swore vases and picture frames moved whenever he passed by. Even with my bedroom door closed, he'd wake me from a sound sleep with his godawful snoring." It was hard to believe I was speaking because the revelations were delivered in the small voice of a boy who scanned the silence for the footsteps of that remembered giant. And even when a lost image of man and boy together broke the silence with the single twang of two lines cast as one, the shadow of the giant overwhelmed the image, inevitably and ruthlessly separating the man from the boy. Anna listened.

"My Mémère seemed so tiny beside him but she wasn't afraid of him…not like I was when I got older. She stood up to him in everything, except regarding my father and mother. Whenever the conversation turned to them, she'd boil water for tea, retreating to some far corner of a world beyond the giant's reach, leaving me to face him alone. Usually, I'd hide in my room or escape to the river. The funny thing is that as often and as much as my grandfather belittled my parents, I knew next to nothing about them."

"How old were you when you went to live with your grandparents?"

"Mémère told me I was just a month old."

"You have no idea what happened to your parents?"

"My grandfather said my father'd gone to sea. Early on when he'd say that, Mémère would shake her head, begin to say something, think better of it and walk away. Later on, silence became her first and last resort. She'd let Pépère talk. Let him badmouth my father, call him a 'quitter,' a 'loser,' 'headstrong,' 'disrespectful,' 'no son of mine,' on and on. Sometimes my grandmother would cry, but she never fought back."

"Your mother?"

"The only thing I ever heard about her was the names he called her…and that she was the one who drove my father away. That, unfortunately, is all I know." Anna stared through my solitary window at the brick building across the alley, from which flashes of sun in windows reflected the intensity in her eyes. I lay there, watching her, wondering but not daring to ask what deep thoughts she was thinking.

"Push over," she said quietly, swinging her legs up on the bed, turning on her side to face me and pressing up against me as I shifted to give her room. Her lips grazed my cheek.

"That's the stuff I could never tell you, Anna…never tell anyone. You know everything else up until you graduated and went away."

"Then?"

"When I graduated, I went to work full time at Tilson's, moved here, started the heavy drinking, and haven't seen my grandfather since."

"What about your grandmother?"

"I'd see her once in a while in town and call her sometimes when I thought he wasn't around. I pretty much knew her shopping schedule and usually caught her coming out of Jake's after she'd bought my grandfather fresh sole or scallops. Early on, she tried to get me to come out and see him. I kept refusing, and she finally gave up and never mentioned it again." As I talked to Anna, she stroked my face, then my chest, kindling in me the fire of her passion, which I still feared more than sunburn…more than death itself. I recoiled at the terror of intimacy with the woman I could no longer pretend I didn't love.

"What's the matter, Tom?" A reservoir of tears, held in check for years, finally gave way. Begun in the middle of my chest where Anna's fingers now rested, the tide of feeling rushed through my body. Wave upon wave. Tears streamed down my face, breaking and bearing away the dams I'd long ago put in the path of love. Anna made no effort to stop me. Her understanding and the respectful silence it inspired fed the fire that surged through me.

"Anna," I began, "the day I left home, my grandfather and I had another of our bitter arguments. I don't remember how it started but probably the way it always did. I wasn't obedient, respectful. I didn't listen to him, wanted to do things my own way. At the height of the argument, my grandfather yelled, 'Thomas, you're just like your father…a coward. He never listened to me, always running away from his duty. Un lâche! You're just like him and you'll turn out to be a coward too.' I almost hit him but didn't…just left without saying a word. I never went back because I thought I might kill him."

The room, echoing the familiar sound of gulls feeding on the bay, had become the recording chamber for a fresh version of an old song. I recalled with unexpected fondness how I had, since I was a boy, been able to tell time by the gathering, swooping, diving and screaming of the gulls. I surmised that the shrill and swelling cacophony on Horseshoe Bay was in response to the last offering of the harvest's waste by fishing vessels.

"Nine-thirty," I pronounced. "Anna, check your watch. What time is it?"

"Nine-thirty on the dot," she replied. "Just lucky. You couldn't do that again in a million years."

"That's what you think," I boasted, remembering with a piercing jolt of recognition how my grandfather had also prided himself in being able to predict events on the river by the sights and sounds his practiced eye and ear pilfered from silences and shadows.

"My grandfather could do it too. That's how he saved my life once." I felt Anna's body shift slightly, though we weren't touching and the bed didn't move. Since I'd cried, every pore in my body was opened wide to her slightest movement. We were more separate than we'd ever been before; and from that tactile separateness, I learned that there was a world apart from me. Anna was there for me to see, to hear, to smell, to touch...to feel. "Anna, I think I know how he did it."

"What?"

"How he saved my life. How he knew precisely when that one huge log would surface, flip and hammer the rock I was hanging onto for dear life. How he knew to make me jump and give him my hand only a millisecond before the log slammed behind me." Suddenly, I was overtaken by the strong eerie conviction that Anna, far better than I, understood how my grandfather knew these things, but she continued to listen without interruption. "He loved the river so much he was able to stand apart from it and let it speak its own mind to him and act out of its own freedom. That's something he wasn't able to do for me."

"Or your father."

"You're right, Anna, not for him either." The sound of our voices, which seemed so separate from and, at the same time, so present to each other, transformed the space between us into a channel, much like Stocking River, wide and free enough for love. I couldn't tell Anna that. I couldn't tell her how she affected me, how she was able, like no other, to make me think I could learn to love.

"There's something in your grandfather for you to love, Tom."

"Oh no, I can't think that. Not yet." But the channel, which continued to flow between us at least as free and wide as the Stocking my grandfather truly loved, prompted me not to reject the possibility. With an inexplicable force of persuasion, another possibility occurred to me...that I could stop drinking. Only hours ago, the chances of that happening were unthinkable. Now the prospect of sobriety partook of the liberating separateness that was there between Anna and me. The prospect had drawn its energy from Anna's fire, the indomitable spirit with which she faced every adversity.

"I love you," she said. I didn't back away from her words. I wasn't even surprised by my acceptance of them. "I love you, Tom." She wriggled closer till our bodies touched. However, the channel remained intact and our touching reveled in our separateness. Her kiss found me, where once I'd been lost to sensations and emotions, free from the captivity of my isolation. By accepting and honoring our separateness, Anna reached me through the layers of my refusal and mistrust.

Almost three weeks after I'd moved in with Anna, I'd settled into a daily routine of long walks, looking for a job and even thinking about going back to school. To celebrate these developments, we ate out at Tyler House, overlooking the inlet. We were seated in a screened porch which, elevated by steel piers set in the rocky hillside, provided an unobstructed view of Tyler Inlet and its southern shoreline. It was evening and, as the sun set, it was difficult to distinguish water from shore. With a warm breeze blowing intermittently up at us from the inlet, we were enjoying each other's company.

"Look," Anna cried excitedly. "See the dogs?"

"Where? What dogs?"

"On those rocks...about halfway out the inlet." She was breathless. "See where that sailboat is?"

"Yeah."

"Well, go out a little further…about thirty feet. To the right. See?" With the hull of the boat already immersed in darkness, I focused on the sail. For the few seconds its brilliance lasted, the sail led to a thin ray of light that cavorted like the scribble of an oscilloscope on the water and vanished.

"I saw something move out there, but it's gone now."

"That's them…the sea dogs."

"You're kidding, Anna. I've been out here lots of times but I never saw one."

"You're teasing?"

"No."

You've missed a lot these last years, haven't you? The voice was not Anna's. There was no mistaking the tone of deep compassion…no mistaking now the similarity between the voice of the invisible woman and that of the Dark Woman. One and the same? I asked myself. *Yes,* she answered. Her words, issuing not from my head but from the outside world to which I was awakening, resounded with the roar of the ocean beyond the confines of Tyler's Inlet.

You had better believe it, she said. *That is the real world, the only one anyone can rely on and be fully alive in. I will continue to speak to you from your heart, but also from the fascinations of the world out there until you catch on. I will continue to remind you to engage in a frank dialogue with that world, as will Anna. Believe me.*

"I believe I've missed a lot," I confessed to Anna.

"Listen," she whispered. "You'll be able to hear them."

I listened. The barking was audible, even when the sea breezes, bringing sound swiftly to shore, suddenly stopped. Though hauntingly low in pitch, each bark came through the screen surprisingly loud and distinct. Anna and I listened with the piety of devotees in ancient cavern or medieval church. *The bark of the dog of the essential fire at the heart of all the poisons the world has ever known,* the Dark Woman said.

"Isn't it beautiful?" Anna asked.

"It is." It was a sad cry from a dark sea. More than sadness, it was irrevocable longing. When the barking ended, a profound silence followed. It was a silence from which I could hear not only Anna's every word, but the longing with which she'd waited for me to return to the world, to her and to myself. The only light left in this world of reality flickered in bowls in the middle of each table. I watched the flame in our bowl glow with the unwavering intensity I'd begun to associate with Anna's presence in my life.

"What are you smiling about?" Anna asked as she leaned over the table, inviting the bowl to dance its great circle of fire in the eager circles of her eyes.

"Nothing." How could I explain thoughts that were undoubtedly not my own and feelings so strange and new that they very well might not be mine either.

"Not a bad nothing," she said, smiling back. "I like it. Look," she gasped. I turned to find a large dragonfly poised on the other side of the porch screen. "Oh," she gasped again, unable to contain her delight. Together we watched the interloper, iridescent with the fire from our bowl. Its stillness drew the fire as the night had drawn stars to my old apartment window. Fire filled its wings with the allure of rainbow. Sea dogs barked their longing. The dragonfly flew away.

"Where I grew up by the river," I reflected, "there were lots of dragonflies. My grandfather called them 'sewing needles.' Whenever I talked out of turn or 'sassed' him, as he put it, he'd tell me that the 'sewing needles' were going to sew my mouth shut. I didn't believe him at first because they reminded me of the way his lures darted in the sun before they dropped with deadly aim onto the target. How could anything that pretty be a threat to me? But the more he said it, the more I got to thinking about what lures actually do to fish. I was scared of dragonflies after that."

"This is the first time I've ever heard them called 'sewing needles.' You weren't afraid of this one, were you?" She laughed.

"You laugh. But you know…as foolish as it seems, I flinched when I spotted it. I can't figure out how such a harmless thing can still make me crazy." Placing her hand on mine with a slight pressure more disturbing than reassuring, she whispered,

"You know I wasn't laughing at you." Sensing the added consternation she'd caused, she removed her hand and sized up her steaming jumbo lobster. The smell of fried clams made me nauseous.

I watched Anna pick apart her lobster with the relish and skill of a "coaster." We lived along the coast; so, we were the "coasters." We named our inland neighbors the "innies" with less reverence than they accorded us. They, we contended, didn't know a lobster from a crab.

"Good?" I asked.

"Delicious."

"Aren't you hungry?" Anna asked. I didn't answer, but glanced furtively at the screen, strangely longing for the return of the dragonfly. The nausea left. With my first bite into the fluffiest crispiest clam, I heard a sea dog bark. I wondered if it was always necessary for poison to inhabit that which we deem beautiful and good.

"Did you make up your mind about your grandfather?" Though Anna's question arose naturally with the ebb and flow of our conversation, it struck me with the same irrational force as the appearance of the dragonfly. Three weeks ago I'd decided to see my grandfather, but didn't follow through. I felt not only guilty, but cowardly. Was I, in fact, the coward he said I was?

"Yes, I'll see him," I stammered.

"When, Tom?" Anna pursued.

"Soon…but I want to see Mémère first. I haven't seen her in such a long time. I do need to see her first."

"Tom, you're not just putting it off again, are you?" From my paranoid point of view, Anna's persistence was becoming harassment. Her eyes were unrelenting.

"Anna, your eyes are burning me up."

"Tom, what in the world are you talking about?"

"They've crossed the line…gone too far." The perplexity in Anna's face begged an explanation I couldn't give. Her gaze backed me against the wall of Cannery Bridge and once again into the inevitability of a decision. "I resent that fire in your eyes. Too probing. Too close. You're getting much too close, Anna."

"Tom, I'm sorry. Whenever you're ready is okay with me. I just want you to know I'll be there when you're ready." With an unfamiliar trust, strangely more powerful than my fear, I placed my hand in Anna's, which she'd not withdrawn despite my earlier rejection. When her hand enfolded mine, the separateness I'd experienced in bed with her three weeks ago returned. Liberating, it enabled me to sustain Anna's gaze and recognize in it the purity of her love.

"I thought I was going to lose you again."

"Not ever." The genuineness of her look, gesture and words made it possible for me to appreciate that calm separateness from which she'd been able to reach me. I looked deeply and deliberately into the blue fire of Anna's eyes, which the Dark Woman needn't have bothered telling me were but another critical threshold on the Whale Way.

"Will you come with me to Mémère's tomorrow?"

"Yes."

"I haven't seen him in so long and I wouldn't let her talk about him. I need to ask her some things before I see him."

"I have to work tomorrow but we can go as soon as I'm done. Okay?"

"You know how much she liked you when we were in high school. She'll be glad to see you again."

"As soon as I get home, I'll change and we'll be off."

"Great." I was relieved that Anna would be coming with me. My grandmother's letter was compelling. "Your Pépère is dying," she wrote. But having reread the letter a number of times, I sensed an urgency that suggested something more than my grandfather's imminent death. I wanted Anna's support when Mémère told me what it was she had left out of the letter.

There were only a few diners left, Anna and I on the porch and two or three other couples inside. When we rose to leave, I lingered, captive to the bright splendor of earthen bowls. They were bearers of another light—eyes of dragonfly, longings of sea dog, stars of a night more benevolent than I'd known these past two years. They filled me with the warmth of pleasant thoughts: of how quickly my burn had healed, how I hadn't had a drink in over a month, and how beautiful Anna was.

"Aren't you coming?" she called from the doorway.

"Coming." I reluctantly left the lighted haven to venture into the darker world of decision and risk. I followed Anna out onto a narrow wraparound deck lit by ship lanterns.

"Watch it," she warned, extending her hand. "That sill's got a steep drop to it." Before I could heed her warning, I stumbled down from the sill against her body, braced and ready to catch me. "I knew you were going to do that," she laughed.

"So you're saying I'm clumsy, huh?"

"No, no," she protested, giggling, "but you've been so pre-occupied, I just knew you were going to do that." She let go my hand and tried to pull away but I wouldn't let her, wrapping my arms tightly around her and forcing her with the full weight of my body up against the rail. "What are you doing?" she squealed.

"I'm not letting you go…ever." I kissed her.

"You mean it?" she asked, squeezing me twice as hard as I held her.

"I was stupid enough to let you go once. Not again." I loosed my grip and pulled away to dare a deeper look into the blue fire obscured by the shock of lantern light. The more I tried to disengage, the harder she tightened her grip. She was sobbing unabashedly.

"Never again?"

"Never."

"Then why are you trying to pull away?" she spluttered between sobs. Again we kissed and held each other as long as it took the silent barking of the sea dogs to immerse our longing in the depths with theirs and transform it into the further separateness our love required. The agonizing touch of that separateness brought our beings together with a longing that would forever exceed the fervor of our love. "I love you, Tom."

"How I do love you."

"Never apart?"

"Never." The joy of that long embrace painfully reminded me of what I'd missed these many years. Perhaps Anna's passion for food, swimming, dancing, idle chatter, flowers, stars and making love was opening my heart faster than I could stand. But I decided then that I'd risk the blue fire of her eyes finding me out when she pressed her desire against mine. I'd risk disappointment and failure when mercilessly she pressed for decisions she refused to make for me. That night at Tyler House, I learned that there was no fire in the heavens or on earth more formative of a man's fate than that of a woman's love.

The following afternoon, Anna and I set out for my grandparents' house. I made a note of the time and date because the visit represented one of the first decisions consciously made since the Dark Woman revealed that my life depended on such decisions. The day was oppressively humid and the sky overcast when we walked to the street where she'd parked her car.

"How do you like the wax job?" she asked, proudly patting the hood of her new red Toyota.

"Looks great, Anna." I couldn't resist teasing her because she looked so smug. "But why waste your time waxing it? Didn't you just buy it last week?"

"You're jealous!"

"Just kidding. It looks great," I brushed a kiss across her cheek.

"I ought to make you wait," she said, tweaking my nose. "Come on, get in." As Anna slid into the driver's seat and drove her knee playfully into my thigh, I was acutely aware of the bareness of her legs without that peculiar distancing of paranoia. It occurred to me that, however staunch Anna was in support of my need to be separate, I couldn't ever again use her as an excuse to run and hide. The fire burning within her leaped to the surface of everything she said, did and was. It made the white shorts and blouse she was wearing glow with an inwardness simple attire and dullness of day could not contain. It made the turn of her breast and the pout of her lips tremble with the same stillness that puts a glimmer into the furthest visible star.

"This is the first new car I've ever owned," she bragged over the roar she coaxed from the engine.

"I know."

She concentrated on making a U-turn. I dared the fire by placing my hand on her knee. She laughed with that bright spontaneity that had always moved me; but, this time, the rise and fall of her laughter, mirroring the dance of white flames in the haze, overcame me with its searing brightness.

"You are beautiful, you know."

"You think so?" she answered with mock casualness. We drove the rest of the way in silence. Although the white sun hadn't managed to burn through the haze on the water, it shone with an intensity that promised an imminent breakthrough.

As I found my eyes drawn inexorably to the poison at the core of the sun, words the Dark Woman had spoken only recently stung me like pinpricks of the primordial fire, irritants I must no longer ignore. "Whale is ever for you and your mother's People the bearer of the first fire; by that light will he walk you and your People into beauty." Who are my People...my mother? I feared that my Mémère had kept secrets that she would finally be forced to tell.

5

A Different Fire

During the twenty-minute drive across town to my grandmother's, haze concealed the bay. Just when the sun was about to break through, a swelter of haze reasserted its tenuous hold on boats, rocks, wharves, inlet and the sea itself. Tyler House shimmered alone in the distance. I turned away from the coastline and tried, with my imagination, to find the spot on the Stocking where the sun of my own deadly lure always lifted the prey out of its darkness.

"You're so quiet, Tom."

"I don't know what to say to her. It's been so long." I'd resolved not to talk about my fears, but found myself divulging them anyway. "She's going to tell me something I don't want to hear. I know it."

"Do you have any idea what it might be?"

"I don't have a clue; but I've got this feeling that, whatever it is, it's going to piss me off. That scares me because she and I have never quarreled. Not once. I don't want to hurt her, but I'm afraid I won't be able to help myself." As we approached South Pearl, I glanced across to Cannery Bridge. It stood out clearly from the blur of the embankment and the anonymity of Tilson's, as though sun and haze had conspired to etch the bridge in gold on insubstantial gray parchment.

"Another threshold," I mumbled, with not a little sarcasm.

"What?"

"Nothing, Anna. Just something someone said to me once. Nothing important."

"Look," Anna called excitedly, pointing toward the dock at Horseshoe Bay. "Wow! They're like little pieces of last night's moon." I looked down at the breakwater where seagulls, slipping into the haze, reappeared incandescent, translucent little pieces of the moon.

"There was no moon last night, Anna."

"There was for me," she said, turning to me with a wry smile. As we passed through the dingy neighborhood where I'd been living, we remained silent.

"What are you thinking?" she asked.

"How lost I was."

"And now you're found?" She laughed triumphantly.

"Something like that."

"Exactly like that! You've been found, no doubt about it. I found you and won't let you get lost again."

Believe it, the other voice added. The Dark Woman's voice…unobtrusive. *Believe it. One other thing…your Mémère, she will not break in two. She, like your mother, is of hardy stock. She is smarter and stronger than you think. Do not be afraid to talk to her, to tell her what is in your heart. Listen to her. Believe!* My grandmother's house was another five minutes away as we approached Sweeney Bridge.

"It's incredible!" Anna exclaimed.

"Yeah, it is." My heart skipped a beat, mindful of the times· its gleaming pierced the clouds like lures into the mystery of life and death through the flutter of poplar on the river bank. I kept looking at "The Sweeney." As a boy, the trees and houses across the street annoyed me because they distorted my view of the bridge. Anna drove to the end of the cul-de-sac where my grandparents' small white cape stood, the last house on the left.

"It's all gone," I said. "The trees are so grown, it's impossible to see anything. Anna, that's the first thing I'd look for when I came home from school…a glimpse of the north bank, a shiny slice of the river and, further down, the northernmost mast of the bridge. That made me feel safe. Gone." As Anna climbed out of the car, her eyes met mine.

"Did you notice how blue the sky is up here? Where'd the haze go to?" she asked, staring into the light.

"Yes," I muttered, not looking up.

"What's that scrumptious smell?" she asked, eyes still on the sky.

"Roast pork. Mémère didn't forget it was my favorite." I looked up at the sky to see what peculiar fascination it held for Anna. I never saw the sky so blue or so bright. "Amazing," I mumbled under my breath, genuinely startled by the purity of blue, imagining it to have been just so when the sky emerged from chaos at the beginning of time.

"Smell those roses," Anna said, inhaling deeply as she started up the flagstone walk toward the house. "Look at them!" She stopped short of the front steps to admire the red rosebushes that flanked the small, gabled portico.

"They're my Mémère's love."

"I've never seen the bushes so full."

"She didn't hear us drive up, otherwise she would've been right out." I pictured my grandmother a dervish of concentration and efficiency amid the hiss and clatter of pressure cookers and the cloud and whistle of her silver tea kettle. My stomach knotted; my feet froze.

"Come on up here, you chicken," Anna called, ringing the doorbell.

"Thomas, Thomas," my grandmother shouted my name in her usual French, pressing her nose hard against the screen and squinting to pluck a blurred image of me from the brilliant sunlight. "O, mon Dieu, Thomas!" When she unlatched the screen door, she pushed it open with such force that Anna was nearly hit in the face. When she realized what she'd done, she cried, "O, mon Dieu" again. "Anna! Anna, is that you?"

"Yes, Mrs. Têtreault. It's me."

"I didn't see you, ma chère. I almost hit you. I am so sorry." Though my grandmother was standing on the door sill, the top of her head barely came up to Anna's chin. She brought Anna's face down to hers and kissed her on the cheek. "I am so sorry."

"You didn't hit me, Mrs. Têtreault. There's really nothing to be sorry about. How are you?"

"Oh, good, Anna, good." She said, peeking around the door, looking for me.

"I'm here, Mémère," I called to her as I stepped onto the porch.

"Thomas, mon Thomas," she whispered as she wrapped her arms around me. When I bent down to kiss her, I saw that she was crying.

"What are you crying for? You're supposed to be happy to see me."

"Oh, I am, I am. Don't mind me. Come, mes enfants," she said, crying profusely, wiping her eyes with her apron, giving me one last squeeze and signaling us to go in ahead of her. "Come before your supper gets cold. It's so good to see you."

Usually my grandmother talked slowly and calmly but today she bumped her words into each other in an eloquent display of affection. "It's hot in here but the breeze from the river will cool us off. You know where to sit, Thomas. Show Anna to her chair. Sit, sit," she coaxed as she hurried over to the stove. Anna turned to me with a smile that said, "See. Everything's going fine." Just as I was about to seat Anna, my grandmother scooted by and pulled a chair away from the table, saying, "Anna, you sit here by the window in Thomas's Pépère's place.'"

Though I thought that nothing could diminish the pleasure of reunion with my grandmother, the mention of my grandfather sent a chill through me. Despite the oppressive heat in Mémère's kitchen, my body iced over as it so often did at the fever pitch of my DT's. No sooner had I sat in my "old place" than I beheld the oak tree where my grandfather had tried to take his life, and to which I would be bound, it seemed, for the rest of my life.

After my grandmother served us the roast pork, with hot carrots, peas and green beans, and a dish crammed with the reddest and juiciest sliced tomatoes, she sat down between us.

"The vegetables are from the garden, aren't they, Mémère?"

"Oui, mon cher," Mémère answered soberly, her words drained of their earlier good cheer. "They come from your Pépère's garden." She too, it seemed, was suddenly revisited by her own secrets and reminded of our unspoken agenda...hers and mine.

"They're delicious, Mémère," Anna said. "Everything is so delicious."

"Thank you, my dear."

"Where is the garden?" Anna asked, looking through her window.

"Oh no, it's not out there. It's by the back door. You can see it through that little window over the sink," my grandmother explained, pointing to the smallest of the two windows in the kitchen's west wall.

"But, oh my, Mémère," Anna cried, "you've got the river in your backyard."

"Last summer, Thomas's grandfather cut brush and supervised the removal of some trees. He knew just which ones he wanted taken down. That's how we got our river back. Did you see, Thomas?"

"No, not yet, Mémère."

"So, you like our backyard, Anna?" My grandmother laughed, having forgotten, at least for the moment, what had been troubling her. "The river has always been our backyard, hasn't it, Thomas?"

"Always, Mémère." She placed her hand on my forearm as she rose to retrieve an almost empty bowl of mashed potato from the table.

"The river will always be our backyard, Anna," she repeated, returning to the table with more steaming mashed potato. "Thomas and I used to pick blackberries on the hill. His grandfather took him fishing every day when he was a little boy. Do you remember, Thomas?" She knew only too well how much I'd loved it all.

I couldn't see the river from "Thomas's window," which my grandfather had named to distinguish it, in characteristic fashion, from "Pépère's window" with its unobstructed river view. The more withdrawn and sullen he became over the years, the more absurdly he invoked a claim on his river and the view from which he seemed to derive his only solace. Despite his yeoman yard work last summer, my grandfather didn't remove the trees that impeded the view from "Thomas's window," denying me access to the river I too loved.

Could he have left those trees there on purpose? I wondered, falling victim to my own deep-seated paranoia. But fond unsullied childhood memories sped to every path, turn, dip and rock on the bank, to every gleam, shadow and eddy in the water. No "Thomas's window," however powerfully invoked by the giant's presence, could hold me back. I was there. It seemed I never left.

"Mange, mange, Thomas, eat," my grandmother urged. "Your supper's getting cold."

"What's the matter, Tom?" Anna asked.

"Just a bunch of stuff going though my head," I answered, continuing to stare out the window.

"What?" she persisted.

"The minute I got here, walked in the house, everything's become so personal. I didn't want that."

Unavoidable, the familiar voice interjected.

"My window! My chair! Always was! Always will be!" I intoned in a voice strangely torn between anger and religious fervor. "Most especially, his window! His! Always was, always will be...forever and ever. Amen." The alien voice trailed in a long inconclusive whimper. Realizing, after my long absence and my striving to forget, that here I could touch and be touched by the river without as much as seeing it, made the smallest thing seem important. I remembered the fervent prayers he said with me every night before I went to bed. Personal. Unchanging. My river. His river. Our river. No matter how hard I'd pray now for things to be different, I knew they could never change. It would always be his river and mine. Ours. The way it was when we'd stand side by side casting our lines from the bank in one effortless motion. Together. I thought my hot tears would burn a hole in my throat.

And so it is, the Dark Woman said.

"Mémère," I said weakly, choking back tears, "I never once thought of the chair you're sitting in now, the one you've always sat in, as 'your chair.' Not once. How come?" Though the question seemed highly irrelevant to me the moment it burst forth, I knew at once that Mémère grasped its meaning. She patted my hand.

"Mon cher," was all she said. Anna was silent. I needed her silence.

The two loves of your life, the Dark Woman said. *And there will be a third…in good time.*

"It's been a long time, Mémère," I said.

"Too long, cher Thomas," my grandmother replied, looking at me now as she had in the past when I returned home late at night after day-long treks along the river. "Are you all right?" was always the question she asked. Her eyes always reflected my hurt. Then, I was made to feel, without resenting it, that she knew everything I did…before my drinking began. I was happy to have her spirit with me as I sat atop a huge granite slab at the tip of the breakwater, letting the breaking waves spray me till I was soaking. Or to be with me when I stood above the dune, guessing which of the moored boats would rise first with the incoming tide. With me when I made up stories of the lands my father, the seafarer, explored. Still with me while I walked home at night with the stars, stomach excruciatingly empty and head exquisitely clear, planning my own escape to sea.

"Mémère, do you remember the nights you waited up for me with supper?"

"Oui, mon enfant."

"I needed those long walks home. They taught me things I never knew before: sounds I'd never heard, sensations underfoot I'd never felt. I'd sit down along the river somewhere, pick a light out from the other side—from a house, a boat, a dock—and follow its trail as far as I could across the water. Then, I'd imagine where it might go if it came ashore, by what inspired and clever path it might show me through the woods. I found a new way home every night. I was happy on those walks."

"I worried when you came home so late."

"I'm sorry, Mémère. I didn't mean to make you worry."

"You made your Pépère so angry."

"I know." As much as I loved how the river talked to me at night, how it made itself heard and understood while I followed its fresh trails into woodland secrets, my stargazing began as a way to vex him. But I'd forget all about him while I watched the stars melt in the river. When I climbed into our backyard, I'd wait until the oil lamp in his bedroom reluctantly died out, convinced by then that he was sufficiently annoyed. Then, I'd pick a star from the sky, draw it down into my hands and carry it into my grandmother. "Do you remember, Mémère, how I'd bring you a star when I came home?"

"Oui, mon cher, je m'en souviens. I remember…"

"And you'd never refuse to take it in your hands, like some kind of treasure. Remember?"

"Yes."

"Then you'd pretend to place it carefully in the middle of the table, tell me to go wash my hands and hurry back for supper. We did that every night, Anna, till I was almost fourteen. Can you believe it?" Remaining silent, Anna shook her head and blew a kiss at my grandmother.

"I didn't have the heart to scold him," Mémère said, wiping her tears away again with her apron. "After all, how many chil-

dren are thoughtful enough to bring their Mémères home a star?"
As I observed with what fondness the two women regarded each
other, I recalled the night Anna found me under Cannery Bridge.
The warmth of their communication transported me back into the
creative sky of our origins and of Whale's procession, to pluck
from the backbone of the great mammal a radiance of my own,
the star from which all the stars of my childhood were lit, the dog
star of my destiny. The quintessential fire.

"Mémère…"

"Oui, cher?"

"Do you think Pépère knew I brought you stars at night?"

"I don't think so," she said so weakly I could barely hear
her. Threadbare voice coupled with a lowering of eyes made me
suspect my grandmother wasn't telling the truth, perhaps—it suddenly occurred to me—to give me the satisfaction of finding out
for myself what she'd always known.

"I think he did," I said, after a long pause. "I think he knew
all about it."

"You think so?" My grandmother's blue eyes were steady
and bright.

"I can't believe I'm saying this…" I was stopped by a sur-
feit of tears caught up more in my refusal to admit anything good
about my grandfather than in the agonizing constriction of my
chest and throat.

"Go on, Thomas." Mémère's gaze was as soothing of my
distress as it was unwavering of purpose.

"I think he knew all about it. I think he helped me carry in
every single star I ever gave you…I think he knew that each was
a glimmer of my destiny. I swear he knew that!" As soon as my
intuition was spoken, the agony of the physical and emotional
constraints I'd subjected myself to eased in a paroxysm of tears.
Mémère and Anna silently watched me cry from the distance
I required.

"I just don't understand any of it, Mémère."

"Patience, mon enfant," she said quietly, giving my hand

another pat before putting the silver tea kettle to boil. Her love did nothing to dispel my confusion, but had already persuasively put me in mind of the fundamental pertinent question. How could I at once both fiercely love and hate this man, my beloved mentor turned tormenting giant?

"Mange, finish your supper, Thomas," Mémère urged. I looked at her, this old woman, my grandmother, and heard her mild exhortation meld with that of past years and reverberate in me with the poignancy of a dear but long forgotten memory.

Diminutive, fair-complexioned, a net taming wild waves of white hair, alert blue eyes, she stood immovable by her stove. As I took in all ninety pounds of her, I was reminded of the stability she brought to a household divided. I recalled her eating little and quickly...being well-mannered, but never fastidious. She wasted no movement in anything she undertook, not in preparing meals, cleaning house, sewing, pulling together the complexities of a bazaar to benefit St. Anne's Church. A woman of few words and decisive action, her flowery dresses and frilly aprons proved statements of her resolve to see difficulties through.

"Mémère," I ventured, steadied by my grandmother's presence at the stove, "what did you want to tell me about Pépère?"

"He's dying, Thomas." I knew that already.

"Of what?" The question seemed harsh to me.

"He has lung cancer," my grandmother answered. "He is in a great deal of pain. The doctor says he will die soon." She lowered her eyes, folding her hands in her apron. The sun's procession westward appeared to tarry on the river. The reflection raged first in Mémère's eyes, then through Pépère's window to transform Anna's long auburn hair into a cascade of blood-red wine. The diamond-shaped crystal twirling in the window above Anna's head cast hundreds of spinning rainbows across Mémère's hands, and the hard whites of apron, stove and kitchen cabinets. The sudden swarm of rainbows reminded me of the times when, with a flick of my grandfather's wrist, rainbows spilled from his line into the river.

"Thomas," my grandmother went on, unrelenting, as she walked through the brilliant maelstrom back to the table, "your Pépère has something he wants to tell you before he dies...something he must tell you," she paused to sit down. "Something only he can..."

"Do you know what it is?" I asked.

"Yes."

"Then, why don't you tell me?" I heard my voice rise in volume and pitch.

"C'est impossible; je lui ai promis. I promised your Pépère I wouldn't tell you."

"It's that important?"

"He is ready to tell you now. You must let him do that before he dies." I looked at Anna's eyes for some sign of what to say or do. Though she didn't look away, she offered no help. I said nothing, convinced that my grandmother too had agonized over what she should say and do. She had the final word; there was no budging her now. Avoiding my grandmother's gaze, which I sensed was as racked with self-doubt as it had been keen with resolve, I watched Anna's hair turn suddenly black with the sun's swift egress from the river. I vowed not to cause my Mémère further pain.

It became clear that the destiny, which I'd begun to feel I could shape, was as completely out of my hands as the implacable setting of a sun. There were, it appeared, family secrets which weighed heavily on my grandparents' consciences. And there was at least one secret which my grandfather couldn't bear to take with him to the grave. Anna brought a cup of Mémère's bone china to her lips, though I'd seen her drain it many minutes ago; she signaled that the ball was in my court. A startlingly cool gust of evening air filled the curtains, the same print of pink and red roses that Mémère was wearing.

Don't worry about your grandmother, the Dark Woman said. *Don't feel sorry for her; she has made her hard choices as you must make yours. But know this about her: she is no fool, this grandmother of yours.*

Know this about her too: she would give her life for you without hesitation. Take to heart the words I offer you now for they are hers. They are words spoken from and held to her heart many Christmases ago as were those of Mary, Mother of your grandmother's God, beholding the son of Spirit in her womb. Hear the words. 'Comme nous nous enfuyons de ce qu'il y a de plus beau parmi nous. Etrangers. En pleine gaité, en plein échange de souhaits, en plein épanouissement du sourire de l'Enfant Jésus, nous rejetons ce qu'il y a de plus beau parmi nous. Nous nous enfuyons de nous-mêmes. Nous nous trouvons seuls. Ca me fait pleurer. How we are prone to run from what is most beautiful among us. Strangers. Even as we rejoice, exchange hugs and best wishes, bask in the radiant smile of the Child Jesus, we reject what is most beautiful among us. We flee from who we are. We are alone. It makes me cry.'

There is a strain of fierce aloneness in your father's people. I do not pretend to know where it comes from…whether the French Canadians learned it by necessity when they immigrated to this country or whether it grew out of the frontier mentality of their forebears, out of their struggle to survive in a hostile environment. I remember their 'coureurs de bois,' the trappers and traders whose lives of often ruthless solitude sometimes crossed the tenuous lives of your mother's People. Trust your grandmother. She knows how to stand alone when she needs to. She knows the pain of having lost that which no one can stand to lose. She would spare you that at the cost of her life.

I remembered how the rainbows had dissolved with the retreat of the sun and the whistle of the silver tea kettle. I winced at the thought of losing Anna, the most beautiful thing in my life. I'd watched her blue sapphire eyes shine beyond the dissolve of the last rainbow as the permanence I knew I could always rely on.

"Mémère," I said resolutely, "it's okay. Don't worry. I'll see him tomorrow." She squeezed my hand but then let it go as though to tell me she understood that what I had to do, I must do alone. I felt, for the first time, feelings of disappointment and acrimony toward her. My grandfather had routinely incited such sentiments, but never before my grandmother. I couldn't bear the thought that my Mémère had kept something from me that might have made a significant difference in my life. What did she know of solitude, I asked myself, overwhelmed by self-pity. How many times did she wake up in the morning with her face pushed up against a foul-smelling curbstone. Woken up wishing she'd died and gone to hell? What did she or, for that matter, the Dark Woman know about being alone?

"We'd better get going, Mémère," I said, rising quickly from my chair, exasperated with the ear-splitting whistle of the kettle. "It's getting late." I started for the door. I knew she was crying, the way she used to when she couldn't stop my grandfather's screaming or pry him loose from his melancholy.

"Everything was delicious, Mémère," Anna said, trying to temper the abruptness of my departure. "Thank you. Can I help you with the dishes or anything?" Anna walked deliberately to the stove to turn the burner off. The sharpness of the whistle subsided into a sharper silence.

"Non, non, ma chère," my grandmother answered absentmindedly. "I have plenty of time to do the dishes."

"I'll see him tomorrow," I called brusquely back from the portico. I left without saying goodbye and waited for Anna in the car.

We remained silent as we drove back toward Sweeney Bridge. The sky turned from golden to crimson as we approached it. "Oh, look," Anna cried, breaking the silence. "It's on fire. Isn't it beautiful?"

"It is," I answered curtly, awaiting a reproof that never came. I wanted the fire of the bridge to leap the chasm between us, but the great lethargy that had come over me became the emotional fire wall I felt could never be breached.

Isn't that the way with self-pity, a faraway voice scolded. *My dear blockhead,* the Dark Woman continued, *you have forgotten, haven't you, that blocks are for bridge-building. Self-pity only blocks the way, whereas facing blocks with courage makes the way.* The woman seemed to relish her wordplay at my expense. *You are my beloved blockhead of the two minds. Your clever Mémère, whom you pity almost as much as you do yourself, has placed you squarely before the two minds. Before your love for your grandfather. Before your hatred of him. Before the two blocks of an inevitably and wholly different cut. For the last two years of your life, you have been consumed by the one mind...your hatred.*

Not until today, when your grandmother confronted you with the reality of the two minds with such force of clarity you felt it necessary to offend her, did you sense how crucial her wisdom is to your Whale Way. She has indeed blessed you, for now you are in a position to seize your life and be rid of the inept poisons that diminish and make it contemptible, even to yourself. What do you say to that?

The Dark Woman's question drew my attention unexpectedly to Anna's calm concentration. It occurred to me, with absolute conviction, that however silently words passed between my godmother and me, Anna heard every one of them. *What do you say to that?* the Woman repeated with mild annoyance. Grasping only too well that she required not an answer but my full attention, I continued to listen.

Now, what do you do with two blocks of a contradictory cut? she asked patiently. *What do you do with the two minds and the maddeningly uncompromising distance your ambivalence has created between them...between your every thought and action?* Absolute silence claimed absolute concentration. *You take the two blocks and rub them together. By so doing, you strike a different fire which, of course, transforms your ambivalence into the openness that alone can bear the thought of forgiveness and grow it tenderly into deed. You see?* This time, her earnestness of tone urged an answer.

"No, I don't see."

Watch! Fix your eye on Sweeney Bridge. Are you watching?

"Yes."

Take your two minds to your heart with the power of your dreaming. You understand?

"Yes." I wasn't at all surprised that I understood.

Now, rub the two minds together...gently. I saw myself—from a great distance but with eminent clarity—pick two perfectly round stones from an unfamiliar shore and begin tentatively rubbing them together.

Good, good, she said, *but don't be afraid to rub a little harder.* I rubbed harder. *Not too hard.* I eased up. *Good. Keep your eye on the bridge.* I did. *Good.* Before long I saw the fire to which Anna had called my attention. *Not so,* the Woman corrected. *It is the different fire...the sacred fire that purges pride from your dreaming and opens your heart to truths beyond contradiction. Watch.*

As I continued to watch the bridge and rub the stones together, the different fire turned from red to white, infusing the bridge with its incandescence till bridge and fire flowed as one through a night deeper and darker than I'd ever imagined.

"Oh," I gasped as I witnessed the bridge turn into an immense and luminous rainbow.

The rainbows you saw in your grandmother's kitchen this afternoon were reflections of this...meant to prepare you for this.

"It seems so close, I could touch it...so real, I could walk across it into Riverton."

That, my godson, you must never do. Never, she warned. A transfixing chill reduced my body to a frailty of being I'd experienced only once before...the instant I chose life over death under Cannery Bridge. *Never,* she repeated with unnerving deliberation.

"Why not?"

It is the rainbow of the Great Spirit, not meant for mortals to mount its sacred back. It rises from the depths of the creation as a reminder of our dependence on the radiant breath of Spirit for our being. In order to live of the spirit, creatures, like you and me, must do its bidding, prostrate ourselves and crawl humbly toward our destinies far below its withering light. Surely you must have had some sense of that, crawling on all fours, the night of your passage under Cannery Bridge?

"No," I responded edgily, before I remembered the brilliant dance of cornflower eyes.

You must keep your eye on the bridge as you rub the stones together.

"Like this?" I asked, trying to find in my rubbing a balance between strength and grace.

Good. Are you still able to see the sacred rainbow?

"Yes."

Now, let yourself down into the river valley. Easy! Very slowly… slowly. Easy…easy. Good. Are you okay?

"Yes."

Whatever you do, do not look up at the rainbow, she commanded as she read my urge to do that. *Kneel down. Down!* I knelt down in the squish of black mud. *What do you see?*

"I…"

Do not tell me, she interrupted before I could answer. *That is not for me or anyone else to know. What you have been given to see is a portent of your destiny. For you alone. Remember it well.*

"I will."

Remember to look down…not up. Goodbye, godson.

6

When Dragonflies Die

W hile Anna fell asleep as soon as we went to bed, I lay awake, unable to shake off the emotional events of the day. I got up and left the room to sit by the window in an adjacent bedroom. Why did everything appear so near and accessible on a night without a moon? Though broad buildings and large leafy trees hid Tyler House and most of the inlet, elongated silhouettes of trees and street lamps stretched out menacingly. Unfettered starlight turned the bay into a second Milky Way, the thick still radiance of which quieted my mind.

Was it, I wondered, the cloudless sky or a new seeing brought on by the vision of the sacred rainbow that revealed the night with unusual clarity? A red brightness just beyond the inlet flickered with an intensity like the votive lamps my grandfather lit in church before early morning Mass; they prayed fervently in our stead, my grandfather instructed me, while we busied ourselves with the "more mundane concerns" of daily living.

When I brought the flicker of red light into focus, it came to me, declaring itself no indistinguishable votive lamp at all but my grandfather's own distinctive meerschaum bowl, the old familiar votive lamp of his personal prayer. The far glimmer became a near seething of red embers, a deep glow and deeper darkness with each inhalation and exhalation of sweet-smelling smoke. With the nightly rise and fall of fire in the dark of the living room and his daily newspaper read and folded neatly on his lap, my Pépère prayed his pipe in silence until it was time to go to bed. What he prayed for I didn't know; it must have been important, I thought, as I watched the same old fire from the window and felt it breathe its same old supplication hot into my face.

I remembered too that my grandmother and I never joined him when he settled into his rocking chair to pray in the darkness of the living room. One summer night when I was five years old, I dared enter the dread sanctuary, drawn by the rhythm of fire in the magic bowl and careful to stay small and still behind the secretary desk. How the fire gleamed in Pépère's eyes! How his eyes seemed to swallow the fire until it uncannily appeared again in the magic bowl! Persuaded by my long vigil in the dark and by my childhood instincts, my grandfather's eyes were actually those of a dragon come from a timeless cave at the center of the earth with the express purpose of breathing the fire of a foreboding mystery into my life.

As I watched the dragon fire flutter in the water beyond the inlet, I recognized the cadence of the dragon's heart as I'd seen it as a child. I sensed that the rhythm of the dragon heart, reflected by fire of warning buoy and magic bowl, was also that of unknown stars breathing their immortal life into mine. When the Milky Way embraced me from sea and sky with its myriad fire-breathing suns, I feared it would incinerate me; but instead, it filled me with the infinite warmth of its compassion for dying dragons and disenchanted children.

I believed it no coincidence that, on the eve of visiting my grandfather in the nursing home, I'd been reacquainted with the dragon. Somehow, it had become my teacher, permitting me with indulgent kindness and good humor to share in its dragon nature.

As the five-year-old who'd seen the dragon in my grandfather, I confronted its fearsome presence in the most obvious and powerful way a child could conceive—I became the fire-breathing dragon. Standing tall on presumptuous tiptoes, I breathed immortality into the light of stars. I extinguished the fire of my grandfather's rage each time he drew on his pipe to revive its embers. I took exquisite pleasure in putting the fire out in his pipe till he put it aside in utter frustration. I was the magician, not he.

"Omer," my grandmother used to call out, peering into my grandfather's darkness from her well-lit kitchen. "Viens te coucher. Come to bed. On ne le verra plus. We can never see him again. You can't bring him back, mon cher."

"Je le sais. I know."

"Jamais. Never."

"Jamais. Je sais." My grandfather would heave a sigh and hold the pipe aloft in his big hand as though willing its power to intercede for him, pleading with it one last time to grant him the one thing he wanted, the only thing he ever asked for.

"Viens te coucher, Omer." Remembering this ritualized scene and cryptic dialogue, I didn't want to be the dragon anymore. I didn't want the power to interfere with my grandfather's last hold on life…his prayer.

Even as a boy, I understood that my grandparents' intentionally vague exchanges alluded to my father. Tonight, before tomorrow's visit, I wanted my grandfather's prayer to be heard. Tonight, I too prayed for my father's return; but having relinquished my moment of dragon power, I conceded that I couldn't breathe life into that dream anymore than I could conjure up a likeness of my mother, which I'd dared hope might at last put my longing to rest. I decided to go to bed, though I knew I couldn't sleep. I made a conscious effort not to look again at the flickering red light beyond Tyler's Inlet; but as I made my way back through the kitchen to Anna's bedroom, it brandished its dragon breath with blinding brilliance. There was no mistaking the chill in my bones as anything but a warning. I must never forget the dragon.

Face him you must…every day of your life, the Dark Woman whispered, *Dragon, the fearless ancestor of Whale. Every day.* I'd grasped that, just as Whale was responsible for the signs of my destiny buried in primordial mud beneath Great Rainbow Bridge, so he'd been for the lifetime of rainbow implausibilities my grandfather coaxed from Stocking River.

What escaped me then was obvious now: each implausibility, born of my grandfather's love for the river, was but a keen Whale eye, one of the millions of keen eyes scanning both land and sea during the millions of years of Whale's watchful existence. I understood that my grandfather was indeed a magician. That his prayers were always heard. That Whale's practiced eye gleamed from the volcanic ash of his meerschaum bowl. That a single neuron of Dragon's fire ensconced in a frail ember of Whale's glance would prove potent enough to illuminate any invisible path and resurrect any lost dream. These were the truths revealed in the mud beneath the Great Rainbow Bridge that I consigned to secrecy at the Dark Woman's behest.

The radiance of the moonless night lifted every whiteness of Anna's room from shadow and made it glow. Translucent scarves floated on the black sea of dresser, highboy and night stand. Luminous sheets set the slice of bed nearest the window adrift on a tide of starlight. Anna remained a part of the darkness until I approached and found her stretched, naked, the full length of the bed. Only gradually, as I watched her, did the stars reveal her whiteness, easing it out of anonymity that I might savor its coming to light and to life. Despite the sharp tickle of the night air, Anna lay perfectly still. How beautiful you are, I thought, as the petals of her radiance unfolded with the measured pace of a white rose opening to dawn, almost like the first time I saw her beauty at Trovert Lake. When I lay down beside her, I knew that her fire was as indispensable to my destiny as my grandfather the magician's, as Dragon's. Unexpected sleep, washing over me, set me adrift on the starlit tide.

I woke next morning to anything but peace and the softness of starlight. "What's going on?" I yelled. "Get off!"

"No," Anna whispered, nibbling at my ear.

"Off!"

"No!" I'd been aroused from a rare deep sleep with the distant sound of waves breaking in my head and the weight of Whale
on my chest.

"What are you doing, Anna?"

"Stupid questions don't deserve answers," she whispered
again, wiggling her tongue in my mouth before I was given the
chance to ask a more intelligent question. I shivered with the
weight of Anna's soaking wet body full on me. She'd run directly
from the shower, dripping, and, according to her later, "belly-
flopped on top of me." I vaguely remembered her laughter
mingling with the splash of water in my head and the squish of
her wetness against my body.

"You can't move, can you?" she teased.

"No," I admitted, surrendering at last to her will.

"Good," she said. "Now try this." She slowly penetrated
one surface of skin and soul after another with inebriating laughter, tender kisses and the ecstatic press of her body. Her hair clung
to my face and shoulders; her breasts fastened to my chest; her
legs sucked mine into hers. My resistance fell away, shimmering,
with the fire of her joy.

"You're crazy," I moaned, pulling her even further down
into me.

"I am?" she laughed, her tongue diving for mine. And with
the slightest touch of her fingers, she searched my skin for the
pleasures I'd forsaken for apathy and the desensitization of alcohol. When she finally found the promise of pleasure in a nerve,
my entire body jumped. "Well, what do you know about that!
You're alive."

"I owe it all to you," I replied in earnest, attempting a kiss
through the strands of hair pasted to her lips. I tried in vain to

push her hair aside as the long, wet curls kept springing back between our faces. Anna giggled. "Only one remedy to that," I said, pulling away and rolling her over.

"Oh no you don't," she roared, wrapping her arms around me and scissoring my legs hard with hers. "Come here..." She wrestled me down into her, and we made love until the last star melted into morning.

"I'll have breakfast at the hospital," Anna said, reappearing at the bedroom door, flushed but prim in her starchy white uniform. "Gotta go. See you at your grandmother's after work." We'd prearranged that.

"Okay."

"I'm sure everything will work out between you and your grandfather."

"You may be right, Anna."

"Love you. Bye." I heard the back door close behind her. I'd tried to answer but couldn't.

I stood a long time on Trovert Lake Road, eyeing the nursing home and listening to the bus whir into silence toward the lake where Anna and I first made love. The anomalous presence of a nursing home on this forsaken road compelled me to imagine it had been cut through wilderness expressly to provide the residents of Gaboury's by the Sea with a proper purgatory to abbreviate their stay in the next.

Gaboury's by the Sea sat ten or so miles inland, looking with its white wings and cupola much the great grounded gull utterly and unalterably out of its element. It swiftly brought to mind the Dark Woman's characterization of my father's people. "There is a strain of fierce aloneness in your father's people," she'd said. French Canadian pioneers burrowed into forest wildernesses with the conviction that too many of them would not survive. What was it that drew them into the unknown of their unique solitary destinies? I thought it must be nothing more or less than a home in a place after their own hearts, the only compass to show the way.

What hidden motive beyond proximity and French ancestry had prompted my grandfather to dead-end his days here? A home and a peace that had eluded him the last twenty or more years of his life? A purgatory in which to make amends for the sins he'd been careful to hide but was now prepared to confess? I shook my head and started up the concrete walk that divided the lawn into two equal rectangles. "There's something wrong," I heard myself mumbling. Then, in a surprisingly loud clear voice, I heard myself ask, "How can anyone expect to find his father in a place like this?"

The question was far more disturbing than the place. Finding my father here or anywhere had been the furthest thing from my mind. "What am I doing here amid this desolation?" I heard my voice ask from a distance far greater than any before. "How can anyone be expected to find a father in a garden where vines, flowers, bushes and trees are forbidden to grow? Where there are no wind-blown sea shadows to soften the glare of a seagull's motionless bald head and stunted wings?" When I passed into the still shadow of the main portico, I felt the sun take sudden drastic leave of me. I shivered violently.

In the foyer of Gaboury's by the Sea, I was greeted by a warmth profoundly different from that which had wafted through bus windows from the sunlit bay, soothing my anxieties and uplifting my spirits. By jarring contrast, this was the warmth of stagnation that compressed walls and transformed the sprawl of red carpet into bloody lens from which everything appeared exceedingly hostile and dangerous. I flinched when the enormous lead crystal chandelier began to sway, threatening to break loose from its mighty anchorage. "Beware, young dreamer. There are no fathers to be found here. Go before it is too late. No fathers here…No fathers there…No fathers…fathers…anywhere."

"Nurse," I called out to a gray-haired woman sitting at the nursing station. She was writing and didn't look up. "Nurse."

"I'm sorry," she said. "Had to finish that note. May I help you?"

"I'm here to see Mr. Têtreault. Omer Têtreault."

"We weren't expecting anyone this morning," she declared from her island. "Visiting hours usually don't start until noon."

"I'm his grandson. My grandmother told me you'd be expecting me."

"Oh yes," she said apologetically. "You've not been here before, have you?"

"No."

"He's taken a turn for the worse in the last couple of days. I want you to be prepared."

"Thank you."

"Just a minute," she said, sounding like the harsh voices in the foyer. "I'll get someone to show you to your grandfather's room." She whispered into the phone, which seemed the only tenuous connection to the breath and stir of the outside world. For some seconds I experienced difficulty breathing. Now that I'd begun to appreciate the magic he wrought in my life, my fishing buddy Pépère was going to die.

When an orderly left me alone at the door of my grandfather's room, it appeared empty. A soft wheezing emerged from the other side of the curtain which divided the room in two. I was immobilized by a terror disproportionate to the sound and seized by the specter of my Pépère dying before he'd been able to unburden himself of his secret.

I listened for another soft wheeze but there was none; I waited, paralyzed in that dark passage of not knowing, for some reassurance, until at long last it came. Then, I waited a while longer, not so much the captive of my fear than of the realization, slowly emerging from the depths of our alienation, that my grandfather had become my Pépère again. I noticed some photographs standing in a row atop the dresser. Though I was too far away to make the pictures out, I recognized them immediately by their frames. The large one in the gilt frame was of my grandparents and me when I was about ten years old. The small black-and-white in the faded cardboard frame was of my father, David, when he was almost nineteen. I remembered my father's age because my grandfather had associated it with the year Jackie Robinson broke into the Majors. My grandfather took the picture in July; my father turned nineteen in September.

Recalling with a pang of regret that my grandfather had never taken me to a baseball game, I ventured beyond the curtained barrier to see what my Pépère had finally become. I gasped to discover a skeletal form sitting in the corner by the window, breathing laboriously from the oxygen that fed him life through dingy plastic tubing. This was not my Pépère, the man of the broad face and noble jaw who'd exerted such power for both good and evil over me. Staring back unflinchingly, this man wore a pressed, dark blue suit that hung loose and long-sleeved on him. My grandfather of old dressed formally for every occasion of living, whether for going to church, doing custodial work at the courthouse, mowing the lawn, trimming bushes, tending the garden, painting the house or praying his pipe. In this respect, he hadn't changed at all. Tenacious mast shrouded by a lax and windless sail, my grandfather stuck out a bony hand and motioned me forward.

Wary of meeting his gaze, I looked around while I walked toward him. Prominent from my point of view were the oxygen canister to which he was tethered for breath, and the rocking chair from which the bellows of remorse once breathed relentless fire into his prayer. The soft wheeze was gone; my grandfather's breath, restored. Avoiding his eyes still, I examined his hands, one resting on each knee, thinner than I'd expected but not as frail as they first appeared. I was almost tempted to smile when he lifted one from his knee and laid it on the bed as a signal for me to come and sit.

"Pépère." When he raised a finger to his lips, I knew I wasn't to say another word. I sat down on the bed. On the bus ride over, I imagined him the giant he'd always been—sedated for pain perhaps—but nevertheless robust and whole. There was no giant before me now, but a man determined not to die until he told the truth.

"Thomas, j'ai de quoi te dire. Ecoute moi bien. There's something I must tell you. Listen to me." His voice was barely audible from weakness but so firm in its resolve that it projected power. Finding the nerve to look at my grandfather, I saw through his dying eyes to sun-drenched fields and woodlands beyond the inadequate looking glass of his large bay window. I saw hidden waterways from which my grandfather's ancestors, the "coureurs de bois" ventured in search of elusive destinies. My seeing, their legacy, placed my footsteps and heartbeats in theirs. Could what I saw be real?

As real as anything you have ever seen before, godson, the Dark Woman whispered. *Otherwise, how could you be expected to find the singular path on which your mother's and your father's people met, the sturdy back of the same dear River Whale?* She laughed softly. *Very, very real. Do not doubt it for a minute.*

As I watched my French Canadian ancestors with the clarity of my grandfather's final vision, I could hear them shouting, whispering and cursing through the forest mazes of their dreams. I clung to their language, my grandparents', as my grandfather to the oxygen he was dependent on to express what he'd striven to conceal.

"Thomas, merci pour être venu me voir. Merci. Thank you for coming to see me," he translated. "I wasn't sure you would come."

"I'm glad I'm here, Pépère," I said.

"I have something I must say to you. It will be hard for me to say and it will be hard for you to hear. I regret only that I didn't have the courage to tell you a long time ago. My silence hurt both your Mémère and me, but I know it hurt you even more." He didn't lower his eyes but shifted them slowly from me to the photographs on the dresser. He fixed upon one of the pictures with the concentration of an eagle eyeing its prey.

"What is it?" My grandfather remained silent for longer than I could bear and made no further attempt to look at me. He'd given his soul over, it seemed, to something beyond the photograph that he could not have back. My grandfather, skeletal, straight-backed, translucent in the sun, spoke.

"Mon enfant, j'ai quelque chose d'horrible à vous dire." No translation this time. I was moved not only by the startling power in his voice but by his calling me "his child" for the first time in my life. "Your Papa was a good son. He would have made you a wonderful father. There is nothing I regret more than not having told him so. When you used to ask me about him, I said nothing. I regret that too...more than you will ever know." With the prey no longer a hapless cod in the shallow but my Pépère's own stubborn pride, I saw the eagle, eyes of his remorse, drop through layers of sunshine, cloud and branch to snatch the last of his obstinacy in the face of a feeble protest. "I made your Mémère promise never to tell you about your Papa. This was for her the agony of mon Jésus crucifié...especially as you grew older and wanted to know." Though my grandfather's words were excruciatingly slow in coming, they were driven by a dire compulsion to confess until every last one had been spoken.

"He did not run off to sea, Thomas." A soft wheeze recurred, the first since he'd begun speaking. "He could never have done that to you." I knew then, without him having to say so, that he was talking to his son, David. Tears glistened in the sunshine of a time and an opportunity lost. Yet eyes and words refused to waver. "Your Papa never left Ingram. He died and was buried here shortly after you were born." The stab of pain in my heart couldn't have been anything but the piercing of my grandfather's by that eagle vision that bore him swiftly off to that other time and place. I grasped at the reflection of Great Rainbow Bridge in my Pépère's eyes, but it vanished before I could hold its healing light to his agony.

"Why, Pépère? Why didn't you tell me?" Tears trickled grudgingly down into the hollows of his cheeks. "Why?"

"David is buried in St. Anne's Cemetery at the top of the hill. He has a small stone there under the big willow tree." The distance that clouded my grandfather's eyes told me he was there now, at the top of the hill, by the small stone under the big willow tree. "He can watch the river from there." It occurred to me that if his eyes grew any more distant, he would die.

"Thomas," he said on the farthest turn of that distance, "your Papa took his own life." There on the hill by the small stone under the willow with his son, David, watching the river go by. I tore my eyes away from my grandfather's. "C'est ma faute, Thomas, my fault. I could not admit it then...but I do now. Ma faute. He wanted to marry your mother but I opposed. He killed himself. Forgive me, David." Though my body could not move, the fierce part of me that did not want to hear the truth fled the room in a panic to hide in the heart of the wilderness where not even my ancestors would think to find me. How long I was away I couldn't say; but when I came back, it was with the realization that the ferocity of an eagle's eye never ferrets the dark for a place to hide, but for the light of life's most unforgiving truths. So I returned to find my Pépère's gaze transfixed by his son's in the faded photograph. "Forgive me, mon Thomas." The supernatural power of his voice, once delivered of its secret, trailed into extinction.

"I will try, Pépère. I will try." Relieved to find that the old hatred did not rush back to consume me, I was confident I could one day forgive him because I knew there was a part of me that loved him. We had nothing further to say. Exhausted, he lowered his head and resumed the regular soft wheeze. I detected a rasp creep into it. My Pépère won't be here for long, I thought. I rose from the bed, placed my hand on the fragile blade of his shoulder and kissed him goodbye in the hollow of his cheek.

When a dragonfly dies, the Dark Woman said, *its light does not. Cherish its carcass as you would your life and it will bear you visions.*

"Goodbye, Pépère." He was breathing comfortably. His silence told me he was grateful I'd come.

"Suicide." When he pronounced the word, how could such clarity, I wondered, issue from that disembodied voice?

In the foyer, I was stopped by something I'd missed on my way in. Under the chandelier stood a sculpture of a whale disgorging Jonah in the high polish of gray-pink stone indigenous to the coastal region. The representation, reminder of the purity of expression that had emanated from my grandfather's gauntness, stabbed my heart again. I stood paralyzed by the same helplessness with which Jonah was being catapulted into the unknown by Leviathan's breath held to bursting at the bottom of the sea. I saw my grandfather's bright hands surge upward through the dark sea and conjure from air rainbow eyes to light dangerous paths.

While I found the heat oppressive when I stepped outside, Gaboury's by the Sea no longer seemed the grounded gull of my arrival. It was more a spirit at rest, awaiting a favorable breeze to lift it seaward to its natural home. I intended the walk to my grandmother's to serve as a distraction from my grandfather's revelations, but the more energy I expended, the more taken I became with the thought of death. I was content to know that my father had committed suicide and that my grandfather was about to die. Death came as the intoxicant, ragweed, to persuade me that its transcendence was the only truth that mattered. It made me feel light-headed; I flew with the ease of the eagle.

At the top of the hill, I stood not only to catch my breath but to follow the crooked line of the street as far as I could through the city below, recalling how many of its bars I'd frequented when I sought out death. Uninvited, it came today as ether, filling me with the lightness to travel other worlds. As tokens of its most recent visitation, it left me with the carcass of a dragonfly, and the urge to visit my father's grave in St. Anne's Cemetery.

Huge, the dragonfly was held aloft by slender blades of grass in a vacant lot between Kettle Street and Stocking Boulevard. It was a marker of sorts, indicating that I was passing from one plane to another. Threshold. Dragonfly. Dried by the sun. Carcass. Before I left my grandfather, the Dark Woman had instructed me regarding Dragonfly.

"Cherish its carcass as you would your life," she'd said, "and it will bear you visions." No visions now, I thought, just a dead and useless thing. I remembered by contrast the beauty of the large dragonfly that appeared on the porch screen of Tyler House. It had been on fire with rainbows. That was a vision; this, a dead-end.

"Ferme ta bouche. You're scaring the fish away. Shut your mouth," I could hear my grandfather caution from the silence on the river, "or the sewing needle's going to shut it for you." Nothing annoyed him more, I recalled, laughing aloud, than a chatterbox at river's edge. Dragonfly. Marker. Reminder that my Pépère would be, from this time forward, party to my journey on the Whale Way. My eyes were drawn to the insect as they had been to my grandfather's lure dropping on target the moment silence had been restored. Was it that same silence that enfolded me now and enabled me to see that the "carcass" was intact from bulbous head to tip of striated body? That its double wings dripped sunlight from their delicate honeycombs? That by their contemplation, my mind was emptied of everything but Dragonfly?

To cherish is to become one with, spoke the Dark Woman from the Silence before the River. But even before she spoke, Dragonfly had superimposed its body on mine. From the crisp blackness of its carcass, Dragonfly called upon the inevitable and sunlit needle of my grandfather's death to trace and bind our two destinies together. Line for line, the two of us, one. The honeycomb of its wings were a match to every cell in my body. Its reality mine, its vision mine, both of us became my father's black coffin to be held aloft by slender blades of grass till our final transformations by this same sun beyond all brittleness and decay. "Cherish," I repeated. We drifted apart again, Dragonfly and I, like a cloud often did from the river at the touch of a distant wind.

7

By Way of "The Sweeney"

My feet dragged as I passed beneath the iron arch of St. Anne's Cemetery gate to look for my father. I used to come here with my grandmother when she came to pray at her brother Charles's grave. She never asked my grandfather to come with her because, for reasons she was careful not to disclose, he and my great-uncle didn't get along. It had been a pleasure for me to escort my Mémère halfway up the hill to a small grove of blue spruce where her favorite brother lay. "How I loved Charles," she'd say each time. "I will never forget him. Jamais. Jamais. He was so good to me." I never refused to go because I knew how much the visit meant to her. This time, though, I walked among the spruces to Uncle Charles's grave with a heavy heart.

I knelt in the grass as my grandmother and I had always done to pray for "Charles Pomerleau, époux, père, frère bien-aimé, né 1894, décédé 1957." I remembered him, but only vaguely, since I was five years old when he died. I remembered his bald head and how, every time I shook his hand, a shiny quarter would appear in mine. Reading his epitaph made me think of my grandmother's maiden name, Véra Pomerleau. She'd actually had a life before she met and married my grandfather. Strange thought; she'd never been anything but Mémère to me. What was she like when she was a little girl and a young woman? With a yearning, unexpected and profound, I wondered what my mother had been like. "Why did she have to die?" I asked my Uncle Charles, sleight-of-hand artist par excellence, trusting—as my Mémère did—that he would know the answer.

It occurred to me, as I resumed my climb up the hill, that, when Mémère came to pay her respects to Uncle Charles, she spent the better part of her considerable time there talking with her son, David. How hard it must have been to conceal his grave site and the fact of his death from me. How did my grandparents manage to hide from me what everybody else in town must have known? How could I explain their conduct as anything but the desperate device of shame?

I was attracted to the stone wall at the summit as it not only overlooked the river, but signaled by its strange compelling invitation the beginning of the Whale Way. It became evident to me, with my unobstructed view of "The Sweeney," that the sadness I experienced upon entering the cemetery was my own secret shame.

How easy it had been to blame my grandfather for everything—a difficult habit to break. But I must, I thought. I must. *Well now, that is a beginning,* the Dark Woman remarked with acrid sweetness. Tempering her sarcasm, she added, *Yet another threshold and another choice. Yes, this is a good beginning, my dearest blockhead godson.* She laughed uproariously. Though the descent into the valley was entirely tree-covered, I recognized landmarks on the other side of the river.

The bright red sawmill, fronted by flat barges laden with logs, marked the beginning of a cove where my grandfather caught cod. No one else caught cod on the river. *Whenever you find yourself blaming others, especially your grandfather, look to the other side of the wall. The truth has a way of riding upstream currents. The other side. Remember.* The Dark Woman laughed again. This time her laughter didn't fade but lingered like delicate wind chimes in the breezes.

Turning from the wall, I found the willow at once even though the laughter had ceased, leaving only a tremor in the slender leaves as a token of her passage. It was the largest in the area, a lofty fountain with a slight tilt to the right for having been squeezed from the other side over the years by what had become a gigantic Norwegian pine.

I walked into the sacred precinct of its shadow. Though it was only the end of July, fallen yellow leaves gilded the tombstones. The River's voice, unerring, led me to my father's grave. No need to read the inscription on the gray-pink stone to know it was so. Like my Mémère at Uncle Charles's grave, I knelt down in grass and willow leaves to pray. Sitting back on my haunches, I closed my eyes and prayed the only way I knew how. By listening, as I always had, to the voice of the River. To what depths the River committed my unspoken prayer that afternoon I couldn't tell; the deep numbness in my thighs told me I'd been on a long and wearying journey. While I leaned against my father's stone, waiting for strength to return, I read his headstone for the first time: "David Têtreault, son of Omer and Véra, father of Thomas, born 9-6-28, died 4-12-52." I touched the engraving and then walked back to the graveled path. How painful it must have been, I thought, as I plodded down the hill, for my grandfather to keep the cross-current truth of the River so devoutly to himself.

I couldn't imagine what I'd say to my grandmother. The image of a shrunken man in a rocking chair pervaded the clouding-up of the afternoon, like one of St. Anne's grimacing gargoyles. How could I have taken such pleasure, as an altar boy, in those gray demons with their malevolent and mirthless eyes? Perhaps because they were the only gargoyles in town, and they belonged to us. The French church had them! We, ostracized and unappreciated Frenchmen, were the only people with daring enough to display the incarnation of evil from the cornices of our defiance and our favor with the Tout-Puissant, Almighty God.

I started at the reappearance of the old chauvinism learned

from my hero, infallible guardian of Superior Court and paragon of fishermen. But "French church" was an expression that evoked forgotten pride and warrior passions. How many boyhood fights had I thrown myself into for being called "frog" or "stupid puddle-jumper."

"Thomas," my grandmother called through the screen door. "Why don't you come in now? It's raining. Viens, cher." I lifted my face to the large raindrops, relishing their coolness after the oppressive heat. "Viens, cher," Mémère insisted, extending her hand. My approach to the house was as tentative as to my father's grave. Anna was waiting in the kitchen.

"Tom," Anna cried. She rose from the chair by Pépère's window. "Tom," she repeated when I didn't answer, putting her arms around me. "Are you okay?" she asked with tears in her eyes.

"Sure," I held her tight and kissed her forehead. My grand-mother sat down in my old place by the second window. "I'm fine," I reassured Anna, gesturing for her to resume her place in my grandfather's chair while I brought another and sat beside her. She took my hand.

"You saw your Pépère?" my grandmother asked after a tense silence.

"Yes, Mémère, I did. You were right...he is dying."

"I will go to him. But it was so important to him that he see you first. Did he...?"

"Yes." I felt Anna's body quiver and turn toward me. Though I focused on my grandmother's eyes, I sensed Anna's, deep blue sapphire, prepared to embrace our anguish. "He told me that my father had killed himself...that he was gone."

"Mon cher." Mémère held fast to my eyes, as had my grand-father to the photograph of his dead son. It was much easier for me to accept my grandfather's silence than it was to understand hers. My grandfather, giant of my youth reduced to a pitiable stick man, was paying the price for his silence. And why shouldn't she?

"Oui, mon Thomas, he took his own life."

"How?" I demanded.

"Your Pépère didn't tell you?"

"No."

"Mon enfant, ton papa s'est échoué…" Becoming aware in mid-sentence that her emotion had taken her into her native French, she stopped and turned to Anna. "I'm sorry," she whispered. She paused and drew a long breath before returning to me. "Thomas," she said in a clear steady voice, "your father jumped from the Sweeney Bridge…into the river."

"My God," Anna exclaimed, letting go my hand and bringing hers in horror to her face.

"You didn't know?" I turned on Anna.

"No, Tom. How could I?" She appeared shaken by the intensity with which I asked my question. Detecting the hurt in her voice, I turned from predator to prey, the cod fish hunted by the eagle, hot with the enervation of flight and cold with an ocean current of danger and deceit from which I could not escape. Is this what the Dark Woman meant when she said that the truth came by way of upstream currents? Against the grain? I was overwhelmed that my father had died in the river I loved. Numbness infiltrated my body like water soaking into driftwood. Searching frantically for safety in the turbulence, the cod was stopped by the sudden thrust of hidden hook.

"Did they find…?"

"Oui," Mémère answered before Anna could finish her question. "They found his body two days later." The tears welled. After a long uneasy silence, Mémère continued. "They found your Papa's body, mon David, in the rocks on the Riverton side of the river. We had a private wake and funeral for him…seulement la famille." My grandmother's tears flowed freely. "We had a terrible time with Father Etienne," she continued. "As soon as he heard that your Papa had taken his own life, he didn't want a church funeral and he didn't want to bury David in St. Anne's Cemetery either."

Anna shook her head. How did she stay so calm? I saw her shine in her white cotton dress against the grayness of a rainy afternoon. Saw her auburn hair caress her shoulders like a sunset flame, day's last headland. Saw her graceful chin jut up and out in protest of priest and dogma. There was nothing angelic about Anna; she was as solid as the well-rooted tree we by chance find alone in a clearing, unremarkable at first, but leaving us with a haunting memory of a particular time and place.

"Si ton oncle, Charles, n'avait pas intervenu…" My grandmother spoke in French again. "It was Charles who talked to Père Etienne and finally made him change his mind."

"How?"

"Charles was an active and influential member of the parish." My grandmother's face lit up. "Though he lived all his married life in Riverton, he remained faithful to the parish where, like you, Thomas, he went to parochial school and served as an altar boy."

"What did he do to get the priest to change his mind, Mémère?" I persisted.

"Your cousin George's garage—that belonged to his father; Charles built the business. He made a good deal of money and was generous to the church."

"So he twisted the priest's arm a little?"

"Not a little. Beaucoup," my grandmother answered with pride. Tears glistened in her blue eyes, like great diamonds.

"I thank him for that," I said.

"There is more, Thomas."

"What is it?" Suddenly the flowered curtains in both windows blew in and a dark deluge swept through the screen into the kitchen. I ran to shut one window while Anna leaned into the squall of the other, bringing the pane down with a sharp thud.

"Sorry," Anna shouted too loudly in the quiet after the bang. She was drenched.

"Thomas," my grandmother went on, staring through me, "ta mère…your mother is still alive." She waited for us to recover from shock.

In the sudden darkness, I felt compelled to register my grandmother's every expression and turned on the overhead fluorescent lights. First one tube, then the other, crackled out bright spasms to mirror the emotional dislocations of the day. In the light, I saw my grandmother's eyes, overwhelmed by the pain she saw in mine, wanting in the will to continue.

"Mémère, you know I love you. It's okay. Go ahead."

Heartened by my words, she nodded. "Thomas, ta maman est venue du Canada." French words, idiom of my grandmother's deepest emotion, struggled for expression against the conditioning of long-suffering silence. "Elle est Indienne." As long as it had taken my grandmother to speak the words, it took my incredulity even longer to grasp them. Indian? Once grasped, the realization leaped from my mouth with the assurance of a truth long known.

"Indian."

"Oui."

"Well, where is she?"

"Je ne sais pas...I do not know." My grandmother's hands began to tremble.

"You don't know where in Canada she came from?"

"Non." I was fighting to stay calm.

"Mémère," Anna interceded, "do you know how Tom's mother came to be here?"

"By bus...the year before Thomas was born. Le mois de Marie...in May. En pèlerinage...they were on their way to a shrine in New Hampshire, je crois. That is what Thomas's Pépère told me.

"What were they doing down here?" I interrupted testily. "That's a hell of a detour! What were they doing in Massachusetts? In Ingram, of all places?"

"Your Pépère said something about a church in Lindsey they wanted to see...a church named after a holy Indian girl."

"Do you know the church, Anna?" I asked.

"No."

"Do you know the name of the church, Mémère?"

"No." Though answers were not forthcoming, I heard the hardness in my voice begin to dissolve at the discovery of another glimpse of the Whale Way.

"But that should be easy enough to find out. Maybe somebody there knows something about that pilgrimage and where the people came from."

"I know you'll find her," Anna said with the conviction of one who'd foreseen the miracle of my recovery.

"Mémère, do you know my mother's name?"

"Non, mon enfant, je ne le connais pas. No, I don't," she translated, glancing over at Anna.

"Do you know how my father and mother met?" The sun set the diamond crystal ablaze in the window behind my grandmother before I realized it had stopped raining. With its constant spinning, the crystal set in motion bright moons and stars to reveal that secret moment in time when lovers first met. "Where did they meet?"

"You know that little rest area on Stocking Boulevard? Not far from the bridge?"

"Yes.

"There."

"How?" I was driven to find a mother thought all my life to be dead, while having lost a father believed for just as long to be alive.

"Your papa was coming home from work one evening along the river, like you used to. He called it 'the shortcut.'" She smiled through her tears at the thought of how far out of his way my father actually went to follow the river bank.

"From George's garage?"

"Oui, justement. Yes."

"Some shortcut!" I was talking to Anna. "My cousin's garage is down on the corner of Kettle and Friend." She nodded she knew it.

"Exactement," my grandmother replied with that tone of

innocent smugness that comes with recognition. "Like you! Didn't you call your walking along the river a 'shortcut'?" Anna smiled knowingly. "You told me that many times when you came home late at night. N'est-ce-pas?"

"I was teasing you."

"Your Papa was teasing too. He teased me all the time." She laughed, remembering. Her hands had stopped trembling. "'What took you so long?' I would ask him when he came home late for supper. 'I took the shortcut,' he would say. Then, he would wink and give me a kiss. You both would have loved him," my grandmother said wistfully.

"What happened that day, Mémère?" I asked.

"Usually he would climb up the bank into the backyard. But that day, he came home by the Boulevard."

"He tell you why?"

"'I met someone,' he said. C'est tout." Bright tears appeared with her reminiscence like dewdrops in the morning sun. "George taught your Papa to fix cars. He became a good mechanic."

"Why didn't anybody ever tell me that?"

"Thomas, later your Papa told me about her. 'She was eating a sandwich under a great big birch tree,' he said. 'Didn't even look up at me when I went by.'"

"What did she look like?" I asked.

"Young and beautiful. 'Beautiful,' he would say, winking and teasing. She had long shiny black hair."

"They must have talked to each other?"

"Not right away. Your Papa said he put his foot up on a picnic bench and made believe he was lacing his boot, but all the time he was watching her. 'She didn't look at me once,' he said, smiling and shaking his head."

"And?"

"He finally got up the nerve to talk to her." Reliving the past, Mémère stared past Anna and me to tremulous images, desperate to hold them as long as possible. I wondered if my grandfather had been able to embrace my father long enough this afternoon to receive his son's pardon, so that he could die in peace. "The leaves were just coming out in the birch tree," my grandmother remembered, "soft, delicate green... Eyes, deep brown... Beautiful brown eyes..." Her voice faded.

"Did you ever see her, Mémère?"

"Oui, Thomas. I saw her once."

"When?" Anna's gentle pressure on my arm urged me to respect my grandmother's obvious distress.

"She came with your Papa a little while after you were born, one terrible night in March. You were hardly a month old. It was snowing hard. When I opened the door, they were shivering so. Pauvres enfants! 'Come in, come in out of the cold,' I told them. I did not see you at first in the dark, mon Thomas, and your Papa had you bundled up so, I couldn't find your dear face until he brought you inside and your mother pulled the blankets away. You in your blue snowsuit. Red, red cheeks. Quelle merveille!"

"You saw my mother..."

"Oui. She was more beautiful than I had thought. Her eyes were full of love for you. Such deep brown eyes." My grandmother closed her eyes, trying to remember. "Brown eyes...almost black. Like yours."

"Did she say anything?"

"Non." Her hands trembled again.

"Your Papa was so proud of you, he wanted to show you to your Pépère. When he carried you into the kitchen, your mother and I followed and stood in the doorway. Your grandfather was playing solitaire there in his place...right where you are sitting, Anna. 'Bon soir, Papa,' your father said. Pépère would not look at him. He would not answer. He kept playing cards until, when your Papa would not go, he took his pipe out of his mouth and put it on the table."

"I know exactly what that meant," I said, turning to Anna. "He was going to make one of his stupid speeches."

"Pépère did not even look at you or your Papa. Instead, he turned around, looked at your Maman and said, 'What are you doing in my house? You have your nerve coming here. I'll have no Indian squaw in my house. Putain, you get out and take these two with you.' I never saw your Pépère so full of hatred before. I could not bear to look at your mother. She was crying. I could feel her whole body shaking. It would have done no good for me to try and stop him. That would have only made him worse. You know, Thomas?"

"Yes, Mémère, I know," I said, angered that she had not stood up to my grandfather, but knowing precisely what reprisals she would have been made to endure.

"'I no longer have a son,' he said, 'and this little bastard is no grandson of mine. Take them both with you and get the hell out.'" I couldn't believe how graphically my grandmother retold that night's events until I realized how compelled she must have felt to leave nothing out in her belated effort to make amends. "Not once did he stop looking at your Maman, not once did he look at your Papa and you. When he finished, he put his pipe in his mouth and played the cards."

My grandmother sobbed. I was troubled both by her story and by my reaction to it. Troubled that my grandfather had been so possessed by hatred that he couldn't let himself be touched by his own flesh and blood, by a love obvious to anyone else, and by a desperate need for his acceptance. Anna went around the table to my grandmother and silently held her.

"I looked at your mother before she left and saw her tears. She did not look down. She stood so tall and still...did not look away from him at his cruel words. I loved her then, Thomas. Her eyes so big...almost black...did not move. I loved her then."

"My father..."

"He removed your hood," she interrupted, "and unzipped your little suit. He tried to have your Pépère take you but he wouldn't. Tête de pioche! He would not look at you. Would not... Your Papa did not speak. He held you out to your Pépère for such a long while... Then, he held you so tight in his arms you started to cry. When he turned around, he was crying too. He said only

'Goodbye, Maman,' and kissed me. I wanted to take you in my arms but he wouldn't let you go. I kissed you and your mother... That was the last time I saw my David alive. I never saw your mother again."

The kitchen was swimming in rainbows, fathoming the outer reaches of the cosmos. It was a ballet of frightening beauty. On the brink of permanent exile from life as I knew it, I took hold of the only fixed star in the reeling universe of the moment. It was a star of such simplicity that I almost overlooked it—the anchoring luminosity of a selfless embrace between two women. The silent exchange between Anna and my grandmother, reflection of the light of love between mothers and daughters that had bridged alienation since the beginning of time. How many times had I been reassured in church by the authenticity of a plain wooden statue of Jesus's mother, Mary, embracing her mother, Ann? Perhaps one day I would put my arms around my mother, the wronged young woman my Mémère had loved for her deep unflinching eyes. The room came to rest. My grandmother's tears subsided. Though the sun behind her took her face into the irrevocable shadow of mystery, it shone in the whiteness of her hair with the portent of a small but important revelation.

"Thomas, I remember now."

"What, Mémère?"

"Your Maman's name...I remember it now."

"What is it?" I asked with unexpected restraint.

"C'est Laura."

"Laura? You're sure?"

"I tried so hard and so long to forget...but it came back. Oh, yes, I am certain. It is 'Laura.'"

"You're sure?" I wasn't doubting my grandmother's recollection as much as I sought assurances in the midst of the rapid and unsettling developments of the past few hours.

"Your Papa. He told me. He was so proud to tell me before he followed her to New Hampshire. He said he would find her and they would be married. C'est tout. He borrowed George's car, came home, washed up, changed his clothes and left."

"You don't know where in New Hampshire they were going?"

"No...only that they planned to meet at the shrine where the group would spend the night."

"You don't know what shrine, do you?"

"Non."

"My mother's last name?"

"Oh, non, non. I don't know."

"Don't worry, Mémère. You can bet I'll find her."

8

Dog Star

nna and I rode home in silence. Despite the day's
revelations, I remained calm. At first, I attributed my
tranquil state of mind to shock, but it was clearly
something else. Though it escaped understanding, it was as real as
the love I felt when my grandmother kissed me goodbye.
It evoked the words spoken by the Dark Woman: "Your grandmother, she knows the pain of having lost that which no one can
stand to lose. She would spare you that at the cost of her life." I
sensed, especially from its indescribable warmth, that my equa-
nimity came from the white radiance around the Dark Woman
when she appeared to me on Horseshoe Bay.

"Why didn't my father go to Uncle Charles that night?"
However fraught with sadness, the sudden question was put to
Anna at the calm insistence of the invisible white radiance. "He
would have helped us."

"Shame?" she asked, in keeping with the radiance that sustained us both.

"Yeah." I knew it was so. "And according to Mémère,
nobody saw either one of us till early morning, the twelfth of

"Oh, I do remember. Look," Anna whispered as boats appeared at their moorings, pilings ran erratically after quicksilver trails, and luminous ghosts fluttered in and out.

"Gulls?" I wondered aloud.

"Do you hear that?"

"What?"

"Listen."

"Sea dogs?"

"No. Listen carefully."

"A sea dog?"

"Isn't it beautiful?"

"It sounds sad to me."

"Sad but beautiful," Anna insisted gently.

"I can't believe I never heard them before that night at Tyler House," I said.

"Maybe you weren't listening for them."

"Maybe." The long silence that followed was interrupted by the Dark Woman who, in keeping with the tenor of the night, whispered to the silence in my heart. *No maybe about it, godson. Learn to listen, as you are tonight. Learn to look, as you do tonight. Look to Sirius, the Dog Star whose beauty indeed matches its yearning. For you, it holds a special brightness.* She left as unceremoniously as she had come. My attention turned to the night sky I'd often scanned as a boy for the one bright star that would guide my father home to me.

"He's home now," I said, knowing Anna knew who I meant. "He's come home to the river he loved as much as I do. That's why..." I recalled his gravestone under the big willow. It would take time to put him to rest in my mind, but I drew comfort from the thought that the peace he sought was the essence of our river. "He can see it from there," I mumbled.

"What?"

"Oh, nothing..." Mystery continued to play with the starlight on the bay. "You've never been to Gaboury's, have you, Anna?"

"No."

"There's a statue of Jonah and the whale in the entrance. I didn't notice it till I was leaving. Big as life! I don't know how I missed it."

"You had other things on your mind."

"I guess I did," I said, recalling my disorientation on my way in. "Jonah was being spat out...as though the whale couldn't bear the taste of him. 'Out, squirt, and don't bother me again if you know what's good for you.'" Anna laughed. "Jonah, that's me," I muttered. "Whale can't stand a coward."

The contempt I leveled at myself was real, different from the self-pity that had driven me to lose myself in drink. Its salutary effect was to lure me into that darkness where the peace of the River abides, where the radiance beyond the stars finds its source, and where the memory of Whale keeps its faith with the world. It was a contempt much in keeping with the way the Dark Woman spoke to me...with truth, not flattery or false promise. A contempt that I might get used to and perhaps, one day, consider my friend. A contempt reminiscent of the grating sounds I heard when I began my recovery, sounds of such profound enervation that they could not have emanated from anywhere but that black fathomless retreat where Whale remembered me.

It was the contempt I once heard in my grandfather's own great baritone when he read to me from the Bible before I fell asleep at night. As the thunder of my Pépère's voice before it succumbed, soul-sickened, to silence, contempt rolled through the caverns of a new hearing. It told of the ocean's claim upon my heart long before it had spilled Whale into my dreams. He began always with the sign of the cross. "Au nom du Pére et du Fils et du Saint-Esprit. Ainsi soit-il." In the eloquent silence only the contemplation of stars can induce, I heard him retell the story of Jonah, filling it to dramatic effect with the stentorian thunder or whispers of wind the sacred text called for. Caught up again in my grandfather's melodrama, I imagined Jonah as my childhood hero, sitting in the dark of Whale's belly, regretting the folly that had made him a prisoner of the deep, and ardently praying for his safe return to father and home:

> *"Around me the deadly waters close, the depths engulf me, the weeds are wrapped around my head; mountain caves I must plumb, the very bars of earth my unrelenting prison; and still, O Lord my God, thou wilt raise me, living, from the tomb."*

However theatrically he rendered the scriptures, Pépère never once deviated from them. "Lord my God," he intoned, "thou wilt raise me, living, from the tomb. Au nom du Pére et du Fils et du Saint-Esprit. Ainsi soit-il."

"Tom, you've been so quiet. Everything all right?"

"I don't think I've ever seen the stars so bright."

"Me either."

"I was thinking about my grandfather, Anna. You know that statue I was telling you about?"

"You mean bad old whale spitting out poor old Jonah?"

"Yeah. How he told me that story all the time. It was one of the things he did that made me love him when I was a kid. Tell me stories. Act them out. Water sounds and all…like being on the river with him. I remembered the words—'Thou wilt raise me, living, from the tomb.' I thought I'd never seen him cry but I'll swear he was crying when he got to that part."

"…your father?"

"Yeah…though he never talked about him except when he was drinking and carrying on about my mother."

"He missed him."

"I guess."

"I'm quite sure."

"I don't worry about my father. His dying in the river makes me feel he's always been home…at peace. But my grandfather, I'm worried about him."

"Why?"

"I don't think he can find peace. Not without my help; and if he doesn't find it, I've got the feeling I'll never find it either."

"You really love him, don't you?"

"For so long I thought I didn't. You know what else?"

"What?"

"I think he wanted me to hate him...did everything in his power to make me hate him. I bet he only let me save him from hanging himself so I could learn to hate him more."

"But why?"

"To punish himself for turning my father away; I don't think he could stand himself for doing that. By not killing himself, he condemned himself to a living hell. That's where he is right now."

"Oh, that's terrible."

"I've got a feeling there's something else they're both not telling us that drove him to disown my father."

"Not your mother?"

"I doubt it. I think it's something else that happened long before my mother came along. And I've got a hunch that sooner or later I'm going to find out what it is."

"It must be something very painful for your grandparents to have kept it a secret all these years..."

"But first, I've got to find my mother; not only for my father and me...for Pépère too."

"No matter how he tried not to love his grandson, he couldn't help himself. He did love you." Anna put her arms around me and held me to the eloquent silence of the stars and of an ancient wisdom. "He took you to the courthouse with him, told you stories, taught you to fish and to love the river. The more he learned to love you, the more undeserving he must have felt. That sounds like hell to me."

"Yeah," I sighed. It was an unhappiness we shared, my grandfather and I, though I'd tried so hard to deny our friendship and our shared destiny. For his sake I must find my mother. It was his dearest unspoken wish. One star distinguished itself from the multitude. Anna saw it first.

"Venus. Evening Star," she said.

"Dog Star," I suggested.

Wrong hemisphere, right star, the Dark Woman interjected with the sarcasm I'd grown accustomed to and almost always expected. Anna laughed as though she too had heard and enjoyed my correction. *Dog Star is that star which dogs you, my dear, the light by which you can be seen as you are, the dawn of your rebirth into that family you thought forever lost. Go find your mother, my child.*

9

Seeing-Through

On August fourteen, eve of the Assumption of the Blessed Virgin Mary, and more than three weeks after my visit to Gaboury's by the Sea, I started the search for my mother. Pépère was still alive. It was my conviction that he wouldn't die until he knew the two of us were reunited. That was his way; once decided on a course of action, he didn't flinch until he saw it through. I was reminded of the time when, while trimming the dogwood in the front yard, he fell from a stepladder in an attempt to cut a dead branch my grandmother had warned him was beyond reach. He excised the branch but paid for his pride with a badly sprained ankle. Bound he wouldn't miss a day's work, he stuffed his swollen foot into dress shoe and limped, ramrod-straight, back and forth to the court-house until he willed the ankle back to health. I was certain that he now spent every waking moment steeled against the diminishing oxygen in his blood and the increasing congestion of his lungs, praying the rosary for the success of my pilgrimage.

I hadn't thought of my journey as pilgrimage until I began pondering my mother's reason for coming to this country and the prospect of my grandfather's remorse, the condition of his return to peace. I sensed that time alone on the road would put me on intimate terms with my mother, who'd already undergone the rigors and transformations of pilgrimage.

"You got your lunch?" Anna asked. It was five in the morning.

"Yeah. I already put it in the car." I could have borrowed a car from my cousin, George, but Anna insisted I take hers for the trip.

"Just don't put any dents in it. Promise?"

"Of course," I said.

"Promise!" she repeated. "You do know I don't love you quite as much as I love this car, don't you?" She pushed her belly into mine for emphasis.

"I promise! I promise!" I kissed her in self-defense.

"Kissing me doesn't get you off the hook. No way!" She kissed me back. Tenderly. "You take good care of yourself. Come back safe."

"I will. You sure you'll be okay without the car?"

"You know me. I'll get around." She had many friends; she was resourceful. The hospital was only a block away. I knew she'd manage.

"Sure you don't want to come?"

"We've already been through that. You know I've got to work. Besides, she's your mother; you have to do this alone."

"I know." She patted the passenger side of her shiny red Toyota and leaned through the open window.

"Love you," she said. "I know you'll find her. I'll be waiting to hear from you. Bye." She turned and disappeared into the apartment building before I could reply.

"I love you too," I called out. Before I'd even U-turned and headed down Tyler Street, I missed her. I hadn't felt the full impact of her presence in my life these past weeks until I began to move away from her. Perhaps she'd made a quick exit to make leaving easier for me, because she was never one to shy away from difficult moments. Maybe she'd already felt all those deeper things I would only begin to feel in her prolonged absence.

I remembered the night we'd watched the stars and made love on the dune. Only now, as I approached Bayview Road, did the taste, smell and touch of that night penetrate my weakening defenses, leading me by subtle resonances to some understanding of how much she meant to me. Hearing, taste, smell and touch— they had transformed from powers of observation and discernment to those of a deeper experience and connection. The more distance I put between Anna and me, the more I realized that she wielded both the power of discernment and experience. But today, she was not my Sirius to show me the way but my Venus to draw me, like tide to moon, into a vaster and more intimate harmony. Morning and Evening Star. Woman. As I made my way north with the shimmer of sunrise about to break loose from the horizon, Venus still shone in the east, more woman than star, shaking me with the tenderness of a night, translating my notion of pilgrimage into passion, rekindling the image of cowled monk who bore the great skeleton of light into the darkness of an unknown destiny. She it was who revealed past my mind to my heart the identity of the solitary monk as my own wretched but beloved grandfather.

The image dissolved in the dawn as quickly as it had appeared; but the leitmotif of Pilgrimage, quickened by the apparition of Venus, Woman, took root in my heart just as Venus, Star, was passing from the sky. *From now on, godson, prepare for an uprooting the likes of which you have never known. For terrors from which I would keep you if I could but from which no pilgrim of any world can escape. Do not despair, however, for you now have your stars to draw and guide you from one threshold to the next, from one choice to the next. The difficulty will reside, as always in life, with what choice to make in the midst of profound uprootings and their consequent bedevilments. For who then, in dire circumstances, can always tell at a glance comet from Dog Star, friend from foe, reality from illusion? And as I have told you so many times, at the risk of turning you away from my instruction, the choice belongs to no one but you. What you will need on this journey, above all else, is to trust your heart. Do this and you will be guided north by your polar star into the southern sky of the Dog who barks the mystery of your River Whale and the light of your grandfather's peace. Trust.*

The Dark Woman's words paled in the brilliance of gold let loose at last by the horizon to flood Horseshoe Bay and electrify "The Sweeney," which loomed ahead. Silence prevailed as Anna's Toyota rolled smoothly onward and familiar sights made their gentle appearances like morning glories opening to sunlight. With a slight trepidation, I approached the bridge from which my father hurtled to his death. It would be my first time crossing since I'd learned of the suicide. Gulls, blindingly white in the bridge's radiance, hovered about the towers and glided along the sweep of cables and between guide wires, more like blossoms than sparks. In keeping with the cloudless composure of the sunrise and my abiding conviction that my father had found peace, the bridge was serene. Bearing no traffic, it floated above the river like the only luminous cloud in the sky. The Dark Woman had introduced me to the idea of Rainbow Bridge, but there was so little yet in my experience with which to convert the abstraction into excitement. When I reached the Riverton side of the bridge, I felt guilty that I'd not felt more of its beauty and serenity. Was I letting my father and grandfather down?

One thing at a time, godson. One thing at a time. Trust.

The Dark Woman's encouragement offered no relief and my disappointment in myself manifested as a profound lethargy of mind and body that closed my eyes and set me swerving from the road.

Wake up, godson, she shrieked in a high-pitched otherworldly voice I hadn't heard before. *Wake up!* The shriek stabbed me in the heart, causing me such pain that I jerked awake to rescue myself from the precipitous descent of rocky escarpment to the river.

It's begun, she said.

"What?" I asked, my heart pounding.

The Uprooting, my dear. From now on, you must be vigilant. You must be prepared with the vigilance of a pilgrim. Never in your life have you confronted anything like this. The Uprooting will attack your faculties singly or simultaneously, moving you from one plane to another with such violence or subtlety, with such rapidity or gradualness, that you will not detect it until you are undone. I will not always be able to intervene. Your only true protection is the trust you put in your heart.

"I'll try," I said weakly.

It was fitting that you crossed the bridge of your father's passage alone. A pilgrim's way is solitary. There is no other way. The Uprooting is necessary but very dangerous. Beware, my Thomas. Pray to your mother and her People. They will teach you to find the south of your grandfather's peace by going the north of your Uprooting. Trust.

The pain of the preternatural shriek had penetrated to the back of my head and lingered as dull ache and reminder of the Dark Woman's unequivocal warning. I was wide awake again and wary of danger. About a half hour into the drive north on a Riverton country road, I rolled down both windows as the air was warming quickly. A glance at the map of New England spread out on the passenger seat indicated I'd be in New Hampshire in another fifteen minutes.

Since my resolution to find my mother, Anna and I had spent many hours conjecturing where in Canada she might be. Though our rummaging in the library uncovered a creditable collection of Native American history and supplied us with a wealth of information about the Indian nations of central and eastern Canada, it brought us no closer to selecting a location for a productive search. Without the identity of my mother's nation, where could I hope to look in Canada? Persuaded by our only clue that my mother had come to Ingram by way of a New Hampshire shrine, we decided to identify some of that state's most popular Catholic sanctuaries. When Anna learned from a library guidebook that one of the nearest and most frequented was directed by the La Salette fathers in Enfield, that's where I decided to begin.

I was heading northwest. When the sharp swing of a hillside wrested "The Sweeney" and the river from the rear-view mirror, I felt that I'd lost touch with the ground and with whatever it was that made me believe my efforts could bridge the chasm of my grandfather's despair. I sensed that the Uprooting had begun in earnest and that I was as much alone in the world as I'd ever been. I began to worry too that I'd heard the last of the Dark Woman whom I once fervently wished out of my life, but who had become such a part of it as friend and mentor that it frightened me to think I might lose her.

Uprooting wears many masks. Do not underestimate its powers. Do not draw conclusions too readily as that will lower your guard and leave your soul unprotected. Uprooting was a being...a person. A Power. *True,* she added with quiet reverence. *Ancient Power that shook the thralldom of the land for the freedom of the sea. Be alert but not afraid, for Uprooting can never be your enemy.*

"I thought I'd never hear your voice again."

I can understand how you might think so since you have entered the sphere of the Uprooting and the vortex of its bedevilments. Though I may not always be able to help you, do not doubt my presence or my allegiance to you.

"Anna!" I called out without knowing why.

You are right, godson, to think of her love as the ground of your deeper entry into the mystery of your People and of your soul. Do not doubt her either. She is bridge to your mystery as you are bridge to your grandfather's peace. A wind rose from the stillness of fields in the east to push firmly against the resistance of will, and subsided into the stillness of trees in the west. In the silence that followed, the Dark Woman spoke from a place far deeper and more serene than ever before. *Understand, my dear godson, that not only to meet but to accept Uprooting in the guise of wind or stagnant pool is the condition of your 'seeing-through.'*

"Seeing through what?" I smiled as I heard my question

arise not from smugness or sarcasm but, in keeping with the silence, from a novel disposition to learn.

Through surfaces, through illusions to the truth of the heart to which Anna and your Mémère are devoted and from which you and your grandfather have unfortunately endeavored to escape. But that will change, will it not, godson?

"Yes," I answered without hesitation.

As I drove through the Massachusetts countryside, I wondered if Anna always saw the way I was beginning to see trees, fields and what seemed to be a pond coming into view with the bend in the road. Under a bright sky, everything slipped past with ease. Objects were familiar, existing as part of my awareness long before I was born.

Uprooting, she said. *As irksome and disorienting as it can sometimes be, it has a way of presenting things as they truly are. It makes both stranger and the strange familiar; for that is what they are. It turns hostile face and land into asylum. With it nothing begs attention, for everything finds a place in the heart. Shiny penny and worn. Polished stone and rough. Uprooting restores to the disillusioned eye the original connections, my dear blockhead. Each block of lowly wood or stone finds another. So you will. And what are bridges for?* The Dark Woman laughed. It was then I knew for certain that she would be along for the ride. *What are pilgrimages for?* Her laughter was of chimes from a nearby willow.

"Trust?" I asked.

Yes.

"I hope I can."

In darkness and in storm, you will always find a hardness of earth to receive your tentative resolve. Take the step you least want to...just as you reached across the unfathomable river for your grandfather's hand. In so doing, you, in your turn, will bridge the danger of its mystery for him. From this moment on, I would be haunted by familiarities that, by the Dark Woman's account, ought to have reassured me but only led to my further bewilderment.

Farm houses appeared at infrequent intervals, sometimes

alongside the road, but more often in the distance. Cows grazed on hillside pastures. A yellow tractor slid downhill between corn-fields in grooves made wavy by a cascade of hills. Bobs and blurs of bright color showing through thicknesses of green stalk belonged, I presumed, to the corn pickers. Crows, perched with edgy blackness at the fringes of the picking, waited, I recognized with unnerving familiarity, for the pickers to go away. Suddenly the crows cawed in unison with a shrillness rivaling the ardor of gulls on the bay, leaping at my approach into the crowns of pine. With their retreat, calm returned as suddenly as disquiet had come over me.

Before ten, I'd found a road with more houses, picket fences, cars, retail businesses and a sign that read, "Nashua, N.H., 15 miles." Quickly in and out of the city limits of Nashua and Manchester.

"N'aie pas peur, mon Thomas, d'aimer. N'aie pas peur." Extending his skeleton hands of city steel across the chasm of my deepest fear, my grandfather told me not to be afraid to love.

"How can he, of all people, say that?" I cried out.

And what is Uprooting for, my dear, but to speak the truth from our deepest fears and the unlikeliest places? When I emerged from the last underpass out of Manchester, the hard geometries of city quickly gave way to the undulation of New England farmland.

I drove into Concord just after noon. While a few broad trees and brick buildings along the main street sheltered cars and pedestrians from the sun, they offered the capitol no such reprieve. Its white granite columns and golden dome gleamed. On the lookout for another landmark on the site, I only glanced at the modest but stately building. Over the manicured hedge and past a cluster of white birches stood the verdigris statue of Daniel Webster, orator and statesman, like gangrenous scar on purity's alabaster brow. My curious perception struck me as yet another cogent reminder of Uprooting's determination to undermine my ordinary way of seeing.

On my way out of Concord, I caught glimpses of the Merrimack River. Travelling parallel to the river for a number of miles gave me heart and made me feel at home despite the distance I'd put between myself and the Stocking. Though every river kept its own mind and put its distinctive mark on the land it by turn loved and cursed, it shared a bond and mystery with rivers the world over that not even its intimates, animal or human, could begin to understand. As long as the river stayed near, there was home; as soon as it wandered off, I was alone.

But the proximity of any river could not guarantee safe haven from Uprooting; it was upon me as soon as I crossed the bridge, an uncontrolled kaleidoscope of thought, image and sensation. I saw the glory of the capitol dome in the sweltering brilliance of August and was filled with patriotism; but more than that, with an excess of patriotic fervor. From one moment to the next, I could not predict what spate of words would possess my mind or what whirl of emotions would invade my senses. It was a condition that, surprisingly, did little to impede my driving. "Oh, say can you see!" Can you see? Can you make sense of the fire and brimstone of Father Etienne's Lenten sermons? Can you see this thing through? This journey? This endeavor? Midst the Pomp and Circumstance of it all? Make sense of the green patina on too perfect a statue? Of Pépère? Of Pépère wearing his dress shirt and tie to paint his house? Pomp and Nonsense! Why am I doing this? Why am I going? Hot tears ran down my cheeks and with them the kaleidoscope ended. I brought the car to a stop by the side of the road. The hot tears continued to fall.

Good question, godson. Why, indeed?

"Uprooting did this?"

Yes. You will not know when or how; but in the end, you will learn why.

"Can't you tell me when, prepare me?"

The best preparation is none.

"Am I going crazy?"

You cannot tell? Trust, godson. Trust. She laughed again but not

at me. It was a laughter of willow. Of approval. Perhaps for having read in my heart the will to go on.

When her laughter faded away, my tears ceased. I noticed a
cemetery across the way. I was sitting directly across from the
gate, seemingly cut from the same white granite that had shone
from the facade of the capitol building. Its solidity, marked by
the breadth and buttressing of stone, ensured fluid grace up to the
cross above, and marked it as a place of peace.

Threshold, the Dark Woman said. With that, the arc of the
gate transformed into Whale leaping the timeless distance between
memory and remembrance. Between remorse and forgiveness.

"Is Whale the Uprooting?" I asked.

No. But a messenger. A light.

"Of the white radiance?" I whispered, word and inflection
so unlike my own.

*No, godson. So it only seems in the final stage of transfiguration.
But no. Your Whale is of the dark and of the deep. Pray. Ask your mother.
Ask your People to instruct you, at the proper time, of his origin.*

As soon as Whale vanished, I entered the cemetery by a
power of vision I'd not experienced before.

*This is where you were meant to be. Whale led you here. Did you
not know that?*

"No."

Never a suspicion?

"No." The Dark Woman unnerved me. I looked up into the
sunlit leaves of maple and oak for reassurance. "Are there willows
here?" I asked in an alien voice. She laughed with the familiar
sonority of chimes in the hilltop willow of another cemetery.

*Do not be alarmed, godson. That is the voice of your seeing-through;
you are growing into it. Enter into your vision as much as you can. Know it
as your own; for one day soon, it may prove the only power standing between
you and the forces of death. The silence beyond the gate did not harbor peace.*

"Is my life in danger?"

Yes. The silence overwhelmed me. *Surely you must have
suspected it; no one ventures pilgrimage without grievous risk. Did you*

really think that your grandfather's place of rest could be found at no cost to you? Without risk?

"I didn't think..."

You cannot afford to think; from now on, you must see-through. Uprooting does not play. You have found two graveyards; there will be two more. Beware the next.

10

Preface at Potter Place

Outside Concord, I found shade near the typical New England stone wall of an apple orchard. Hunger postponed fantasies of "the next graveyard" and the mortal danger awaiting me there. Sitting on the wall to eat my sandwiches and drink in the scent of green apples warming in the sun, I felt the wall move under me.

Sturdy, unbroken, it followed the slow bend of the road—until it became a thin line and disappeared in a far turn. Moving again, almost imperceptibly, it seemed to gather momentum along its length in the distance, transforming into my Pépère's fishline skimming surfaces for an unwary victim. Then, it became the pursuit of Whale after that uncompromising memory which, if captured, would bring me safely home, as the poison at the heart of a flower produces healing light.

You remember still, don't you? she asked.

"What?"

At the heart of your running away, you remember, don't you? The Dark Woman seemed to be teasing me and I was becoming desperate as Whale failed again and again to capture that one uncompromising memory.

"Who?" I demanded with exasperation.

The Old Woman. My Mother.

"I don't remember."

Yes, yes. I know you do. See now. See with the power of your grow-ing vision. See-through. I felt the same dull ache at the base of my skull that followed the near crash in Riverton.

"The beach?" I stammered. "When I was sick on the beach?"

When you almost burned yourself to a crisp.

"The woman? Not Celia. The woman from the sea? Her face was dark and her eyes were ablaze with white fire. She was beautiful. Her?"

Yes. There now, you do see, she exclaimed. *You can avail your-self of your new vision of power. You are learning to see-through...because you are beginning to trust. Because you are beginning to let your Mémère and Anna love you. The Woman you saw that morning...She is your uncompromising memory. You must never forget Her because She alone knows the heart of Uprooting.*

"But I thought all along that you were that woman."

Oh no, no, my dear godson, she protested, laughing. *Most assuredly not. No, no. No!* She laughed with such glee I thought the chimes in the willow would not cease till every silence in the world had been filled with the shiver of their ecstasy. *Since you have only begun your instruction, I excuse you. No, She is my Mother. My Grandmother. And yours.*

"I remember everything she said."

Good.

"But she sounded so much like you."

You must not make that mistake again. It is She who sent me to you.

"She called me 'blockhead'?"

Yes. Why not? But not only because She knew you as slow to trust, but because She was calling you to bridge-making. In Her name and out of my own affection for you, I call you 'my dear blockhead,' do I not? Take no offense.

"I don't."

She laughed softly. *What you must not ever forget of this uncompromising memory is what Grandmother confided to you without the intermediary of words...from Her heart to yours. Do you know what that was? See-through, godson.* I was beginning to feel the otherness of the puppet again. Words rose from depths of soul not mine to utterances at the tip of my tongue clearly understood as having never been mine.

Speak.

"Each drop of water, a distillation of the sun. Each a revelation. Each a poison I must drink both to die and to live again." I was trembling, I realized, with whatever it was that made every willow of remembrance in the world laugh and cry.

Good, godson. Do not forget. Remember what manner of poison you are called to drink. Beware what manner of death you choose among the gravestones next. Trust your Grandmother, dear blockhead. Trust her. With that final exhortation, my attention returned from the distance where mystery dwelled and danger lurked to the warmth and support of the stone wall I was sitting on. I examined the texture of one of its big round stones with my fingers, finding that rains polished the granite and limestone of this country road as ably as waves burnished the breakwater on the bay. With a heightened awareness of the cooperation of farmer and element in the making of this solid place, my peace returned, only to be broken almost at once by an uproar of flapping behind me. A huge crow swooped across the road to light upon the largest branch of a small red maple that stood alone in a clearing.

The branch, bright ember in the high sun and chilling premonition of fall, pointed northwest to the distant purple hills of Vermont in the direction I'd be heading. In the time it took to follow my grandfather's fishline and the wake of Whale to the point at which they vanished, I was ready to leave. As I drove off, I noticed that the crow had abandoned the tree. Ominous flame, it stood alone once more. And long after it had disappeared from view, I knew we would meet again...not along this road, but surely on another.

It wasn't long before I turned further north. I wasn't surprised that nothing of the beauty of the place touched me. By now I was getting used to Uprooting and tried to brace myself against its powerful incursions. Nothing of the solidity of the land, my initiation at the apple orchard, remained. Even though farmland was garrisoned by the growing regularity of rock formations, its reality seemed compromised. As I proceeded, earth gave way to water. Water of the Merrimack pushing from behind in the east. Water of the Connecticut pulling from the west. And the maelstrom of the Stocking below. Anna's red Toyota, makeshift canoe, rode turbulent waters.

The more I tried to control my craft, the more ungovernable it became. Perspective, breached by surges of sunlight from the steel and glass of passing vessels, degenerated into a branching of blinding pathways and improbable choices. Terrified, I cried, "Abandon ship!" and prepared to let go the wheel.

Do not let go, the Dark Woman cried. I hung on. *Not so tight. Have you not learned? Seeing comes with trust. Looser, looser!* I loosened my grip on the wheel. *Good. Again.* I obeyed. *Very good.* The canoe responded to my slightest touch. The Whale Way was revealed.

Do not doubt your experience, godson. That would be rash. You would be made all the more vulnerable. You said, 'Abandon ship,' did you not?

"Yes," I answered sheepishly.

I do like that, she said, laughing with the abandon of willow.

Soon after the repair of cornstalks and trees fractured by the earlier torrent of light and the reconstitution of reality from the tattered sheathing of a dream, the road reappeared as the one River powerful enough to restore a grandfather's vision from the ravages of shame. It was also the River that would reclaim from the ruins of my own blind and shameful deeds a truth I'd written off for its simplicity and to which I must now devote my life. A truth of the heart, it went directly to my fear of not being able to bring the red canoe of my destiny to shore.

Smell the land, it suggested with the detachment of yet another puppet voice. *Smell the land.*

Recalling the little red maple, I smelled its essence with the power of seeing-through. From a place beyond the shallowness of its planting and the solitariness of its existence, I smelled the musk of the black earth out of which it grew. I smelled the pepper of its root and the faint oleaster of its leaf. I smelled it as concoction of the essences of ragweed, goldenrod, lichen, mushroom, moss and grasses. Intimately related to my experience of the one River flowing in an ever-mindful direction, the little red maple exuded the smell of the land Whale loved before leaping after mystery into the sea. There were deep essences of an unknown earth on the brink of discovery, teasing my trust at the end of a grandfather's fishline and on the tip of a dark whale's flaring nose. Essences of a land to be loved. Whale knew the Way. "Trust the essences. Trust them," I heard the puppet voice say.

I laughed as heartily as the Dark Woman had ever laughed when I discovered myself guiding my red canoe downriver with the speed of a turtle in the mud. My feet, it seemed, had punched through the floor of the canoe and were walking the river bottom, propelling me slowly but surely home in the wake of some unidentified creature who knew the way better than I. So, this is what trust is, I marveled.

So it is, the Dark Woman of the willow chimed in. *So it is.* Then, a hundred feet away, the quiet waters of the river quaked and, in a tumult of sunshine and foam, rose the trailblazer. Soared the fearlessness of a dark woman astride the mammoth blackness of Whale. I stopped, ankle-deep in mud, to wonder at the spectacle.

"Is that you?" I asked, trembling.

No more than it is your mother or Anna or any woman of earth, the Dark Woman answered from her invisibility.

"Is it she?" I asked, shaking violently.

"Yes, *it is She,* the Dark Woman confirmed. *Neither young nor old. Neither living nor dead. It is She. Not of water. Not of earth. But of all that is. From beyond the sky where Turtle grows the tree of truth and peace. It is She.* Woman and Whale sounded as one to rise again only when the river had calmed. The pair swam to the mouth of a shadowy cove, silently inviting me to follow.

"Should I?" I asked my companion in a guarded whisper.

Yes. Follow. Unexpectedly freed from the suck of mud, my feet moved just as easily over the riverbed as the canoe glided over the stillness of water. The instant I entered the cove, Whale and Woman disappeared, leaving me alone to discover what they intended I should find among the rocks of the furthest shore.

Climb, the Dark Woman instructed as I approached a ledge that rose steeply from water's edge.

"I can't," I protested. "Not with this canoe wrapped around my waist."

What canoe? It vanished. I looked back and found it resting on the stillest of waters in the exact center of the cove. "What's going on?"

Climb. When I reached the top of the outcropping, I looked thirty feet down the other side to discover an assemblage of loose rocks below.

Climb down, was all she said. I picked my way gingerly down the wall of moving stone till I reached the bottom. *Do you see?* With an intuition that I recognized immediately as one of my puppet alter egos, I identified the human bones scattered among the rocks as my father's and grandfather's remains.

"Yes," I answered. "But my grandfather, he isn't dead. Is he?"

Though he continues to cling to the thread of his physical life with an iron will, he has been dead these many years with the enormity of his shame.

"I don't..."

No need to understand. Not now.

"What is..." I was going to ask a question about the gentle stir of the bones in the pit when my earlier trembling resumed so that I was unable to speak.

Be still, the Dark Woman whispered as I watched the bones slowly rise from the ground and assemble themselves into the skeleton of the Whale that had hovered over me that fateful day by the railroad tracks at Cannery Bridge. No sooner had the skeleton appeared than it burst into flames and was consumed. From its ashes emerged a large lustrous white stone that looked unpretentiously like a loaf of bread. I felt warm all over. I smiled.

Remarkable in its simplicity, is it not?

"Yes."

Cherish the carcass, the Dark Woman whispered from a great distance. At the bottom of the pit, only inches away from the white stone, I trembled again in the shadow of birches on the hill. *Reliquary*, she announced from an even greater distance.

"Why have I suddenly turned so cold?" I asked, my words rendered unrecognizable by the quivering of my voice.

Do you know what a reliquary is? she demanded, ignoring my question.

"No."

It is a repository of relics. This white stone is a reliquary containing the ashes of your father and grandfather. It is Dragonfly. It is Whale. It is sacred stone. Your sacred stone. Gift from Grandmother. You are to wear it around your neck, my dear blockhead. As long as you live.

"How do I wear that around my neck?"

You mustn't try to figure it all out at once. Continue on your path of trust. A last word, she added thoughtfully. *You might remember that your grandfather knows something of reliquaries. You must ask him someday.*

I awoke in a rest area from what seemed only a dream. Propped against a boulder that overlooked a woodland stream, I saw that I'd parked the car by the entrance fifty feet away. No cove, no pit, no white stone. No unpredictable river, I thought, as I watched the stream ripple along in the dapple of sun.

We are cocky, are we not, godson? Do not dare Uprooting lest he loose your most perilous fear upon you. To avoid any such confrontation, I freed my thoughts to flow with the stream under a small wood bridge. When I rose to go to the car, I found that I'd already laid the map of the northern New England states and Canada out on a nearby picnic table. Despite my efforts not to let my apparent memory lapses bother me, concern over what might happen next nettled me more than the mosquitoes that, having lulled me at first with their leisurely drifting up from the water, now dove in earnest after my blood. I wondered when Uprooting would strike next.

Tracing my itinerary thus far, I was struck by the name, "Potter Place," which I'd seen on a sign at the junction of two roads. Village? Town? Surely not a city. But why was I so taken with the name? Why did it sound familiar and make me feel such an inexplicable kinship with it? Had I been here before?

Yes, the Dark Woman answered with an inexplicable casualness. *You know you have.*

"Are you sure?"

You were here from the very beginning, my godson. You have always been here. As dumbfounded as I was by her assertion, I was even more perplexed by the displacement I experienced at the core of my being. I felt that at any moment I might disappear not only from this place but from the face of the earth. The fear of vanishing, as had an entire cove only minutes ago, overcame me.

Face your fear, she said calmly.

"How?"

Trust, my dear. Trust Uprooting. I stood insecurely by the picnic table, attempting to hold my ground against the onslaught of fear.

The outcropping. You see it, don't you?

"I don't know…I think so," I said, barely able to make out a vacillating structure in the midst of darting mosquitoes.

I know you do. Concentrate, godson. Do you see it now?

"Yes," I answered with growing confidence as I began to recognize the distinctive contours of the outcropping above the cove. "Yes," I echoed in a puppet voice reduced to a faint whisper.

You also heard the change in the sound of your voice, did you not?
"Yes."

The weakness you detect in your other voice signals the strengthening of your seeing-through. There will soon come a time when you will not experience your voice as other; for then, you will have begun to see-completely-through and your many voices will have become one. I didn't try to puzzle out the Dark Woman's words but focused my attention instead on the clearly visible details of the outcropping. *Juncture,* she whispered with an unsettling solemnity.

"Of roads?"

No.

"Threshold?" I ventured.

Yes, my dear. The Potter Place beyond the one you perceive with ordinary eyes is the perception of your Uprooting. It is Threshold. Now, press the white stone of your seeing-through to your fear until such time as you can wear it about your neck as emblem of its permanent residence in your heart. With your seeing-through to this new Threshold you are preparing for the next. And the next. The perception of each succeeding Threshold will require a deeper seeing-through until you have attained the last and have become both cornerstone of and bridge to your grandfather's peace.

I was astonished that the particulars of the Dark Woman's enigmatic explanation hadn't set my head spinning. Instead, I found myself embraced by the pacific stream and musings of my mother and father. It was in a rest area such as this that they met and fell in love. I saw my father bring his beloved down to Stocking River to court her in the shadow of Sweeney Bridge. I entertained no unpleasant thoughts, feeling only tenderness for my parents and the times I'd watched the bridge melt in purple sunset and reappear among the stars. The sound of the stream reminded me of the little noises the Stocking made curling around Noah's Crag. But there was something more. Like lullabies sung by a woman to her child, miniscule chutes and eddies spoke a language of such softness I thought I would cry.

Language beyond language, the Dark Woman said.

"My mother's language?"

Yes. And beyond the language of your mother's People, it is Grand-mother's language to which Uprooting grants you brief audience. Be glad.

"It does make me glad," I heard myself say in an inaudible puppet voice. "It is beautiful." The peace it sang, like that my grandfather aspired to, I wished on all the babies of the world. "Where did that come from?" I asked.

Need you ask?

"What is my mother's native tongue?"

When it is time, you will know. For now, be patient and trust.

I knew it was time for me to leave. A last glance at the map confirmed my turn west, which would lead directly to Enfield and La Salette Shrine on the south shore of Lake Mascoma.

Walking to the car, I recalled "Merrimack" and "Connecticut," both Indian names for New England rivers. "Mascoma," was that Indian too? I remembered reading that the founders of Concord had first named the settlement "Penny Cook" after "Pennacook," an Indian word which meant crooked place. For the first time in my life, I felt that I'd always inhabited Indian country. Despite Uprooting or perhaps because of it, I was beginning to feel more and more at home.

It is good, is it not, my godson, to return home to who you are? Though I found it hard to leave the place where my Grandmother had given me my sacred stone and the essence of my mother's language, I drove off.

Not quite a mile away, my eye was drawn to the whiteness of a lone house on the left-hand side of the road. It seemed the more solitary for its contrast to the green ribbon of trees that unfurled in lazy undulation like a ceremonial introduction to the jewel it bore. While slowing down to take a good look, I had no intention of stopping until I read the sign above the windows at the side of the building—"Potter Place." That was enough to make me turn sharply right and stop the car across from a structure like a restored but abandoned railroad station. It was empty, and so were the flower boxes beneath every latticed window. And not a soul anywhere near it. "Not a soul anywhere," a re-invigorated puppet voice kept repeating with a purpose and meaning that eluded me. Why, then, was the place so well kept? Like my grandfather would keep it up if he were living in it, I thought, with its green trim and white gingerbread frieze. The peaked twice-gabled roof appeared somehow separate from the main structure and a building in its own right.

Twained, the Dark Woman said offhandedly. I laughed. That's the way I would have said it when I was a kid. I could not pronounce my "r's"—train was always "twain." I laughed with a giddiness and irrelevancy that overpowered me.

Two, she said. *Made two. Like a double star.* I wasn't laughing anymore. Was she trying to confuse me?

That is not difficult, my dear. But do you know what a double star is?

"No. What is it?"

Listen carefully, godson. Understand that there are two very different kinds of double star. Two realities. Two meanings. To your situation, both apply. Pay attention. There are the two stars that, often separated by enormous distance, appear as one. Do you understand?

"Yes, godmother."

In this manner, your Dog Star may, in fact, be a series of stars leading you back into the mystery that is the source of your destiny. Then, there is the other double star, which is a system of two stars revolving around a common center of gravity. In this instance, the white stone by the cove and this little station are the two stars having a common center of gravity, namely the purpose for which you have undertaken pilgrimage. Do you understand?

"Yes, godmother."

By your Grandmother's design, the station assumes the role of double star in a unique sense. Its magnitude, which consists in its capacity to twain, is derived as much from its apparent loss of function as from its diminutive size. That is your Grandmother's way. Behold the twaining, godson, as revealer of the essence of stone and the engine of pilgrimage. Twaining. Training. Profound feelings of division and divisiveness returned.

138 • *Dance the River Whale*

"Uprooting?" I asked.

No matter. See this defunct railroad station as you first saw it. As the jewel held up for your seeing-through by the green ribbon of pilgrimage. The jewel of doubling and of multi-faceting given to you here at Potter Place by your Grandmother is not for your undoing but for bridge-making. Fear not the mirror images of the jewel, for they are nothing less than the reflections of your talisman, the white stone. Your guides. Torches held to the dark paths of your soul. Stone and jewel are one. To be worn about your neck with the lightness of an eagle's feather. Trust.

"I will," I muttered more as prayer than as conviction. "Is this the third graveyard?" I asked, surprising myself with the question.

No. But it is its indispensable preface. Heed what you have seen here. The gravity with which she made this pronouncement was new and menacing. *I do not threaten you, godson; you know me well enough for that. What I stalk with a ferocity you have not yet the eyes to imagine is the danger that lurks ahead. Danger within as much as without. Heed.*

I braced myself behind the wheel for whatever it was Uprooting had in store for me. Suddenly, with a flapping of wings, a thousandfold more uproarious than the crow in the orchard, the roof of the train station flew off and over the trees in the background.

Trust, I heard her say clearly above the thunder of wings. I tried; and with that, I floated from the car and hovered over the station like the child who, having removed the top of her doll house, looked down into the interior. With an intuition spoken by an altogether unfamiliar puppet voice, I selected a casket.

Double star, she whispered. There appeared two caskets, side by side, in the middle of a highly polished wood floor.

"For my father and my grandfather?" I whispered in keeping with the solemnity of the moment.

Shhh. Watch. The two caskets became one without any discernible movement. Then, the one grew with a redoubtable creaking and groaning until it filled the station, leaving hardly room on either side for mourners to kneel and pray. *Yes, they were your sires. Would you like to see what they have become?*

"Yes," I hesitated. With the same uproarious flap of wings I'd heard earlier, the lid of the casket swung open. "Whale," I gasped. Dark and foreboding, it filled the casket to bursting. "Look," I cried, "the walls of the casket are giving way. It's going to break." I panicked.

Whale is both contained and container, flowing with and through the land, through the People and through the infinite and infinitesimal fissures of a single life. It is ever contained by the Mystery and holds us ever to it. It is Grandmother's message and messenger both. Ever Her gift to your mother's People, She now gives it to you, godson. She gives the seeing-through of its Dragonfly eyes. She gives the luminosity of its primordial bone as sacred stone to be worn about your neck with the lightness of an eagle's feather.

The Dark Woman's ceaseless repetitions began to wear on me because they reminded me of the mortal danger she was preparing me for. *Training,* she said, her inimitable laughter riding the soft thunder of wings in circles to the sun.

"But it feels like Whale will crush me in the process."

Oh no, godson. Twaining. Remember the double star. No little station this. Threshold will seem at first a suffocation. But now you must remember the next star and the next and the next. Threshold is a vast universe given us by Grandmother for freedom of movement and of choice. It was so at Cannery Bridge. It is so in this little railway station of no visible consequence. Your feelings of constraint reflect nothing more than your inexperience with the power of Threshold. Trust will avail you of its power to open the heart to Mystery and to the ultimate choice.

"What ultimate choice?" I blurted out anxiously.

Whether or not to abide Mystery. Her intemperate laughter grated on raw nerves.

"You're just making things worse...confusing the hell out of me."

Good. Good. More lyrical irritating laughter. *And to add to your delightful confusion, my dear, hear this: Mystery sends Uprooting to elicit Thresholds from the heart; Uprooting, in turn, sends Whale to point you in the direction of Threshold and its temporary but necessary confusion.*

"What do I do now?" There ensued an interminable silence, more unnerving than the earlier laughter. "I know...I know. Trust."

Trust the messenger, Whale. Though he cannot help you abide Mystery—for that is a solitary task—he can prepare you to face the danger of the third graveyard and teach you how to make powerful allies of Uprooting and of your destiny.

"Just in the nick of time." I sighed deeply out of an inexplicable sense of relief.

No. Oh, no. The timing is just right. Whale times everything right. He has allowed himself more than enough time to teach and prepare you. The cowled monks from the ominous sky over Cannery Bridge came to kneel by the casket. Whale provided them with ample space to bow their heads forward and to stretch their legs backward. Whale provided them with more than ample space to pray. I could feel their freedom stretch their hearts for prayer. I could feel their freedom stretch mine into a vast universe of unknown trust and prayer. It hurt.

"I can't..."

Abide the Mystery. See-through the demeanor to the unspoken prayer the heart aches to speak. Who is it?

"Pépère." I wanted to cry out his name, but could not.

Your grandfather, your father and you.

"I know." The heartache grew in proportion to the expanding dimensions of a vast universe.

The three generations.

"I know."

A fourth.

"I know."

The seventh.

"I know."

See how the prayer of the heart, Anna's and your grandmother's, has stretched your heart for pilgrimage and love. With your new heart, you are stretching the length and breadth of your grandfather's pain. By the light of your seeing-through will your grandfather span the darkness of his shame.

"But why a train station in the middle of nowhere?"

Where else the conjunction of pilgrim souls? Of apparitions? Aspirations? Of forgiveness and remorse?

"Threshold?"

Indubitably. Struck by a disturbing flash of intuition, I realized that my grandfather, father and I had been kneeling to mourn the death of Whale.

"Is it true?" I asked, voicing my alarm.

Yes. She remained calm but was clearly becoming impatient with my slowness to learn. *And no.*

"What?"

It is well the Enemy think him dead.

"How?"

Later.

"But why the wake in a god-forsaken train station?" I heard the Dark Woman's breath labor in a silence of exasperation.

God-forsaken? she began in a tone much calmer than I should have expected. *How else does Whale travel so deep into a land it still loves from the distant but enduring memory of that love? Remember always, god-son, that Threshold transcends our limited conception of space. Remember. Double Star. From the perspective of seeing-through, a train might very well be a river. No?*

"By twain? Traveling by twain?"

You are learning faster than I thought. She laughed with the unrestrained merriment of willow.

"Double Star?"

Of course. Before I became too comfortable with my trifling progress, the Dark Woman added gravely, *Beware. You can never be well enough prepared for the hazards that lie ahead.*

"The graveyard?"

No rehearsal next time.

"Soon?"

No matter. What matters is that you keep your vigil with Whale. That he readies you to see-through to both the promise and peril that spring from the heart. You see more clearly now why he comes to you at this modest but critical junction? I couldn't answer. *To show you that as great as he is, he too wisely submits to Grandmother's unpretentious ways. To teach you, godson, how to pray.*

11

The Twin

The further northwest I traveled, the more hills turned to mountainous ascent. The heights of the White Mountains to the east and the Green Mountains to the west affirmed what the depths of the Merrimack River and the Connecticut River had intimated with their subterranean whispers. That, having freely chosen to proceed this way, I was being ushered through a Pilgrim Corridor from which there was no escape and no turning back. I felt as though Whale had flipped in his coffin and landed with the brunt of his weight on me. I recognized the feeling as the claustrophobic self-pity to which I'd succumbed earlier.

Good, godson. To have recognized the feeling so quickly represents a significant and critical improvement. Self-pity is undoubtedly the first weakness the Enemy will want to exploit.

"Why?"

Because it is the surest path to shame, the supreme inhibitor of life.

"What can I do?"

Beware the subtle suggestion that anyone but you is at fault here. No one made you drink. No one robbed you of your trust. Not even your grandfather. No one made or makes you do anything. No one forces you into pilgrimage. To assume so puts you, body and soul, in extreme danger. When I informed you that pilgrimage was a solitary undertaking, I spoke the fundamental truth. There is nothing more solitary than taking responsibility for one's life. That is what is at stake here. Your life. No one can make you choose life. That, you must do on your own. It is you who ultimately decide to evolve your life by crossing each successive threshold of your destiny. You alone.

"But what about you? You're helping me. Without you, I could never have made it this far."

Illusion.

"You're no illusion. You're real, aren't you?"

Oh, yes, my godson, I am real. The illusion is that I have made the choices for you. No, no. You have made your own; and without making them, you could have not come this far. You could not have entered the Pilgrim's Corridor where you alone must choose to face your Enemy. When my voice is silenced, remember that it was you who chose to move on from Cannery Bridge...to get well...to visit your grandfather...to brave the incantations of Uprooting...to heed the teachings of Whale at Potter Place...to move into the Corridor where death awaits you. The Dark Woman's words resonated in me no less powerfully than had the initial sighting of mountains in the distance. Both vista and teaching transformed my usual awareness into an ambivalence of such intensity that I couldn't help but think of the mother who receives her child into the incalculable danger and beauty of this world. "Twaining" did not seem amusing anymore; I was torn by the pristine guile of seeing-through.

Have the courage to see-through to the Enemy, godson. Not to do so will cost you your life. The volume and pace of her teaching and the earnestness with which she delivered her latest warning drove home the imminence of her leave-taking. *Not leaving, godson.*

"What then?" I asked with unprecedented calmness.

I will hold my tongue and not interfere; but I will not leave. It was difficult for me to imagine that, having invested so much time and trouble in my reclamation, the Dark Woman would not bring her vision to bear on what she herself had characterized as a life-death struggle. I determined that, in keeping with the strategy of Whale, her silence would be more ploy to deceive the Enemy than an abandonment of me to the naiveté of my own devices. She laughed the gentlest chimes of willow yet. However inscrutable the laughter, it deepened my calm and drew Anna near. The stillness and starlight of Anna's body on the beach and in her bedroom. The scent of her perfume made haunting by the heat and humidity of August. The tenacity of her presence and of her love. Anna with me, however many miles her precious Toyota put between us. Anna teasing and joining in the willow's laughter as I neared Lake Mascoma's south shore.

It was only a ten-minute drive from the start of the lake to La Salette Shrine. As I approached the entrance, my heart began to race. Could this state of heightened alert signal danger? Can't be, I told myself as I drove uneventfully into a car-filled parking lot.

Smug, are we not, godson? Too sure of yourself for one who knows so little.

"I..."

Do not indulge in or bore me with pitiful excuses. Tell me, does danger have a look? Does it? Come, come, tell me what danger looks like? Relieved that the Dark Woman had not yet made herself inaccessible, I didn't much mind that she was lecturing me.

"I don't..."

Of course, you do not know. The danger of which we speak has no look, nothing to distinguish itself, no way to alert us until well into the throes of our dying. Do not question the appropriateness of the doubling and its seeing when they come to you. Accept them with graciousness and they will serve you well in every instance, whether for your protection, your enlightenment or the pure pleasure of seeing-through.

I followed her instruction while I searched for an empty parking space. It was a bit of luck, I thought, when a car suddenly freed a space near the end of the first row of cars. Eager to park, I bumped against the island of grass, which not only appeared a buffer between the road and traffic I faced, but a barrier to impending danger. I knew with absolute certainty that I would be granted asylum here.

Luck, godson? No luck here. Asylum, yes; but that will not always be the case. It is a rare gift to be certain of sanctuary and, thus, be able to concentrate on the lessons at hand. You do realize that?

"Yes," I answered with genuine gratitude.

As I sat in the car with eyes closed, pondering how I knew I'd be safe within the precincts of La Salette Shrine, I was startled by a slight pressure on my left shoulder.

"Are you okay?" a deep, gravelly voice inquired.

"Yes," I answered, rubbing my eyes in a pretense of having just awoken. When I looked up, I found a baldheaded elderly gentleman leaning inquisitively through the window. "I'm fine. I've been on the road since early this morning and was just taking a nap."

"Oh, I'm sorry," he bellowed his apology as he pulled away.

"No need. It was time I got going anyway. Do you have the time?"

"Sure," he said, looking down at his watch. "It's almost five o'clock." Bewildered by the occurrences at Potter Place and having subsequently lost interest in time, I panicked when I remembered my purpose in coming to the shrine.

Relax, the Dark Woman said. *You will be given the necessary time to learn that which is essential to your pilgrimage.* Still unconvinced that others couldn't hear her speak, I scrutinized the man's face for a sign of his having heard. There was none.

"My wife's always telling me to mind my own business but I never do," he offered, laughing hoarsely and pointing at his wife who stood, smiling back at us, near the end of the row. "Where are you from, young man?" he asked.

"From Massachusetts," I answered as I stepped out of the car. My legs felt stiffer and heavier than they did when I stopped at Potter Place.

"We're from Morristown, New Jersey. Came on a bus from church. It's amazing how many people know about this place. They come from all over, you know."

"Is this your first time?"

"No, it's our fourth," he answered, looking at his wife waving for him to come along. "We're always glad to come back. It's so beautiful." I nodded, gazing over the sizzle of auto rooftops and past a gray barrack-type building to the serenity of a green hillside. "I've got to go," he declared, "before she comes and hauls me off by the ears. They're about to start the rosary up at the pond. Nice meeting you. Sorry for being a nuisance." He shook my hand hurriedly and trotted off after his wife.

I walked slowly to the nearby gray building to look at the register in which pilgrims record their visits to the shrine. I dared to hope past registers might provide an indispensable lead to my mother's whereabouts.

First things first, the Dark Woman whispered as I neared the main entrance. *Look,* she urged with startling energy. My eyes leaped to a statue of Mary which appeared to grow, like a delicate white flower, from the middle of meticulously pruned evergreen bushes. The sun was just high enough to immerse her raised crown in blinding light while softening her face and transforming the folds of her tunic into the gentle shimmer of a woodland waterfall.

"'Twaining,'" I heard a weak puppet voice utter with a reverence I did not expect.

Accurate and with the proper respect to boot. You have acknowledged the doubling of that which has always been and will always be one for seeing-through to its ultimate truth. Now, child, look again at the woman's crown and tell me what you see.

"The radiance of eagle feathers," I heard myself shout ecstatically. Then, feeling extremely foolish, I looked around to see if anyone had heard my outcry. I was alone.

Why should you care what others think? You see Eagle scream the truth of suns and you preoccupy yourself with what others think? No, god-

son, no! Seeing-through gives you what is essential for your life. Do not allow yourself the deleterious distractions born of shame. If in the face of the Enemy you forgo your vision, you will surely die. Cling to the radiance of Eagle for your very life! I watched the headdress shiver in the excess of light until it vanished in the twilight of the waterfall.

I stood a long while alone by the statue, wondering how in the world it could appear to me at once so alien and so familiar. Remembering Mary, Mother of God, familiar of my night dreams and sole confidante of my childhood loneliness, I saw the Woman, my Grandmother, ever young and ever beautiful, emerge from the deep memory of a darker sea. I saw her, radiant in the headdress of revelation, ride the Whale over rapids and across currents to a shore of reunion and redemption.

"Are they one and the same?" I asked, torn between feelings of expectancy and disloyalty. "Mary? Grandmother? Are they the same person?"

Why do you doubt your question? How many times must you be reassured of the truth and the power of seeing-through?

"It doesn't feel right."

That is because it is new to you. You must not doubt your vision, my dear, for the double-star of the soul, unlike that of the physical universe, is not illusion. Its unique power is to return to oneness that which has been falsely perceived as many. We must not create divisions where there are none, for, then, we are blinded to those differences and diversities that, when perceived, constitute the threshold starways to the peace of our one Medicine Wheel, the Earth. She paused until my head had cleared of the clutter of her instruction. *Your Mary and my Grandmother are ever the One Woman who falls from the sky of Her promise into the want of our loneliness.*

Long after the Dark Woman had finished speaking, I could hear her words until interrupted by a low droning. I was reminded of the trains that wheeled out of Tilson's freight yard and gathered speed on their approach to Cannery Bridge. I imagined them hurtling past highway and through countryside until they slowed and glided into the sanctuary of Potter Place. The more insistent the droning, the more I recognized it as prayer from the Rosary Pond on the hill. The low sun and the rhythmic click—passage of railway car from one set of tracks to the next, passage of one bead and Hail Mary to the next. Sacred passages, each. Two yet one. Unrelated and incongruous but for the grace of Whale's seeing-through to the original truth. Demonstrating how every part is connected to every other distant part by the unseen rivers of the world. "The neck bone connected to the shoulder bone, the hip bone connected to the thigh bone...and that's the way of the Lord," I was reminded by the spiritual. "That's the Way of the Lord."

By the beating of the drum and of the heart. To bear the burden of the other's shame and be touched by the ecstasy of the stranger's love, the Dark Woman whispered before the squeals and laughter of young girls consumed her words. I saw them scurry up the hill to the pond to pray.

I listened in that profound silence that anticipates revelation. *And now the people that went about in darkness has seen a great light; for men abiding in a land where death overshadowed them, a light has dawned.*

For our sakes a child is born, to our race a son is given, whose shoulders will bear the sceptre of princely power. What name shall he be given? Peerless among counsellors, the mighty God, Father of the world to come, the Prince of Peace. Ever wider shall his dominion spread, endlessly at peace...

I waited in that profound silence that embraces and mulls revelation. It was the silence that enveloped Whale when love prompted its return to a land and a people divided. It was the vastness of silence that elicited the deep drone of the collective "Ave" echoing from the Rosary Pond and commemorating the first spoken by an angel almost two thousand years ago, many centuries after Whale began making its way back through our dreams and into our lives.

"The prophecy of Isaiah?" I asked nervously, still stunned by the anomaly of solemn revelation provoked by the giddiness of adolescent girls.

Yes.

"You've read the Bible?" I asked stupidly and even more nervously than before.

I have not.

"How did..."

Godson, these are the words your Mémère has held to her heart since she was a little girl. Words sustained by the silence of every prayer uttered since Whale began to contemplate its return.

"But..."

Do not doubt your seeing-through, Thomas. You did hear your grandmother speak the prophet's words.

"She didn't know any of that stuff. I never saw her read the Bible."

That is how little you know your grandmother, child. Do you not yet know that the silence of seeing-through transcends all barriers? Your grandmother has long held the prophet's words to her heart and knows their meaning well. She has long known to what end the words are planted in a young girl's soul. Heed their promise at sundown in the giggles of girls off to pray. Heed their promise in the sunrise birth of a virgin's first-born son. 'Ave!' 'Orenda!'

As I walked toward the first of twin white porticoes, my head still swimming with revelation, two young girls, running with their heads down, bumped into me, tossing breathless "sorrys" behind them and racing around the corner. I headed toward the door they'd come from, hoping to find someone to talk to.

"Hello, father," I called to the lone person behind the counter of the shrine's religious articles and book shop. My greeting lurched out almost in self defense as the cassocked priest seemed to glower at me over his horn-rimmed glasses. I thought that perhaps he'd chased the girls out of the store to the Rosary Pond and was wondering why I wasn't up there praying as well.

"Hello," the priest said curtly.

"Father, perhaps you can help me. I'm looking for information concerning my mother. I believe she might have paid you a visit in the summer of 1951."

"Not I," he replied. "Well now, you're going to have to talk to Father Têtreault about that…" Seeming to have anticipated the sudden queasiness brought on by my astonishment, he bolted around the counter more deftly than his portliness ought to have allowed, and grabbed my arm just above the elbow. "How about a seat, lad? I'll get you a chair."

"No thanks, father. I'm okay. Maybe a little hungry. That's all."

"I can fix that," he said. He placed a white shoe box down on the glass countertop. "A couple of tuna sandwiches and some brownies," he smiled with the twinkle in prominence over the horn-rimmed glasses. "Just a little snack," he added, laughing till he was red in the face. "Come on now, take it. You'll not be refusing my hospitality, will you? I've had my fill for one day," he said, splaying the fingers of both hands across his paunch.

As I walked toward him in disbelief of his agility and with renewed suspicion, I could have sworn I heard him laugh the laughter of willow with a forthrightness I hadn't heard before and a preternatural power that belied his eccentric affability. Was he party to the conspiracy I'd suspected earlier? Was he perhaps an accomplice of Uprooting? As I took the shoe box and bid him goodbye, I was convinced he knew much more than he let on.

Perhaps, the Dark Woman interjected. *Who knows the ways of Uprooting? Certainly not I. Trust, godson. Trust.*

"He will find you," the priest said.

"Father Têtreault?"

"Yes," he replied, grinning widely. "In the meantime why don't you stop in the chapel just behind the store where the current register is kept. And before you leave, don't forget to stop next door for something to drink. Tell them the 'Leprechaun' sent you; they'll know you're my friend. Be well, my son." Before I turned to leave, he'd lowered his eyes, taken up his pencil and busied himself among the thickest of his catalogues.

As soon as I entered the dusky chapel, my first thoughts were of Pépère and of my conviction that he was still alive. It was as though he and I were entering St. Anne's Church together just as we had so many times when I was a boy. It was his hand, as sturdy as the Leprechaun's, that ushered me down the center aisle past the wood benches toward an altar draped in white linen. I could no more avert my eyes from the altar than I could withdraw my hand from my grandfather's death grip. I had no choice but to be led on.

"It's begun, hasn't it?" I asked the Dark Woman, certain that she was a witness to my ordeal.

Yes. You must remember that you are approaching the heart of Pilgrim's Corridor.

"Like a lamb being led to slaughter," I muttered, overcome with self-pity, feeling myself powerless to resist being dragged forward.

Did you think you were going on a picnic when you chose to do pilgrimage? Histrionics will not serve you well here.

"Trust?"

Precisely, my dear.

"But who do I trust?"

Your experience. Go where your feet take you, where you know you must go. Where you are impelled by a destiny to which you were born and from which there is no honorable escape. There is choice in that, godson. You will see. It became clear to me then that while my grandfather was accompanying me to predestined sanctuary and altar, he could not, now or at any other time in my life, divest me of choice and responsibility.

Now you must choose whether or not to go on, she said solemnly. My hand was released; my grandfather, gone. I felt terribly alone. *As it must be,* she intoned to preface the silence that enveloped me. I looked nervously about to find that not only was the chapel empty, but that it had darkened save for the sanctuary, which shone with a light from another sky. I stood in complete darkness before an altar bathed in blinding light. To proceed with pilgrimage and embrace the danger it preordained, I must choose to climb both of the two steps before me. The silence of my first choosing was as deafening as that from which I thrust my hand into my grandfather's when the river, which had already claimed his son, threatened to wrest his grandson from him too. I climbed the first with a momentum begun with the clout of Whale's fluke against the unknown of Cannery Bridge. A free and necessary choice. Mine alone.

Standing in a darkness more complete than any I'd ever known and on the Threshold of giving up my life as I'd narrowly imagined it, I dared not breathe for fear of disturbing the balance of this last and awful silence. As suddenly as a meteor erupts in a night's sky, the light of the altar struck through my eyes to my heart, urging me to take the white shoe box from under my arm and open it. Inside I found a miniature of the reliquary Grandmother revealed to me on the other side of Potter Place. The three—box, reliquary, altar—were the one Canicula. Dog Star. The one bright cornerstone.

Common stone of the Rainbow Bridge, godson. Three in one: Redemption, Reunion, Vocation. That your grandfather may die in peace. That your mother may know you are well. That you may realize your destiny. Say it.

"What?" I asked, taken aback.

Your name. Say it. Speak your name and choose your destiny.

"How..."

Now or never, godson. Say it.

"Wait by a bridge..." I stammered.

You have known it all along.

"That's my name? 'Wait by a bridge'? That sounds stupid."

Keep still! The Dark Woman's voice rang out in the excessive silence like a gunshot to my head. *How dare you question Grandmother's wisdom?*

"But..."

Not another word before you ruin everything it has taken you such time and pain to accomplish. It is your name. 'The Little One Who Waits by a Bridge.' It is the name by which your Grandmother knows you. How can you hope to be the grandson of She Who Makes Peace when you cannot accept with grace and gratitude the name by which She has called you to her bosom since before the beginning of time? It is not the name that is 'stupid' but the snot-nose—your grandfather was right about you—who bears it. Do not ever again deny what you have known from the beginning. This very night you will desperately need to say and be who you truly are: the little one who waits with trust by the bridge not immediately apparent to minds and hearts devoid of peace. Help your Grandmother make peace by waiting near the little bridges of life and trusting that reconciliation is always possible. Now do you understand?

"Yes."

Tell me your name.

"Wait by a Bridge." By simply saying my name, I passed through the terrible silence into what I knew to be the blazing sanctuary of no return.

Lamb to slaughter, you said. There will be truth in that, godson, only if you forsake your name, indulge your narrow view of death and lose yourself in the melodrama of false inevitabilities. Do not think for a moment that Great Spirit did not require of the boy, Isaac, as much faith as He did of his father, Abraham, as both were clearly called to the altar of sacrifice. Do not think yourself any less challenged by the choice you will be called to make between unknown powers that spring from the heart. I must go now. I leave you to trust and suffer alone the freedom and burden of your choice. Goodbye, Little One Who Waits by a Bridge. Goodbye. I was suddenly overcome no less by the light than by the darkness of the name I'd been given lifetimes ago. I would be given quarter by neither. I knew that I would live or die by the power of seeing-through. I knew that if ever I were to hear from the Dark Woman again, it would be only after having survived the test of being true to my name.

The first thing I did when I left the chapel was check the shoe box. Just as the Leprechaun had told me, it contained two tuna sandwiches and some brownies. That didn't surprise me as I was gradually learning how quickly appearances, especially since I'd entered Pilgrim's Corridor, could put on their unusual but essential faces. It was with just such a face that the sky looked down on the throng that encircled the Rosary Pond. The blue eye of the one pond in the world that generates stars opened wide to my seeing-through the cerulean secret of prayer. How blue can blue be, I wondered, looking up at the sky and sensing that it was the locomotion of prayer, like that of the rosary, that sustained the floodbirth of stars since the beginning. Standing alone on the central path that led up to four visible crosses on the hilltop, I was overwhelmed by the wistfulness with which I tried to grasp my stars in the corner of the window in my old apartment. Dog Star, I thought, waiting in vain for the Dark Woman to wisecrack about how much I still had to learn. She said nothing.

Viewing the circle of prayer between two of the tall cedars that lined the path, I thought of the murmur of the stream at Potter Place, an ancient instruction spoken both here and there in stillness to the soul. It was like the idle chatter from backyard porches by women who'd known, suffered and embodied life. It was the mindful language of my mother's People. I was told so by the inner voice that bore no trace of puppet rote or pause.

"Il faut prier pour tous nos péchés," I remembered my grandfather saying as he forced me to kneel on the hard wood of a kitchen chair every night to pray the rosary. "We must pray to be forgiven our sins." While my mouth had moved in pretense of prayer, my mind was preoccupied with other things—with finding groves of lady's-slippers in the woods, catching the biggest and meanest bass in the river, watching a monster tide swallow the breakwater on the bay. My grandfather used to close his eyes when he prayed, his face turning as red as the embers he sucked on in his meerschaum bowl. He gripped his beads as though to pulverize them. He was fighting for the life of his soul. Between his Hail Mary's he'd mutter, "Il faut sauver son âme." Watching my grandfather pray, I learned not to. As one grown up as much a Catholic as any around the Rosary Pond, I felt myself an intruder at La Salette Shrine. I was alone.

"Is everything okay, my boy?" I was startled by a voice at my back.

"I'm fine," I answered, turning around.

"You seemed preoccupied. You apparently did not hear me coming."

"No, I didn't, father," I said, looking up at a hulk of a priest with a full head of white hair and steady blue eyes. "I suppose I was daydreaming."

"Perhaps praying," he said in a rumble that suggested thunder in the distance. His smile came easily, broadening his cheeks till they made his eyes disappear. "This is a pretty good place for dreaming, isn't it? The mountains, the lake, the pond, this hillside. All good places for praying and dreaming." The old priest spoke English fluently but with a decided French Canadian accent that I detected immediately for having heard it all my life. "I'm Father Têtreault," he added, sticking his hand out for me to shake. When I felt its strength, I was reminded at once of my grandfather guiding me safely across busy Stocking Boulevard when I was a small boy.

"That's my name too, father," I informed him almost with the glee of that boy on the street corner spying his Pépère get off the bus after work. "My name is Tom...Tom Têtreault."

"Good name," he said, patting me on the back, his eyes disappearing again in the wake of a smile.

"Did the priest in the bookstore tell you I was looking for you?"

"Oh no, I haven't had the chance to see Father Quint yet. I'd just returned from preaching a retreat before I came looking for you, Tom."

"For me?" My knees buckled.

"Come, let's walk," he said quietly, taking me by the arm and escorting me up the path. "You're looking for your mother, aren't you?" His directness made me quake from head to foot.

"Yes, father. I am."

"Well, you've come to the right place...Do you know her name?"

"My grandmother told me her name was Laura."

"Do you know her last name?"

"No, father."

"Well then, I'll tell it to you. Her maiden name is Martin...just as it appears in the register. There is no question that she was here on the feast day of the Assumption of Mary, August fifteenth, 1951, our inaugural year. Twenty-five years ago tomorrow. By the way, Tom, do you know how she spells her first name?"

"I'm guessing it's spelled L-A-U-R-A."

"You guessed wrong. It's L-O-R-A. Different, isn't it?" he added with a fiery twinkle in his eye.

"Do you know where she was from, father?"

"Yes. Kayanerenhkunis, Province of Quebec, Canada."

"You're sure?"

"There is no doubt, Thomas." He laughed heartily at his serendipitous association of me with the Apostle who doubted that Jesus had risen from the dead until he placed his hand in the gaping wound of his Master's side. It comforted me to know that the Dark Woman, who'd felt the need to admonish me unceasingly for my lack of trust, was laughing too somewhere close by.

"How about my father?"

"He too. I found his name in the register five or six lines below your mother's. 'David Têtreault, Ingram, Massachusetts.'"

"My mother was here. I can't believe it. They were both here...together. I might very well be walking in their footsteps."

"Undoubtedly, Tom, for they were pilgrims too." We had made it three quarters of the way up the hill by great slabs of granite which, thrust equidistantly in the near verticality of the incline, served as stairs and respite for those who attempted the climb. It was well after seven o'clock and the gathering at Rosary Pond had dispersed. The priest and I stood alone on the hill, looking past a grouping of three white marble statues to the pond below. The sun had cleared the trees behind us and was only visible by the light it cast on the hillside, Mascoma Lake and the mountain beyond. It gilded the white marble.

"I couldn't see the statue of the Blessed Mother in the pond before," I said to Father Têtreault.

"No, not from down there with all those people standing around. But you could have easily seen her from up here, crowd and all."

"Father, what's the story about Mary and those children?" I asked, pointing at the golden group of three.

"On September the nineteenth, 1846, she appeared to an eleven-year-old boy and a fourteen-year-old girl who were watching over some cows on the slopes of the French Alps above the village of La Salette. When they first noticed her, she was sitting on a rock, crying. They were struck by the light that shone from the strange crucifix adorning her breast. Like the one I wear," he whispered. He took into his great hand the facsimile, which hung from his neck by a slender black cord.

"Note the hammer on one side and the pincers on the other. The hammer is the instrument of sin by which we nail her Son to the cross; the pincers, the instrument with which we release Him into resurrection. By the exercise or repudiation of our faith, we ever choose the outcome of life's essential drama." I heard the thunder, deafening, in the caverns of my ears as I'd heard it on Horseshoe Bay, like the alarm of the St. Bernard waking me from the torpor of my dying. It rolled down the slope of our watchfulness, the priest's and mine, across Mascoma Lake into the foothills of the White Mountains. And through its other-worldly intonation, without being able to make out all of Father Têtreault's words, I heard it proclaim, "Reconciliation."

"Reconciliation with one another is how I have always understood our Mother's message," he said.

"Redemption? Reunion? Vocation?" I asked, daring the shorthand of the Dark Woman's teaching on a whim while doubting the priest's ability to translate.

"Thomas," he replied, laughing with peals of thunder which shook the willow of another hilltop to its roots, "I get it. Just so.

Just as your godmother taught you." The laughter dissipated in ripples of chimes on the lake.

"You're his twin, aren't you? My grandfather's twin." The dawning of that improbable notion coincided with the reddening of the priest's white hair and hands that held the crucifix up to the dying of another day.

"This is not just another day," he said, overshooting my question. "This is the day of your pilgrim crossing. Golgotha." Only then did I realize that the four blurred crosses at the top of the hill constituted the Way of the Cross my grandfather had walked every Good Friday as far back as I could remember. "Have faith," the priest said.

"I'll try."

"Your life depends on it." The words resounded as thundering echo to the Dark Woman's quieter warning. "Trust in your seeing-through."

"I will."

"Remember the River of the Fourth."

"What's that?" I asked, perplexed.

"I am sure she told you of it." He offered no further explanation. "Follow the thunder of oracle to the end; your life will depend on it." Father Têtreault vanished as mysteriously as he had appeared. White marble turned crimson. The group of three was a raging fire. The statue of Mary flickered on the Rosary Pond, vigilant votive candle and restive ember in my Pépère's meerschaum bowl. Silence swallowed the last of light for a solemn meditation and final preparation.

12

Death Cry

When I left the grounds of La Salette Shrine, I was struck by the coincidence that tomorrow, Sunday, August fifteenth, the feast day of the Assumption, would be the twenty-fifth anniversary not only of the shrine's inauguration, but of the launching of my parents' life of pilgrimage together. Despite the despondency that had me view their fate as star-crossed lovers, I was persuaded by a deeper objectivity to see it by the light of the double star. From that lucid perspective, I was able to realize both the gravity and opportunity of this night. This is it, I thought. Had I not chosen to go forward in the chapel, I would not have met Father Têtreault. Had I not met him, I would not be on my "merry" way—the Dark Woman's humor was not lost on me—to meet the Enemy. For a moment a tiny red ember breathed a Dragon fire from the black cavern of the lake.

This marked the end of the sanctuary I'd enjoyed at the shrine. Danger of a sinister kind lurked, I sensed, in the unpredictable loops of the road ahead. On impulse I removed the cover of the white shoe box. To my dismay, there was no talisman there. No white stone. No ultimate weapon. Dimly I saw brownies and tuna fish sandwiches for which I had no appetite; my stomach turned at their sight. I couldn't imagine eating tonight, or for that matter, sleeping either.

However, my mind wasn't racing as I'd expected it would; it was flowing, instead, with the power and ease of a River I'd not known before. River of the Fourth? The River of Kayanerenhkunis? What exactly was this place Father Têtreault said my mother was from? Village? Town? Reservation? I'd been so absorbed by this evening's experience that I'd not asked the priest the obvious question. "Gayanerenhgunis." He'd pronounced it with such fluency, giving the "k" a soft guttural "g" sound and muting the "n" to render "enh" with a nasal twang not unlike the "enh?" with which my grandparents translated the American "huh?" I couldn't help laughing at the comparison, despite my driving deeper and deeper into what felt like Enemy territory. "Gayanerenhgunis." The way I pronounced it didn't do justice to the gentle beauty of the language I'd heard spoken this afternoon by the stream at Potter Place. It sounded harsh in the isolation to which I condemned it. With so little in my experience to offer it a context, I bruised the name in my hurry to find a place and a meaning for it in my life.

The moon, no more than three quarters full, became my welcome guide. It reminded me of the winter night it followed me while I rode in my Great Uncle Charles's car, a memory I'd forgotten until now. As a four-year-old, I'd tried to figure out how the moon could be so bright on the bay, yet powerless to light a path so my father could come to me. As inconstant as it had appeared up till then, that night it brought such a constancy of light to the snow in fields, on rooftops and tree branches, I was convinced that my father had never once stopped looking for me. As reassuring as the moon had been in my childhood, its promise, unrequited with the passage of years, served only to deepen my adolescent loneliness. That winter's night moon, like Kayanerenhkunis, had in later years lacked the necessary context until Anna appeared in its afterglow to reflect its constancy and renew its promise. By the light of the double star I saw that the three—

Anna, moon and Kayanerenhkunis—provided the invisible landscape where pilgrimage inevitably takes place with all the context I would need: Anna from her impassioned heart; moon, its inner light; Kayanerenhkunis, its plain-spoken eloquence.

Despite the mystery surrounding Father Têtreault's appearance and disappearance, I didn't for a moment think his existence the product of hallucination. To do so would have been an affront to the Dark Woman and a renunciation of the seeing-through, without which I would not survive the night. So, with absolute trust I received the vision of the Woman who'd appeared to the two children in the French Alps, sitting on a moonlit rock at almost every turn in the road. She shone with the inner brightness of the moon. As she cradled her face with her long, slender hands, translucent tears squeezed through her fingers and rolled down the chiseled flumes of sleeve to the ground. Their abundance flooded the road with a brilliance that bore Anna's Toyota along like the sleek and swift canoe I'd wanted it to be. No more plodding through the muddy river bottom. This was the power of the River of the Fourth, generated by the Woman's tears. At the next turn, she removed her hands from her face to show me her brown-eyed, dark-skinned radiance. It was my mother.

I remembered my grandmother saying how powerless she felt in the face of my mother's sorrow when my grandfather would not acknowledge her beauty and her worth. While I experienced my mother's tears as an expression of her sorrow, I saw them by seeing-through as the medium of her abiding love for me. I understood that she'd not abandoned me, but transformed the sorrow of separation into the river of her prayer as my access to Grandmother and Whale. And at the next turn, she stood with arms folded and face resplendent in the feathered radiance of her headdress. I soon realized I'd gone too far when my mother no longer appeared in the turns and the way became increasingly murky.

Turning back, I glimpsed the moon through a copse of tall, wispy trees on the right-hand side of the road. The moon had been waiting for me just beyond the trees that revealed themselves, in the sweep of headlights, as starkly white birches. I drove slowly into a clearing where the light of the moon transformed the mica of a great boulder into glimmering stars. There was no trace of the Woman…of my mother. Filled with the premonition that I should not leave the car, I drove around the boulder until I came upon what seemed an impenetrable wall of thickets and trees.

Convinced by the exact alignment of the moon above with the concentration of mica stars below that I'd found the Threshold of my reckoning, I waited patiently for a sign of what to do next. Intuitively I looked for an opening in the wall. "There it is," I cried, my joy of discovery changing almost at once into the panic of being discovered. Too late, I thought, remembering the words of warning pronounced by the Dark Woman upon her leaving. How could the Enemy not know of my coming and of my present location? Would Uprooting know any less?

Directly behind the boulder, not more than fifteen feet away, a luminous slab of white granite declared the opening and proclaimed the way. The Whale Way, I thought, reeling from an ambivalence that momentarily stopped both my breath and my heartbeat. Nevertheless, I proceeded, shifting into second gear, advancing carefully over the slab and settling finally into a smooth channel no wider than the car. I found it unnerving that the path was such a precise fit on the way down into the clearing below. Sensing the encroachment from every side of a silence not unlike that with which Father Têtreault's disappearance had left me, I stayed still in the car.

How fervently I wished for the Dark Woman to speak and relieve the unbearable tension; but no, she was true to her word and let the silence be. I sought feverishly to remember everything she'd told me, but couldn't recall a single word. Then I realized that it wasn't the instruction upon which I must rely, but the seeing-through for which it had prepared me. Having reached that inescapable conclusion, my body sagged into a profound relaxation, the car's engine came to a gradual stop, and the headlights faded out. Every effort I made to return the car to function failed. The time had come for me to step outside.

While I stood by the car and looked at the illumination of moon and stars, I was astonished at how poorly they lit the clearing. Two worlds. One above, bright and well-defined; the other below, dim with the brooding of chaos. My guiding stars would be of no use to me here. Cut off as they were from the foreboding of this place, how could they hope to penetrate to the obfuscations of the Enemy? The silence was as thick as the gloom that cast the distance of eternity between me and any chance of escape without a struggle. No call of bird from the birch trees, no crackle of twig by rabbit or squirrel, to fathom the distance. I knew I was on a sea where my father had been before and could now name it the "chaos" of sons being lost to fathers who despair of forgiveness. Being able to name it made me inexplicably serene; I heard myself cry, "Pépère," with his anguished fear of dying before he was forgiven.

With my cry, the Woman appeared. Though she stood at a great distance, I could plainly see that, while her tears had subsided, she remained disconsolate. Whereas the moon and stars had failed to reach the clearing, she illuminated it with such radiance that the magnitude of my peril was clearly revealed for the first time. The compactness of pine beyond the tall birches defied escape.

"Fort Apache," I thought, wincing at the random but essential thrust to the heart of my vulnerability by a ruthless seeing-through to the essential question of my identity. Was I among the whites who held the fort or the Indians who sought to take it? I was cut to the quick by the terrifying inference that I was among those of either side whose fears prompt and pander division and whose cowardice compels intransigence. Was this cogent vision of a fortress the reflection of the fearful posture of shame from which I'd barricaded myself against the world? The likeness of my grandfather's face superimposed itself on the Woman's, transient as a single frame in a movie, but lasting as luminous link to its meaning. I grasped for the image, desperately wanting to believe in its power to reconcile my mother and grandfather.

She waved me on. "Come to me," were her unspoken words. Uttered in mystery with the foreknowledge of what I, inexperienced, was facing, I heard them as warning, urging me to survey the clearing as though it were a field of combat. From the perspective of warrior, I viewed everything in the clearing, including the Woman, with unsparing skepticism. The arena was barren but for the great boulder upon which she stood. Not a bush, another stone, a dead branch. The car was gone. The grasses, shorn by winter kill, shone silver in her radiance.

I walked toward the Woman. Raising her hand in admonition, she cautioned me to approach with more care. The vast silence held an unidentifiable sound that grew louder and more unsettling as I advanced. Alarmed, I turned to find that the grasses had begun to grow into long, slender snakes writhing silver in the Woman's expansive radiance. At first confined to the area directly behind me, the snakes swiftly gained the entire perimeter and were now moving in force toward the great boulder at the center of the circle. When I realized that I would soon be surrounded by hissing menacing snakes, I suspected the Woman of having betrayed me. Was she the Enemy? Had she lured me to my inevitable death?

A blow to my stomach was of such power that I fell to the ground and lost consciousness. When I awoke, I was crouched on my knees. The Woman had vanished. I was convinced that she'd humbled me in retaliation for my doubting. "Thomas," I could hear my grandfather's twin thunder in gentle reproof. With that, I remembered the last thing he said to me: "Follow the thunder of oracle to the end; your life will depend on it." The boulder loomed over me as shadow and forceful reminder of Her who promised the children, praying in the shadow of the French Alps, reconciliation as the fruit of their prayer.

When I stood up to evaluate my situation, the snakes had advanced to within twenty feet from the boulder, the magical center of the circle. What else but magic could restrain the luminous energy that bridled against the invisible circular line that separated them from me. Prayer? At that thought, the viperous quicksilver, braced for mortal combat, struck such a light against the sky that I feared the moon and the stars would flee in fright forever. Bracing myself too, I resolved not to stray from the shadow of the boulder, which I took to be the Woman's final word and indispensable augury.

The hissing and the heat were intolerable. When would the Enemy show? Intolerable too was the waiting. With my back to one of the boulder's four massive walls, I waited until worn by vigil, I succumbed to exhaustion. Shortly, I was struck with such force in the middle of the back that my body lurched forward, landing barely an inch from the reticent perfection of my last line of defense. Only when I dared lift my head a little to look into one snake's piercing blue eyes did I see myself lying face down at the edge of the bristling circle.

With every bit of strength remaining, I resisted naming the Enemy. That decision served me well as I then recognized the doubling of seeing-through that the penetrating blow had initiated. With my back still braced against the boulder, I saw-through to my body lying within an inch of death. Earlier I'd turned to "Stone," which I named refuge and friend in fierce though unspoken opposition to "Snake," secretly but vehemently declared the Enemy. When I finally declared "Snake" friend too, all hissing ceased and every last snake was gone.

Baffled but having at last learned the foolhardiness of prematurely naming an unseen enemy, I waited. There was an invaluable lesson in this because waiting, I admitted, had always been the most difficult thing for me to do. Running to the river had been easier than abiding my grandfather's pain; drinking, easier than facing my own. It became exceptionally difficult now as the pain deep in my back not only increased with the waiting but began to permeate the rest of my body. I stood there until Stone, having emptied itself of its radiance, poured it into my waiting. Throbbing with the rising tide of Poison, I was filled with the brilliance of Snake until I thought I would burst. "Hold your ground. Abide your pain," I heard my own loud, un-puppet-like voice command. "Remember that the Enemy is within," I shouted. As often as I'd heard that admonition through the years and as much as I'd disdained it for its overuse and seeming triteness, I wasn't underestimating it now. I believed it with all my heart.

"The Enemy is within," I declared with enormous relief as I prepared to die. "That is my battle cry, the truth of He Who Waits by a Bridge," I proclaimed from the memory of Whale sailing back to the People through the bloody gurgle of a broken heart. "Twaining," I faintly remembered. While I calmly stood my ground, my radiant body split in two. The transformation of pain to anger was made manifest by the simultaneous transformation of my divided body into two great snakes, each with a trunk of silver, a head of gold and a pair of blue sapphire eyes.

"Face to face with my Enemy," I shouted with a conviction of life stronger than my expectation of death. From a detached but nearby place, I watched the two giants glower at each other while their upright bodies swayed in a slow fascinating unison.

"Fascinations are the sapphire eyes of the soul," someone said. "When you see from your soul, you no longer speak with forked tongue, do you?" At first, I thought the Dark Woman had spoken because her restructuring humor had always been at the crux of her instruction, making fresh and acceptable those indispensable and difficult truths. From the amused gleam in their sapphire eyes, I deduced that it was the snakes who had spoken with a single voice. Suddenly and incongruously, I was reminded of the stream at Potter Place and the warmth of a language that flowed from the truth of the earth's heart.

"Do you know what language that is?" I asked.

"That is Mohawk, one language among the many of the Iroquois people," the great snakes answered with one voice.

"Is that the language my mother speaks?"

"Yes."

"Do you know where I can find her?"

"Kayanerenhkunis," they said with what seemed the perfect pronunciation. "But you know that already. Why do you ask us unnecessary questions?" They expressed their displeasure with a formidable and frightening hiss.

"But I don't know how to get there."

"Find the road to Montreal...if you survive the night. Then, listen for the voice of the River of the Fourth. There is no mistaking the sound of its voice. But first, you must survive the night." There was a finality in the temper of their last answer that I knew well enough not to question. They resumed their glowering at each other, their militant posturing and their magnificent swaying. I entertained the persuasive thought that they, no less than the Woman, bespoke augury.

"Do you not want to know more about your grandfather?" the Snakes asked with one formidable hiss.

"Yes," I answered meekly.

"When your grandfather was a boy, he wanted to be a priest. You did not know that, did you?"

"No."

"Nor did you know that, in fact, he had studied for the priesthood. Did you?"

"No, I didn't."

"Did you know that he would have given his life to be one?" Apparently in vigorous competition to be the first to divulge the secret, they preempted my reply, blurting out once again in perfect unison: "He would never recover from the shame of being dismissed on the eve of his ordination." I was shaken to the foundations of any trust I'd built up in preparation for this defining moment of pilgrimage. "You know the source of your mother's shame, do you not?"

"Yes," I answered, unable to contain my tears as I recalled those the Woman had shed for me.

"Do you know that shame breeds contempt and hatred?" The hissing reached such a pitch I thought that, at any moment, the Snakes would lunge and strike each other dead. "Do you know that your mother and grandfather hate each other so completely and so irreconcilably that their mutual hatred will be the death of you tonight?" The two great Snakes glowered at each other with such intensity, I thought their deaths imminent and inevitable.

Instead, the passion by which each was consumed effected unimaginable transformations. The one snake became a stag; the other, a whip. The stag tried to spear, and the whip to lash, an invisible and constantly moving target. The performances were of rapid fire metamorphoses: from whip to snake and back with the glint of fishline slithering into shadow for the kill; from stag to snake and back with the gleam of needle-point antler poised in the sun for another kill. This was a kaleidoscopic dance of incredible speed, horrific intent and deadly consequence.

"Be the boy who waits by the bridge," they taunted with the one voice as they filled the void between them with lightning strikes. "Help us reconcile. Teach us to ease each other's shame. Mediate our hatred and our contempt. Make us friends."

"How?" I asked, quivering.

"Show us only that you care."

"How?"

"Catch our lightning flashes with your teeth." Their hissing laughter signaled a despair beyond the reach of caring. "Drink from the cup of our unforgiving shame." The smell of sulphur, issued from the chasm where Stone, emptied of its radiance, once stood. Deathly sick and afraid, I vacillated at the brink of another decision. Waiting, which I recognized as essential to seeing-through, deferred action, whereas earlier I might have delivered myself to the lightning before I was prepared. I waited interminably. "What are you waiting for?" the great Snakes asked with a sputtering hiss that exposed their own extraordinary impatience. I waited.

My uncharacteristic patience drew from the void bolts of lightning that unnerved the Snakes as much as they pacified me.

They're "rattled," I thought, surprised but encouraged that, at a critical time, I should be filled with the Dark Woman's playful and debunking spirit. I listened to the rattles as they trembled with confusion. Soon tremor increased to roar of thunder. "Follow the thunder of oracle to the end," the Twin had counseled. I waited, listening intently to the thunder as it moved swiftly and randomly about to brilliant flashes of lightning. "How can I follow that?" I cried, desperately hoping that the Dark Woman would come to my rescue. Instead, I heard my own consolidated voice speak with unusual calm. "Dismiss Lightning, decoy of the Two. Hear the thunder only to know what you must do." I waited, concentrating on the thunder until I was assured that it emanated from the depths of the void beyond the confusion of rattles; it was only then I realized that listening had always been and would always be at the heart of my every waiting and seeing-through. As stunned as I was by the realization, I was not at all surprised that I could now follow the thunder as it rose after the lightning from the depths of the void. In wave upon wave, it came, influx of another time and another world, summoning me to hear. "I must wait upon the ebb and listen for its oracle to follow," I said with utter confidence.

How long I stood at the brink, hearing the slower, deeper thunder past the brilliant glib show of lightning, I had no way of knowing. I waited and listened past the futile glowering of the Two until the thunder began to roll back. I was certain the lightning was receding as well by the reliability of my seeing-through. But unlike superficial Lightning, Thunder left me with something of its truth to echo in my heart long after it returned to its origins. "Je vous salue, Marie…" I heard my grandfather pray the rosary. "L'amertume," I heard my grandmother punctuate the toll of his beads with the softest, most heartrending cry. "L'amertume." Bitterness. While the thunder simply murmured "shame" upon its retreat, I recognized the word as the oracle I must follow to its bitter end. Inching as close to the brink as I dared, I prepared to die.

"Come to me," the first Snake cried, "and ease your Pépère's pain."

"Come to me," the second vied, "and avenge your mother's name."

Heed Thunder, wait by the bridge and live, I heard a third voice calmly counsel.

"Come!" hissed the first.

"Come!" spat the second.

"Come!"

"Come!"

"Come!"

"Come!"

"I choose no sides," I answered dispassionately, "only the poison of both their shames." Remembering my father's leap to freedom, I dove into the void after Thunder's dying breath.

Despite the acceleration of my descent, I was able to distinguish the hiss of Thunder's breath from that of the Two as the authentic trail back to the precise moment when Whale leaped back into the lives of the People for love. As tenuous as was its breath, Thunder pierced the depths of Grandmother's love as truly as Whale pierces to the depths of a destiny lost. Pierced the great boulder I thought I'd left behind to the infinite brilliance and velocity of mica, another universe of guiding stars. Pierced to the dark pupil of the sky-blue pond, destiny's eye, by which Whale enters the lives of my mother's People from the prescient birth of their individual stars. Pierced to the truth that Thunder's breath was my grandfather's last. To the truth that before its expiration, I must grasp from the luminous dust of spiraling galaxies the bridge of forgiveness between my mother's and grandfather's mutually unforgiving shame.

"How will I find it in this mess?" I asked myself, listening for the last burst of air left in Thunder's roar.

Look for the spark of recognition, the anonymous voice interjected once again. *The one and only familiar light you will see as Thunder passes from the sky. Listen with your whole heart and see-through to reconciliation.*

"I will," I said weakly, hoping against my utter loneliness to hear the voice again and wondering if perhaps my impending death had not forced the Dark Woman's hand.

You must react instantly. Upon recognition, seize the star of your destiny and you will live. Hesitate and you will surely die.

"I won't hesitate," I promised in a powerful voice. I waited, listening.

Be ready now, godson. Be ready. It was she. Before I was able to thank the Dark Woman for returning, the last of Thunder's roar burst in my ears like an enormous balloon. Just as destiny was about to pass me by, I clawed with fierce recognition at the fizzle of a shooting star and cried, "Pépère, mother, I love you." Darkness prevailed.

I awoke the following morning from a profound sleep, face down and shivering from a dank coldness that seemed to emanate from deep within the earth. "The pit at Potter Place," I exclaimed with the discovery that my head was hanging at a painful angle over the edge of some steep precipice. Darker than the previous night of moon and stars, the penumbra before sunrise prevented further exploration. I crawled backward into what I thought was the great boulder. Sitting down and propping my back against it to support a severely strained neck, I rested until daylight. Slowly the sun rose, loosing from the black sky one long, stringy shadow of birch after another.

Good morning, the Dark Woman whispered from the clearing just the other side of the pit. *How is your neck?* I couldn't feel any pain in my neck but flexed it to make sure. There wasn't any indication of discomfort, but I couldn't say so because the chill in my spine had turned to violent shudder through my entire body.

No need to answer, she continued. *The chill is not from the night but from your near-death experience. Be glad, as I am, that you are still alive.* The announcement triggered a sobbing, which I made no effort to control. *There, there,* she said with the gentle mocking I'd grown accustomed to, which had come to epitomize her affection for me. I laughed. *Do you hear it?* she asked.

"What?"

The laughter of willow. Do you hear it?

"No."

But I do; and so will you, when body and emotion settle. It has become exquisite; for, at long last, its leaves contain the silver of tears shared and the gold of forgiveness exchanged—your mother's and your grandfather's. Their sorrows and joys intermingled. Warmth was returning to my body; stability, to my emotions. I could hear the chimes faintly. They flew straight to my heart.

"How?" I asked, skeptical still of what I had so fervently prayed for.

Thomas, she scolded. *It was you. You made it happen. You gave them that which was at once most dear to you and most difficult for you.*

"What did I give them?" I tried without success to stand.

Sit. You are too weak to stand; you have not yet been able to appreciate the nature and implications of last night's ordeal. Sit and remain quiet. I fell back against the stone.

"I..."

Shhh. You are only to listen now. Trust. Your hard-earned trust is what you gave to each in equal measure. Not to one more than to the other. You prized their shames dearly and equally. Not the whip of your grandfather's self-flagellation any more than the crown of thorns of your mother's self-imposed exile. At the risk of your life, you trusted and chose the path of seeing-through into the void and bitterness of their two shames. At one and the same time, you claimed your name and secured your destiny as reconciler. Be glad for you have put your mother and your grandfather on speaking terms and made them confidants to one another in your heart and in the hearts of those who seek reconciliation and peace. The pale light glimmered in a cloudless sky, turning the surround of treetops into a ring of emerald fire.

"My grandfather's dead, isn't he?"

Yes.

"When?"

The moment you wrested for deliverance the emblem of his shame.
"Last night?"
In the deepest part of it.
"What was the emblem?"
It is within your grasp as surely now as it was the moment of your reckoning. Remember.
"I can't."
Try.
"I was blinded by an awesome light."
Before that.
"I opened my hand."
That was your trust, godson. Now, open your hand once more. When I'd done so, I watched the dawn inscribe an incandescent lattice into the quivering flesh of my palm. *Do you see?*
"A ladder?"
Do you remember?
"Yes, it was a ladder."
What ladder?
"The one my grandfather used when he tried to hang himself," I answered as the sun rose in revelation.
Trusting, you were able to transform the emblem of his shame not only into the sacrament of his reconciliation but into that of your bridge-making. Today and always be one who waits with trust no matter how irrelevant the true bridges, testing faith, make themselves seem. She paused briefly. *Come. See what you would have become had you not believed.*
By the light of the newly risen sun, I found the pit.
Do you see? she asked in a tone more severe than any she'd used before.
"Yes."
What do you see?
"Bones," I whispered squeamishly.
The bones of hapless pilgrims all. I laughed nervously. *You laugh? Seeing the skeletons of doubt and fear by the light of your Jesus's and my Hiawatha's vision, you dare laugh?*
"I didn't mean…"

Exactly your fate, my dear, she said, enunciating the epithet with slow sarcasm, *had you not believed.*

"You're trying to scare me, aren't you?"

What I tell you is not for effect. Do you understand that you could have died last night?

"Yes."

Do you understand that waiting by an invisible bridge in the face of others' fears and doubts can be dangerous?

"Yes."

Then, know that what happened last night can happen anytime and anywhere. Do you know that?

"Yes."

Then, know that you may be called at any time to snatch the stars of seemingly contradictory destinies and make for them a rainbow vision from your trusting heart. Though others may refuse the opportunity for reconciliation you offer them, your life is nevertheless challenged each time you intercede between opposing stars. Do you understand?

"I think so."

I do not think so. She laughed softly. The incandescent host of the sun was lifted high. The Great Boulder loomed over me, a shadowless and sprawling universe of mica stars.

"I swear it's growing," I cried.

You must leave, godson, the Dark Woman warned, *but first, look again into the void.* I returned to the pit and scoured its depth for bones.

"They're gone."

Hurry! Look again!

"Ashes?" I asked, doubting what I'd seen.

Do not doubt your seeing-through!

"They're blinding me."

They are the ashes of Whale, bright with the incandescent dawn of another sun.

"Grandmother's?"

Yes. But now you must leave before Her sun, eye of the Pilgrim Corridor, incinerates you with its excess of vision. Remember the instructions of the Two, your fortunate double star of Shame. Run, godson, run! Hurtling across the clearing, I saw the Toyota suddenly appear, then ripen to vermilion with the incandescence of the other sun. I prayed I was right to think the Dark Woman's riotous laughter meant the car would start.

13

River of the Fourth

However questionable the Dark Woman's laughter made the danger in the clearing seem and whether or not she'd resorted to tricks of magic to hasten my departure, I would not presume to question her command. So, on Sunday morning, the fifteenth of August, I drove away early from the eye of Pilgrim Corridor before it waxed inexorably white with the vision she'd warned I could not withstand. After crossing from Hanover into Vermont, I headed north along the Connecticut River, passed through customs into Canada at the Rock Island–Derby line, then turned west in the direction of Montreal. I estimated that, in another two hours, I'd be near Kayancrenhkunis.

The moment I left the clearing, my body was overcome by a heavy numbness that soon lifted with a rapidity to rival the sudden clouding up of a bright blue sky. It was as though my lethargy was being siphoned into the sky as thunderclouds and I was free to ponder the two convictions that sped my heart to Kayanerenhkunis long before the storm. The first was that my grandfather had not died before having reconciled with my mother; the second, that Anna, my love, had accompanied me every step of my pilgrim way.

With uncanny swiftness and purpose these certainties came to me as soon as I took the straightaway home. Home, I had no doubt, was that timeless place between the moment I stuck my hand out to the unknown and the moment I received the emblem of my grandfather's shame, the ladder from which he reached out to my mother, placed his hand in hers and received her forgiveness. Kayanerenhkunis was home because my mother and Pépère were now walking along the River of the Fourth, talking, laughing and making peace. I was on the direct road of the heart, the way of peacemaking. This was the way Jesus had taken too when, for love, he embraced his cross. The shortcut home.

As I remembered my grandfather making the Way of the Cross in St. Anne's Church on Good Fridays, I shuddered to think that every step he took in the shadow of his isolation prevented him from carrying the cross of his shame to salvation. Taking the crooked longest way home. Push. Push away. Push the cross always to the next hill, to the next highest hill, putting yet and always another valley between himself and forgiveness—until last evening at red sunset, when in the company of his twin, he found and embraced his cross on the final hill. How free I felt, knowing my grandfather had embraced resurrection.

And Anna. The freedom of knowing that my beloved was nearer and dearer to me than she'd ever been. How futile seemed the scurry of darkening clouds to Kayanerenhkunis in racing a heart home. Traffic crawled as I flew with the luminous memory and flutter of eagle feathers and the persevering stillness of ember on a pond. Anna. Anna and I making love in the starlight of the new moon. The radiance of mystery peering through and piercing darknesses with the incomprehensible sweetness of intermingling destinies. Breathlessness of dawn anticipated by a night of endless discovery. She'd pulled the sheet away to reveal the most secret stars and the warmth of a heartbeat that fathoms the distances of a cold universe.

Her abandon. Her laughter stirring the last of the numbness of my nipples and in my groin. Her tongue finding places where sensation barely lived. Her lips teasing, teaching me love's intimations and its tenderness between long kisses. Anna had made it possible for me to find my grandfather in his shame and love him for it. There could only be one direct road to Kayanerenhkunis—the way of Anna's love for me.

Thoughts only for my grandfather and for Anna. The bittersweetness of loves once lost and now reclaimed. Only a whisper of a thought for my mother. Why had she not been more a part of my joyful experience and appreciation of the straight-away of the cross and of the heart?

Her prerogative, godson, her choice.

"What do you mean?"

She has done what many mothers find it agonizingly difficult to do, let their children go.

"But she never had me. How could she let me go?" I heard self-pity and bitterness creep into my voice.

Not so. She carried you all the deeper in her heart for having lost you so young to her despair and to her own youthful inexperience. Do you know what our People call your mother? She is called She Who Dreams by the River. It was always there, by the River, that even as a child, she sat and learned to be dreamer for her People. It was there she returned, after having lost you, to dream and dance your destiny, to learn the love that frees you to dream and dance your own destiny, fight your own battles and claim your own victories. To be what she knew from her dreaming she could not give you. Your name.

"Waits by a Bridge?"

Yes. The fierce flame of a mother's letting go had transformed my self-indulgence into fledgling fluff, freedom fresh from a fire generated by the flap of an ancient eagle's wings. *Tell me, godson, how can the drag of self-indulgence or of cloud compete with the fierceness of Eagle, especially in a race for the homeland of Kayanerenhkunis?* She laughed the uproarious laugh.

"I don't know what to make of all this," I said, giddy with the liberating fire of transformation.

It is called seizing one's destiny, godson. She laughed long with a new laugh, one which rose from the rootedness of a great willow sprung from the heart of a grandfather forgiven. Time bore no relation and relevance to traffic or clouds standing still or to eagerness of eaglet for fiercer seeing. Time didn't matter. What did is that I was on the straightaway home. *Straightaway is an apt name for it*, the Dark Woman said. *There are others, you know. Names I urge you to ponder in secret when I am gone.*

"You're going?"

You know that I am.

"For good?" I knew it would be so. I was not afraid.

I know indeed that you will not be afraid anymore than you need to be.

"Will you tell me the names?"

You tell me.

"I don't know them."

You do. See-through, Thomas, to the time of the wind-fire beyond the time of our plodding in mud, to the precise moment when you opened your hand, without knowing, to your destiny. Name what you see.

"Ladder?"

Yes, Ladder is Straightaway. What else do you see?

"Backbone of Whale," I answered without hesitation.

Yes, she said. *Absolutely. Straightaway is no other than Backbone of Whale. What other?*

"Rod," I again answered without hesitation.

True. No truer name than Rod for Straightaway. Good, godson. Is there no other?

"No," I affirmed. "No other."

True. There is no other.

"But what is the meaning of these names and their connection with the Straightaway to Kayanerenhkunis?"

I know how eager you are, my dear, like the eaglet, to fly the luminosity of the great eagle. Impossible. When you chose life in the shadow of Cannery Bridge, I was summoned to guide you through the subsequent Thresholds of your initiation to destiny, including that of the chasm, the last. I but offer you the rudiments. The rest is for you to learn without the crutch and coddle of my voice in your darkness. When I depart, you will need to learn your lessons from the shadows of life which, more often than not, will hold up to your nascent seeing-through the faintest of the emblems of reconciliation.

"What will I do?"

You will learn. For now, while my voice lasts, I must offer you the rudiments and you must acknowledge them for what they are...a modest beginning. Do you understand?

"Yes," I answered distractedly, still buoyed by the freedom of the Straightaway and only vaguely aware of the diminishing power of her voice.

Our time together is short, so pay attention to the fundamentals of peacemaking. It is different for each mediator of Grandmother's peace. For you, who are called to reconciliations of the heart, it is a matter of seeing-through to the emblems of forgiveness in conflicted lives and relationships; and by the power of trusting your visions, making them the Straightaway, Ladder, Whale's Backbone and Rod of reconciliation. Far from drowning out the Dark Woman's words, the rain, which had come without warning and soaked me before I could raise the windows, pelted the car against distraction and made it a cocoon for their contemplation. "Dance" was the last word spoken. Not by the Dark Woman. It was from the time of the fire-wind and from an earlier rain than this, yet a gentle and familiar word. My own.

I glimpsed through the downpour a highway sign that read, "Kayanerenhkunis, 39 kilomètres." I didn't beat the clouds, I thought.

Oh, my dear, how you underestimate the directness of the heart. You dance! How can you not already be there?

The freedom of connection I experienced between the rainy world of the road and the fire-and-wind world the other side of the chasm was only one of the strangenesses that I encountered on this stretch of road. There was my familiarity with place names and the layout of the land. Magog, Lac Massawippi, Lac Memphremagog, Bromont, Rivière Richelieu, La Prairie and finally "Kayanerenhkunis." All known to me. I anticipated landmarks, a purple house on a hill, turns in the road, lake views, a river crossing. Known. I saw a river where there was none.

River of the Fourth was all she whispered. I'd begun to realize how her words had seeped into my soul. Had perhaps always been there. Nothing obsessive or peremptory about them. I knew they'd always be there. Essential to twaining and seeing-through. "Rod, Ladder, Backbone of Whale, Straightaway." Whale Words spoken by Grandmother to my soul in the time of Wind and Fire.

River of the Fourth, she whispered. There was the word and more than the word, "Dance." I danced without ever having learned to dance, without knowing how to dance. I danced.

Dance. It is pilgrimage in place, she said, her voice still fairly strong. *It is your mother's People's way of journeying the heart to the source, to the spirit spring of the common rock. It is prayer Grandmother hears; as the rain on your car and the beat of moccasin on the earth make a cocoon where we and our Mother talk alone for the good and promise of all the People. Dance.* I danced between an interior homeland and that which was unfolding before me. Danced the trail of my origins with the time and care for detail that defied the speed with which I'd traveled. Strangenesses of the most familiar and ordinary kind.

I hadn't given much thought to what I would do in Kayanerenhkunis—just to get there as soon as possible to find my mother. My heart beat faster in anticipation. It seemed as though I'd been awaiting this moment all my life when, in fact, I'd learned only weeks ago that she was still alive. Though I'd only been able to catch glimpses of the great Saint Lawrence River through the rain, I felt its attraction. Is this the River of the Fourth? I wondered.

Perhaps, the Dark Woman said. *Time will tell.* Her ambivalent answers annoyed me. *Time and timing are of the essence,* she answered my disquiet patiently. She laughed the sweetest and most light-hearted laughter of willow yet. The Saint Lawrence River. What was the influence it held over me? With a paranoia reminiscent of my former DT's, I attributed malevolent powers to the river that had once appeared a thin lifeless scrawl along the fold of a map.

Convinced that my state of mind could not be ascribed to the benign mischief of Uprooting, I braced myself for what lay ahead. I questioned whether or not I'd chosen the path of the lesser danger. The series of sweeping overpasses ahead seemed creations of toothpicks and clay as I visualized the river leaping its bounds and carrying them along with it into the chasm I'd been fortunate enough to escape with my life last night.

The sense of freedom vanished. An asphyxiating terror struck as soon as I'd emerged from the third underpass, compelling me to stop in the middle of a huge rain puddle.

"Am I trespassing?" I asked meekly, much as I would have asked the Dark Woman a question earlier on in my initiation.

You have still to learn through experience when felt boundaries are Thresholds and when they are dead-ends. When to stand and when to pass.

"I feel that I don't belong here, that the river itself is saying, 'Turn back.'"

Boundaries are by far the best teachers of waiting. Tell me. Did you not think of Uprooting a short while ago?

"Yes."

Well, what does Uprooting teach?

"That he is not the Enemy?"

True. What else? I was stumped. *To wait for the opposing sides of a conflict or ambivalence to come into view, for the antagonists to show themselves so that you may see and hold the middle for them, the reconciling emblem of your vision. The Rod.* Godson, *mediators of Grandmother's peace, must learn to wait with the Rod.* Confused, I looked through the window at high grasses and cattails dripping gold. The rain had stopped; the sky was clearing; the sun, shredding clouds.

"Waiting for?" I asked, thinking it a stupid question but compelled to ask it anyway.

Not a stupid question at all, my dear. One which sooner or later must be asked. Wait with and not for because Rod is always there for you, the mediator, to find. Rod waits for your waiting...for you to take hold of when you have truly found and clearly seen both ends of a problem or a divide. Rod is your vision to take and to hold with all of your might as a mirror to both antagonists that they may discern in one another what is still possible to respect and to love. Think of your grandfather as you wait for your vision. Wait as he waited. Time as he timed. Seize the Rod as he did when he perceived the light in the fish's eye and straightaway reeled him in. Do you remember what you did last night when you leaped into the chasm?

"Yes."

What did you do?

"I grabbed my vision?"

Exactly. With the Straightaway of your heart, you seized the Rod. And what was the Rod?

"A ladder," I answered with more authority.

The Ladder. Ladder of your grandfather's shame become the emblem of his forgiveness and of his reconciliation with the world. I marveled at the gold in the grasses and among the cattails multiplying, and felt a gentle pressure on my left shoulder. I dismissed the sensation until I felt it again. Then, I turned to find an old man standing by the door. When I rolled the window down, he placed his hand on my shoulder and said, "You look lost, son. Is there anything I can do to help?" As I stared up at him, his dark, crevassed face became so bright I couldn't see it anymore.

"Is this Kayanerenhkunis?" I asked.

"Yes." In his voice, I detected the rumble of distant thunder; his hair shone white. My grandfather's twin? When the light gradually faded and I could see again, my hunch proved wrong. This wasn't Father Têtreault but a much older Indian wearing jeans and a faded plaid shirt. Now that his face was visible, I judged it quite ordinary but for the penetrating eyes in which, it seemed, no insidious and evil intent could be kept.

"You're in the right place, my son," he said after an easy silence. "Keep on going. Up ahead...just around the bend, you'll see a tunnel. Pass through. In Great Spirit's good time, you'll be told what to do." With a final pressure on my shoulder, he lifted his hand away in a slow, measured arc reminiscent of the final blessing Father Etienne always dispensed at the conclusion of High Mass. I started the car and headed slowly for the bend in the road. In the rear-view mirror, I saw the old man standing on a gold-studded island where the huge rain puddle ought to have been. I saw him turn and walk toward the first of the three bridges, his long white hair tied in a ponytail, bobbing brilliantly in the sun.

Stop, the Dark Woman commanded when the tunnel came into view. Once more I pulled over to the side of the road. *Permission granted*, she offered wryly, *to him who has learned to wait. Do you see?*

"Yes."

If it were not in your People's best interest to proceed, that would have been made known to you as well. Do you understand?

"Yes." The Dark Woman's voice had become weaker. *My time is short, Thomas, as your observation has been keen enough to tell. There is so much to say in so little time. And now I leave for good. My part in your instruction will soon be at an end.* I felt the kick in my stomach I'd had so many times before when left to my own devices.

This time is different, she said. *This time you are prepared. But you must listen well to the last of my teaching. Do you hear?*

"Yes." So fast was her voice fading, I feared there would not be time for her to tell me what I needed to know.

Trust, she said, laughing with barely audible breaks in her voice. *First, I want you to take a good look at the tunnel before you. What do you see?*

"It's a small tunnel."

Yes?

"Built into a grassy embankment."

Like?

"Cannery Bridge," I blurted out with the exhilaration of discovery.

The fourth... she began.

"...bridge?"

Yes. The fourth bridge. The three behind you and the last that lies ahead."

"River of the Fourth?"

Exactly, my dear Thomas, River by the Fourth Bridge. And this little tunnel is identical to that of...

"...Cannery Bridge?"

Yes.

"Twins?"

No.

"Twaining?"

Absolutely. Despite the noticeable breaks in her voice, the laughter of willow was whole in every golden raindrop on the field, the marsh and the grassy bank. *And if my mathematics of the twaining are correct, here we have double fours. Tell me, godson, what is the quotient of four divided by four?*

"One."

One bridge. The name of which is?

"'The Sweeney?'"

Yes. It takes four bridges always...four sides of a stone always, to make a Rainbow Bridge. For you, there will always be the glimmer of Sweeney Bridge and of your father's triumph over death by way of the River of the Fourth in every Rainbow Bridge you hold up to the promise and the challenge of Reconciliation. Remember.

"I will." Though it was approaching noon and this mid-August day was characteristically hot and humid after the rain, I trembled with cold.

Thomas, the Dark Woman continued, *look to the top of the embankment and tell me what you see.*

"I don't know what you mean. I don't see anything but grass."

Trust and see-through, Thomas. See-through. Now what do you see?

"Railroad tracks."

Like the ones you stumbled across when you entertained thoughts of killing yourself?

"Yes."

What did you learn of railroad tracks in the lessons of Potter Place?

"They return Whale from the sea."

For what reasons?

"For love?"

Yes, Thomas, that is one; but there are two reasons. What is the other? Intermittently the Dark Woman's words disappeared in whispers.

"I don't know." My body shook uncontrollably with cold.

You know that I cannot pass with you through the tunnel?

"I know," I answered, my teeth chattering.

I have come full circle, godson. Then I found you by the tunnel below the track. Now I leave you by the tunnel below the track. I found you dying and without a glimmer of vision; I leave you thriving and initiated to vision. Tell me, what is the second reason for Whale's return?

"Vision."

Just so. Without Whale and its Dragonfly eyes, you would lack the vision of bridge-maker. So, be ever mindful, godson, of Ladder for it is as much track by which Whale comes to you as it is emblem by which you reconcile, in the name of your grandfather's reconciliation, the conflicting forces of your People's universe. As the Jacob's Ladder of your grandfather's tradition is the path and means by which angels from heaven visit vision and healing upon the earth, so the Medicine Wheel of your mother's tradition is the path and means by which the messengers of Grandmother make friends of enemies and life force of venom. These messengers will make themselves known to your vision in many guises: old man, snake, boulder, leprechaun, reliquary, ember, all of which are recognizable only by the power of seeing-through. Godson, be ever mindful of Ladder.

"I will." The violence with which my teeth chattered was becoming more than my body could contain.

You must hear me through to the end, howsoever the cold inclines you otherwise. Do you hear?

"Yes." I was just beginning to realize that the increase of cold throughout my body was in direct response to the decline of the Dark Woman's voice. It was as though she were dying inside my body.

Vision requires each of its four sides at once, she lectured in a throaty whisper. *Do you understand?*

"Yes."

First, Straightaway, the heart of vision. Then, Ladder, the emblem of vision. Then, Rod, the power of vision. And finally, Backbone of Whale, the courage of vision. All four. Together. Like the white stone the other side of Potter Place, like the altar in the chapel of La Salette Shrine, like Father Quint's shoe box, like the Great Boulder in the middle of last night's clearing. Do you understand?

"Yes." It didn't seem so much a question of understanding as it was of hearing the Dark Woman's words. Whispers thinned almost to vapor. She was dying; and the chill to the marrow of my bones was my mourning. As I began to understand the searing articulation within each of her dry gasps, it became clear to me by the power of seeing-through that she was fulfilling the ancient and necessary ritual of the death of the mystagogue, which heralds the birth of the neophyte into vision. This would be her dearest and most authoritative legacy.

Finally, the courage of your own vision, the leap, she gasped. *Backbone of Whale.* Wisps of cloud left to be burned away by the sun approaching zenith. They would last, I knew, only as long as she. *You may not remember clearly enough and I no longer have the luxury of time to tease the memory from you. So I tell you now the final truth of the Fourth. When you reached for Ladder, the emblem of the Fourth, with the power of Rod, you consummated the first of your many pilgrimages to come.*

For the first time in your young life, dear godson, you trusted completely. There was no dawdling, no hanging back, no toehold on the brink. You let go of the narrowness of your certainties and plunged headlong into a vast chaos from which there was no guarantee of return. At the moment of release, even before you secured Emblem in your hand, the courage of Whale came up under you. Do you remember?

"I remember a powerful jolt followed by the incredible lightness of my body. Something like what happened to me the night Anna found me under the bridge."

Precisely that and more. This time Whale carried you back to its origins where Grandmother turns the virulence of our most bitter shames into medicine for our deepest fears. Be grateful, godson. Her voice was entirely gone. There was nothing left of it but a fierce grating, which I knew was marking my soul for bridge-making.

"Don't go," I pleaded.

Do not let appearances deceive you, she whispered with unnerving determination. *The River of the Fourth is the River of your vision which springs from the depths of Grandmother's heart. Trust that River to take you where you must go. Be He Who Waits by a Bridge. Straightaway! Ladder! Rod! Backbone of Whale! Trust the River of the Fourth, my dear. Dance!* Her last word was the least audible but the most grating of all. Every last cloud in the sky was consumed by the sun at zenith. The ice melted in my bones. The thin outline of tunnel through which I must pass alone gleamed gold.

14

The Great False Face

As soon as I passed through the small tunnel of red stone and cool dampness, I intuitively looked for the museum where I would get my bearings and perhaps some information about my mother. "Museum of Kayanerenhkunis," the sign that fronted the one-story log building read. I was truly here; but not for long as I sensed that the old Indian had granted me only temporary passage. It seemed obvious that staying would be dangerous. The adrenaline that discharged through my body turned my new-found resolve into a quicksilver of doubt. Nevertheless, I left the car, at the Dark Woman's insistence that bridge-making meant facing the possibility of danger and death every day of my life.

The ground under my feet was much more substantial than I expected when everything inside me shuddered with the expectation of peril. Not so the letters of "Kayanerenhkunis," carved with simple majesty in a great slab of oak over the front door; they trembled, despite their stoutness, as violently as I. Only when I began to focus on the soaring totem pole by the entrance did I feel the solidity of the earth pass through the soles of my feet into my body. As the animal faces in the aging wood peered at me from a time predating the exile of Whale, I was mindful of the power of Uprooting and seeing-through, for which it was primarily responsible. Watching luminous strands of primordial wood unravel from the pole, flow into the earth from which they'd originated, and return through the tissue of sapling growing from rock in a near-by field, I knew I was home.

In the totem pole, I saw the patience of Mohawk heart harbor the stillness of the land of whales, and the reverence of Mohawk hand release it for my vision and my dance. How could I be in danger here, where I felt Mohawk artists as midwives of my destiny? As I watched, the eyes of my seeing-through were drawn to the brightest strands of the unraveling at the top of the pole where an eagle's broad beak protruded into space. Guided by the discerning look of ancient eyes, what a bite of space and stillness it took! Below beak and eyes, Eagle entrusted its span of wings to Stillness, which made of every fibrous feather and steely cut a swift prayer on behalf of the entire People. For only an instant, I saw wings of Eagle become flukes of Whale, a great undulation on the River of the Fourth, bringing back as swift an answer from the heart of Grandmother, a blessing on all the People.

I felt desperately alone; compelled by a growing sense of vulnerability, I decided to enter the museum, persuaded by the eerie stillness that I would soon be crossing yet another pilgrim Threshold. Squinting through the screen door into the gloom of a small vestibule, I was reminded of the tunnel through which the Dark Woman had been forbidden to pass, unable to guide me through this next darkness. Beyond the door was a dimly lit anteroom. The luminous eyes of wolves, turtles and bears, deeply chiseled into the low ceiling, followed me from the overarching mystery of Grandmother's heart.

I had the disquieting awareness of being led into a primeval setting by an unseen presence. I had entered unexplored territory where the sun dwelled in treetops and rarely slipped through twilight tangle to forest floor. I was unable to see to the end of the room but knew that a mysterious presence lurked there. While I waited for it to appear, I inventoried dolls, moccasins, jewelry, books, jackets, headdresses, stones, shells, carvings and the like displayed on a nearby wall and in adjacent cases. But the attraction of these objects gave way to the supernatural stillness that filled the room. I waited, as I'd been taught by the Dark Woman.

It wasn't long before I knew that the presence had taken me for an interloper. I felt its alarm, that I'd encroached upon its retreat. While the shrillness of that silent alarm urged escape, I chose instead to study the texture and grain of the wide-planked flooring beneath my unsteady feet. Then, I glimpsed, floating through shadow, shimmers that became realities—of rattle, gourd, handle and horn. In their midst danced a huge grotesque red mask. Confronted by the visible presence of what might well have been the Enemy, I waited, aghast, for it to reveal the truth of its nature and its intent.

As it danced toward me, I saw it shoot incandescent rays through shadow from the dark centers of its two yellow eyes. Its gyrations flung its mop-like black hair straight out like a multitude of darts in search of a target. It looked like a tragic clown: its nose, bulbous; its mouth, the taffy-pull of a contortionist's grief. While every part of it displayed virtuosity of terrifying imagination, I was especially intrigued by the contortions of a mouth on the cusp of cannibalism. Lurching in my direction, the mask made a pretense of devouring everything in its path, opening wide its maw to show me the very chasm from which I'd escaped with my life last night. Suddenly it leaped at me, and with jaw sprung to its obscene limit, it spat a star of the second magnitude in my face. The bright star turned into a little dog yipping, somersaulting and pissing meteors into the chasm. "Dog Star," I cried, laughing my first uproarious and liberating laughter of willow.

The red mask had transformed from terror to entertainer, reminding me pointedly that throughout her instruction, the Dark Woman insisted I not take myself too seriously. She'd taught that the grandiosity of creating importance where there was none blinded vision to the genuine emblem and interfered with the authentic power of Rod to see-through. From the sputtering of the last of the meteors, a tiny spark fell by my feet. Dying, it gave me the light of its truth in the guise of a red deer. A large doe, she snorted and clattered her hooves on the hard yellow pine floor until Stillness absorbed her restless spirit, and she quieted my eyes with her steady gaze. Then, she turned and walked slowly through the forest to the river bank where she disappeared. With her went the twilight and the tangle of branches that had held the sun captive.

"Hello," a voice called out to me. "Can I help you with anything?"

"I don't know," I said, spotting a young woman behind a counter and reeling still with my visions. The sunlight, pouring through a window behind her, set her apart in the blaze of her white blouse from the penumbra of that darker world that I had experienced. Her dark skin and braided black hair, though, bespoke a beauty and mystery separate from and impenetrable to the sun's searching rays. "I'm looking for someone," I continued, unsure that she was the one to whom I should look for guidance.

"I know. She is waiting for you." I trembled almost as fiercely as I had when I first realized that the Dark Woman was leaving for good. "She has been waiting for you a long time." The young woman was as calm as I was flustered.

"My mother?"

"No, your grandmother." Since I'd learned of my mother's whereabouts from Father Têtreault, I'd thought of no one but her. Not of a grandmother or, for that matter, of anybody else. In an attempt to hide my disappointment, I lowered my eyes only to discover the single string of purple sea shells the woman wore around her neck. From their strange shining, I knew that she was some kind of intermediary...perhaps one of those "messengers" the Dark Woman had told me about. "Your mother is not here just now," she said in answer to my unspoken question.

"Where is she?"

"You must ask your grandmother that." The more forth-coming she was, the more she became part of the mystery that enfolded this place of transit or—more likely and truly—this transitional state. Like Potter Place, the museum encompassed more than its external appearance indicated. Like Fathers Quint and Têtreault, this young woman, perhaps a counterpart to the angel of Jacob's Ladder, ran errands of a very different kind. The Dark Woman had alluded to powerful spirits turning medicine to venom and venom to medicine at critical junctures of an Indian's quest on behalf of every creature on the Wheel. Was the young woman to vanish as had Father Têtreault?

In fact, she did not; but the deer head mounted above the window directly behind her took on the unearthly aspect of the antagonist stag of the clearing. Antlers worn smooth by the rub of tree and battle, it watched over the ominous world with which the young woman seemed well acquainted. Dankness of forest floor, thick with the night prowl of predator, cloyed my nostrils. The young woman's brown eyes gleamed with an other-worldly light of recognition. She patiently awaited my question.

"How do I find my grandmother?"

"Do you see the deer who watches over my shoulder?"

"Yes," I answered timidly.

"Go back there and follow his tracks into the trees," she advised, pointing through the window to a stand of pine the other side of a meadow. "Past the trees, you will see a cross. Take a left there. Your grandmother's place is on the right-hand side of the street...last house. An old white house. She will be waiting for you."

"Thank you."

Sensing some urgency in her voice, I turned and headed

for the exit. "Good luck," she called out just as I was stepping into the obscurity of the entryway. I looked back only to reassure myself that she was still there. The young woman smiled and waved.

The deer's path began on the westerly side of the museum as a deep furrow through tall grasses, readied with apparent care to receive the solitary steps of a mother's lost child for the furtherance of his vision. I didn't doubt for a moment that my mother had a hand in all this. As I hurried across the field toward the pines, I noticed how much more hot and humid it had become. Though the sun still shone, high cumulus clouds were gathering in the northwest. I saw no one, but suspected that I was being watched. I glanced back to see whether the young woman was watching; she was not. Perhaps my mother peered from a thicket blind to assess my progress without wanting or being able to influence it. No, I determined; they were the eyes of a greater power that drew me past the museum to the totem eagle's jut of beak and stretch of wing. Crickets announced my entry into the wood with a sharp yammering from clumps of goldenrod.

When I emerged from the wood, I saw the cross. Where the two steel girders were raised in blessing against high wind and dark cloud, I crossed the street where my grandmother lived. But before I reached the other side, winds drove the clouds down from an electric sky, pushing me back and turning me by force around to face the cross. Lightning revealed the steel grillwork to be the jeweled radiance of a crucifix, the illumination of Dragonfly's carcass streaming resurrection through the pinholes of his agony and death. I turned and ran against the rain toward my grandmother's house.

She'd pushed the screen door open in anticipation. "You look like a wet rat," she said as she shut the door behind us. "You bring this rain with you?" I searched the gloom in vain for the woman behind the straight words and abrasive manner. Slowly my eyes adjusted and I saw a fieldstone fireplace and on either side of it, shelves full of books. "Come on," she directed. "You can't stay in here dripping wet. This is my study. Where I do my work. I won't abide you mucking it up." As I wiped my feet on the doormat, my eyes were drawn to brightly colored circles in the middle of the floor.

"You like my carpet?"

"What carpet?"

"The circles…"

"Oh…yes," I answered, straining in the dark to see the ground from which the circles glowed.

"Follow me," the woman commanded.

I walked behind her into the kitchen that seemed brighter than the other room because of the fiery curtains hanging in three small windows. My eyes flew to the expertly woven zigzags of red, yellow, beige and forest green. They were flames that defined the woman when she turned abruptly round to take her measure of me. Strangely, this incisive action rather than her earlier words put me in mind of the Dark Woman. It became obvious that my grandmother would be painfully truthful with me.

"Did you make those curtains?" I asked partly out of curiosity and partly from the anxiety that both house and woman aroused in me.

"Yes."

"You wove them?"

"Yes." I guessed that somewhere in the obscurity of her study stood my grandmother's loom, and sensed that her weaving represented more than the means of making a living or passing time away. Unexpectedly I pictured in my mind the luminous tapestries Whale wove into the iron-gray sky of Cannery Bridge in response to my childhood longing. "You'll do," she concluded, looking briefly into my eyes. "Come over here and sit down."

She lifted two chairs from the shadow of a corner and toted them on her hips to the middle of the room. "Sit," she ordered. She sat quietly across from me with her hands folded in her lap and resumed gazing into my eyes. I didn't flinch as I found her face not only pleasing but reassuring to look at. I saw nothing in her features to confirm my initial qualms about her. There was a youthfulness that shone from her weathered face, reminding me fleetingly of Father Têtreault. In it there resided no disposition to smile but more than a hint of complicity in a mischief she intended to keep from me.

The large black-and-white chessboard squares of the linoleum invited my seeing-through, as I continued to look her calmly and directly in the eye. The game, I knew, was in her eyes and I was drawn willingly to it. I couldn't help but be amused at the thought of another Threshold coming on.

"Before we go any further with this," she said casually, "do you know what 'Kayanerenhkunis' means?"

"No," I answered.

"It is essential that you know from the start the meaning of your place of origin. Do you want to know its meaning, Thomas?" I was startled that she knew my name.

"Yes."

"Oh, I know your name all right and its true meaning...and what it implies for the rest of your life. You are He Who Waits by a Bridge. And for whom do you wait?"

"I don't know."

"You wait for your Grandmother, Kayanerenhkunis. She Who Makes Peace. To be bridge-maker, you must know this. Do you understand?"

"Yes."

"For whom do you wait by a bridge?"

"For Kayanerenhkunis, my Grandmother."

"And what is the meaning of Her name?"

"She Who Makes Peace."

"Good. Now, do you have a question for me?"

"Yes, I do," I said meekly, hesitant to ask it.

"Do not hesitate to ask important questions."

"Grandmother, are you the Dark Woman?" Raising her hands in a gesture of disbelief, she laughed a remarkably uproarious laugh but one lacking the color, breadth and depth of willow.

"No, no, no," she protested as she laughed. "The Dark Woman is someone else. An immortal. One who has taken an interest in you beyond any I, despite my undying love for you, may aspire to. Try to understand and trust as completely as you can everything she took upon herself to teach you in the time Grandmother gave her to be the initiatress of your vision. Do you understand?"

"I think so." In fact, I was overwhelmed.

"That's good enough for me," she said to my relief. "Then, let us proceed." As she was talking, I wondered why there was no table in the kitchen. "I like the space," she answered. "I like being able to move around without bumping into things. Furthermore, I like eating on the move and wherever I please." I tried not to think of anything specific because I suspected the game consisted of her reading my thoughts back to me. "Is that so?" she asked. "Sounds sort of simplistic to me. Do you think I would trouble myself to read the thoughts of a novice even if he happens to be my grandson?"

"I..."

"Absolutely not!" She laughed. I observed that she hadn't smiled once. Either she laughed out of control or appeared grim.

"'Grim,' is it? And 'out of control,' is it?" She laughed. I blushed with embarrassment and swore to think only trivial thoughts from then on. Such as...her kitchen was smaller than my Mémère Têtreault's. "I like it small," she countered. "Just three small rooms. That's plenty big for me." She paused a moment as though she were giving me time to outthink her, to play my end of the game better than she did hers. "When I have company," she continued, "I set the card table up here where we're sitting. It's sturdy enough for what I put out to eat." Anticipating my every thought and question, she played two or three moves ahead of me; and when I tried to calculate from move to move how many she'd actually planned in advance, she sought to keep me off balance. We both laughed enthusiastically and the laughing together consolidated my trust in her. She could never hurt me, I decided.

"True," she affirmed emphatically. The only light visible in the kitchen was shed by the zigzag flames of the curtains; only when I'd warmed to that light did I ask about my mother.

"Where is she?"

"At last," she exclaimed, exhaling a sigh of profound relief. "I thought you'd never put to me the question I couldn't recognize as the true one until it was asked. You've won, grandson. The game is over."

"I've won?"

"Yes. You finally asked the one question I could not anticipate, the crucial question I could not put to you and to which only you could give a voice. The asking alone has made the truth of Kayanerenhkunis accessible to you. Now we may proceed. Are you ready, grandson?"

"I am."

"I am not your biological grandmother." I believed that the game was still on and resolved to steel myself against all possible deceits, however innocent and playful they might be. Nevertheless, my resolve to stay that course faltered when my eyes fell upon the beads my grandmother wore around her neck. While they resembled in size and luster the single strand the young woman in the museum wore, they consisted of four strands, each strung with seashells of a different color: white, pink, lavender and black. They made a bold statement.

"I am a clan mother," she said in anticipation of what would have been my next question. "Everybody's mother and grandmother. That's how we do it here. All mothers and aunts, fathers and uncles to the young. Given my office, it falls upon me to look out for the children in a special way. That was true of Lora when her mother, your biological grandmother, died bringing her only child into the world." While these were momentous words, they didn't surprise me, as I'd begun to anticipate them long before they were spoken.

"I know," I said with the inexplicable conviction of having been a party to this truth before I was born. "You looked after her?"

"Yes," she said. "She was barely a day old. The midwife brought her to me and I raised her like my own."

"What about her father...my grandfather, where was he?"

"Who knows, Tom. That's what they call you, isn't it?"

"Yes."

"Jake, your grandfather, was an iron worker. He traveled all over, building bridges and skyscrapers. He'd go where the work was—New York, Montreal, Chicago, San Francisco. His father was one of the men working on the Quebec Bridge when it collapsed in 1907. Jake was two or three years old then. A lot of our boys died there. Your great-grandfather was one of the boys who came back." The rain pelted the low roof and washed against the little windows in waves. As the rhythm of the rain underscored the rise and fall of her story, the old woman spoke in a monotone that suggested the ritual retelling of a much older story from a far different time. "Did you see the cross up the street?"

"Yes."

"Well, that was built in memory of the Mohawk men who died lugging and stringing steel up in the sky."

"What happened to my grandfather?"

"Like his father, he couldn't help himself. He went after the challenge. Of course, there was money in it too. He sent some to your grandmother once in a while. Then, about three months before your mother was born, the money stopped coming. We didn't hear from Jake again. That's ironwork...a tough business." She shook her head. That was the only time she'd budged during the entire recital. "You know, your mother never once asked me about her father, but I'd catch her, when she thought no one was looking, standing by the cross. She never looked up at it...just stood there with her back to it as though she was waiting for somebody or hunting for something she'd lost on the ground." I peered over the old woman's shoulder at a mask I'd noticed. The rain had stopped slapping at the windows and now leaned hard against them in a steady torrent.

"Is that what I think it is?" I asked, fidgeting in my chair.

"You've seen it before, haven't you?" My answer stuck in my throat at the sight of fiery zigzags leaping like ecstatic lightning to set the red mask free.

"It's a great dancer, don't you think?" The old woman seemed to laugh more at my consternation than at the antics of the mask, which cavorted uninhibitedly about the room.

"The museum! I saw it in the museum," I sputtered.

"The same." Red-faced, crooked-nosed, black hair flinging darts, jaundiced eyes flashing incandescence, it danced. "No difference at all?" she asked.

"It smiles more," I exclaimed, proud of my perception.

"And what does its smiling teach you, grandson?"

"It has teeth," I said, examining the mask's crooked smile. "Enormous teeth! Grinding...clamping down like the teeth of a vise..." After one last wicked smile, the mask retreated back to its place on the wall.

"The enchantment of a smile." The old woman mimicked the mask's most hideous smile.

"What?"

"A ploy, grandson. Distraction. With all your attention given to the exquisite contortions of a smile, you are wonderfully diverted from the mask's essential truth. Come, grandson. I'll show you." I followed her to the mask. "Now, put your left eye up to the Great False Face's left eye." She detected my misgiving. "Yes, grandson, you have been confronted by the Great False Face, well known to you not by name but by association with one of your powerful familiars. You must not fear him since he is the brother of your benefactor, Uprooting. Come." I approached the mask cautiously. "Don't be afraid, Tom. Closer," she instructed, giving me a gentle push from the back. "That's good. Now, look into the pupil, the very center of the eye." I obeyed. After a long silence, I was overcome by a deafening roar of wind and the sensation of being sucked into the tunnel of the mask's seeing.

"God!" I heard myself screaming from a great distance. "Here I go again!" echoed back at me through the rush of wind until I could see my own body somersaulting in the cyclone of the deeper silence.

"Over and over again," I heard my grandmother announce with extraordinary clarity. "Every day of a bridge-maker's life."

"God!" reverberated from the great distance through the uproar of my grandmother's laughter.

"Do you see it yet?"

"What?" I called back as my body was catapulted by the cyclone into the sea.

"Float and wait," was all she said in response to my desperation. "Wait."

"I'm sick of waiting," I retorted. She laughed back at me with an unbridled hilarity.

"I see something," I shouted.

"Tell me what you see."

"It's only a blur now...way out there." The blur squiggled toward me and assumed a more definite shape midway in the tunnel of the Great False Face's seeing.

"Do you see it yet?"

"A whale?" I asked incredulously.

"Can't you tell?" Past the midpoint of the mask's vision, Whale breached into full view, liberally spraying great beads of light about with the splat of its mammoth flukes.

"It's Whale!"

"Are you sure?"

"Yes."

"Do you see it still?"

"Yes."

"Then, look and remember it well, for this is no ordinary

whale. This, my dearest grandson, is River Whale. This is the Protector and Benefactor of our People. This is the only Whale you can ride to vision. Did you know that?"

"No."

"If you had not asked about your mother, you would have returned to Ingram no better off than when you left there. You would have witnessed but the one manifestation of the Great False Face and been deprived of this second. You would have failed to learn that the way to vision is not by his omnivorous maw but by his left eye alone. Not by appetite but by discrimination. Do you understand?"

"No, I don't. Not everything."

"That's as it should be. I will explain. To enter into vision by the maw is to take the exclusive path of emotion. Your feelings can take you only so far. More often than not, that path, which relies on the narrowness of one's instincts, swallows an initiate whole. You must enter into the vision which surpasses your understanding by the eye. By the left eye of transcendence alone. It is only through the spiral of the Great False Face's seeing that River Whale will find you and bear you safely through the chasm to the source of Grandmother's healing and reconciliation. You understand?" Unerringly she took my silence for a no. "What now?" she asked with seeming impatience. "I'm not impatient with you, grandson. It's that we have so little time, but go ahead. Ask." The room was smaller and darker than ever, a tight cocoon against the roar of a great waterfall.

"I don't understand what you said about my mother. How I would've been sent back home if I hadn't asked for her."

"When you asked for her, it was not simply because you love her. It was from the heart of your seeing-through that you asked. It was not solely for your biological mother that you were asking. You inquired after the woman her People call 'She Who Dreams by the River.' In so doing, you asked after the prayers and blessing of the People for whom she dreams. In deference to her, they pray that you be given the medicine and vision of River Whale. They accept you as son, brother and bridge-maker for your People. Do you, in turn, accept these roles for which the Dark Woman saw fit to prepare you?"

"I…"

"Stop wasting time, grandson. Do you accept? Yes or no?"

"Yes." The room was so dark I couldn't see my grandmother but so close I could feel her breath through my clothes. I was soaked through as though I'd been out in the rain from the beginning of the storm. This was another kind of cocoon. Not that of the Straightaway on the road where Stillness couched me in safety against the turbulence of the world.

"Now do you know why I made a point of telling you that I am not your biological grandmother?"

"To teach me that I belong to a People?"

"And that what you do, however removed from this homeland you happen to be, is either blessing or curse upon all your People. Do you understand?"

"Yes."

"Do you also know why it is that the Great False Face showed you his teeth?" She didn't pause for an answer, driven, it seemed, as the Dark Woman had been, by a constraint and imperative she would not name. "To show you that, at all cost, you must enter vision through the discrimination of his eye, not the allure of his mouth, however sensually gratifying he makes that organ out to be. Never by his mouth. Never. Do you understand?" I nodded, knowing she wouldn't allow me the time to respond. "For whatever star you find calling out to you from the maw will, in its hurry to embrace you, burn from your memory any recognition of your true name and destiny. Alcohol was such a star. Lucky for you, River Whale came along in answer to your mother's prayer with the fond deeper memory of your name from the time before the sea. Do you see him still?"

"Yes."

"What is he doing now?"

"He's still coming toward me."

"Do you see his eyes?"

"Not yet."

"Good. Since you must not ride vision with impunity, you will return from the tunnel of the Great False Face's sight not a moment sooner or later than River Whale makes contact with your eyes. Do you understand?"

"Yes."

"By this gesture alone can you adequately express not only your utter dependence but your willing reliance on him for your vision. Use the power of discrimination his Dragonfly eyes will transmit upon contact. Return a moment too soon and you will never see again; a moment too late, never see-through again. Never."

Suddenly a multitude of flying pinwheels erupted in the night space between River Whale and me, spinning out red, yellow, blue, green and white tracers until the tunnel became one immense, brilliant and multicolored pinwheel.

"Talk about your distractions," I cried out, despairing I would be able to detect the eyes of River Whale at the precise moment he made contact with mine.

"Rely, grandson, on the prayer of the People and on the power of River Whale to make the moment known."

"I can't see..." The streaming carnival of lights continued, unabated.

"There are but five circles of light between you and the River Whale now." Just as I was about to protest, my grandmother cut me off. "Listen. Only five. Circles of red, yellow, blue, green and white medicine—each a remedy for a specific shame to be healed and a reconciliation to be effected. If you come to any one of these medicines by way of the maw of your presumptuousness, you will make of it a poison for your People. If you come to them by way of the humility of the Great False Face's left eye, you will truly be He Who Waits by a Bridge and your father will not have leaped for his life in vain."

The very instant she mentioned my father, the maelstrom of lights reverted back to the original five pinwheels which, in turn, transformed into translucent pools of red, yellow, blue, green and white light. To my astonishment, the blue pool began to pulse and became more luminous than the others.

"Why…"

"Your mother will always make herself available to you from the blue circle. When she goes to the River to dream and to pray for you, she approaches the blue pond in the sky and beseeches of it a new and a true star for your vision." As soon as my grandmother concluded, the brilliance of the blue circle diminished and that of the white circle increased.

"What's…"

"That is the circle from which all the stars are born and to which they return with the glorious news of the earth's healings."

"But…"

"Rely, grandson. Wear your name well. Be prepared to return. Do you see?"

"Not yet."

"Rely lest your arrogance turn Grandmother's five medicines into poisons of misgiving and doubt. Do you see?"

"The circles are dissolving."

"Rely!"

"I see!"

"Quickly! Turn! Follow my voice back to me!"

15

She Who Makes Peace

Back to the gloom of the kitchen and the safety of my chair I followed the unwavering sound of her voice. Hot and soaking with the sweat of purification, I felt the room shake like a great rattle with stones flying and bouncing from ceiling, floor and walls. The din became unbearable until my grandmother prevailed upon room and stones to be still.

"River Whale is your animal of power, grandson," she proclaimed. "It dreams the first dreams. Let it take you where it will." When she'd completed her injunction, the rain ceased and the sun filled all three windows with a fierce luminosity.

"Come," she said. As I rose to my feet, I noticed that our chairs had been placed diagonally in two corners of a dark brown carpet, the ground of five large circles. Four—the red, yellow, blue and green—each adorned a corner; and the white, the perfect center of the square.

"That's not the carpet from your study?" I asked.

"Come," was all she said. I followed her out the back door onto a big slab of stone, slick with rain. "Watch your step," she snapped, not looking back. "I don't want you breaking your neck on my property." She laughed. Stuck between the doorway and the screen door which had sprung back and pinned me against the jamb, I felt my feet giving way.

"What's the matter?" she yelled from a distance.

"The step's slippery."

"A little clumsy, are we?" Unsympathetic, she laughed more of that riotous laughter that nettled and unsettled me. "Just make sure you shut the screen door. You have to lift it a little to get it tight." By the time I closed the door and jumped down from the stone, she'd disappeared. I didn't call after her because I knew she wouldn't stop for me.

While I ran downhill in the wet tracks she'd made through the field, I marveled at how quickly the sky was clearing. Though the runoff from above made the descent treacherous, I pushed ahead at breakneck speed, grabbing at trunks and branches, trying to stay on my feet. With the thinning out of trees, I was able to get a glimpse of the St. Lawrence River. My love for the Stocking wavered in the light of this expanse.

After scanning Montreal's shimmering spires beyond the river's north shore, I let myself down slowly by the seat of my pants in the new mud of a steep embankment.

"What took you so long?" my grandmother asked from the top of a gray chunk of granite fifty feet away. "And, my God, how did you get so dirty?" She looked pert and dry in her dark purple dress. "I thought you got yourself lost," she added, smiling for the first time. I smiled back. "Oh, I let up once in a while. And what you are about to experience gives me good reason to smile. Come along now. See the shadow; it's starting to slide this side of the river. Means we have no time to lose. Come along."

"Wonder what time it is," I said, checking my wrist. "It's gone. My watch. It's gone," I cried out with some alarm.

"No need for a watch," she responded calmly. "We are pressed by another time here." She leaped to the ground from her four-foot perch with an alacrity that defied her years, and disappeared into the brush. Vowing not to lose her this time, I scrambled after, trying in vain to keep in step and managing scarcely a purple glimmer of her through the glut of leaves. She paced me on a clear-cut path among brambles of blackberry to a narrow bridge of logs that breached a deep ravine. "Cross," she commanded as she placed a hand on my shoulder. The sharp contrast between command and gesture unnerved me.

"Won't you go across first, grandmother?" I asked, confident she'd traversed the bridge many times before.

"No, you must cross first, for she is your mother." My heart began to pound violently.

"She's here?"

"Grandson, cross the bridge." I studied the three logs that constituted the short span over the precipice. Lashed together with hemp, they seemed newly shaven and glassy with rain. I knelt in the grass to scour the bridge for gouges where a foot could grab hold.

"Now I know why she called you Doubting Thomas." She laughed a deeply annoying laugh. "Tom, there's only one way you can make it across that bridge. Do you know what I'm talking about?"

"I think so."

"What then?"

"Trust?"

"How so?"

"I must rely completely on River Whale for my seeing-through."

"It's a hard lesson, isn't it? But that's the only way. You must cross with your eyes closed."

"But that's impossible," I protested with a whine that infuriated me.

"Not if you rely on River Whale and allow your mother to help you. Close your eyes and call out to her by her true name, 'She Who Dreams by the River.'" After my eyes had been shut for a while and I'd called my mother's name numerous times, a red doe appeared between me and the bridge.

"Follow me," I heard the animal say in a voice I recognized immediately as my mother's. "Put each of your steps precisely in mine without hesitation." I did as she said, placing each of my steps precisely in one of hers without a moment's hesitation.

"Open your eyes," the harsher voice of my grandmother directed. When I did, I found that I'd made it safely over the precipice. The doe was gone. I watched the old woman glide across the narrow bridge with the grace and agility of a cat. I wondered who she truly was.

When she passed me and disappeared into the rampart of blackberry bushes that deprived me once again of the view of the river, I tried in vain to detect the glimmer of her purple dress. I dove into the blackberry thorns, pressed by the irrational fear of losing her forever. But when she reappeared, she remained well within sight, walking slowly along the bank toward a narrow peninsula that protruded a hundred yards or so into the river, like the acute angle of a badly broken arm.

"Come along, Tom," she called out from fifty feet away. "That's Uncle's Broken Arm," she shouted more loudly than necessary, pointing at the peninsula. I followed her out on the furry green arm to the crook of the elbow where Uncle's forearm took an alarming turn to the east. "Come," was all she said as she led me on an easterly path though sedge grasses and thicknesses of scrub pine and blue spruce. I couldn't see the river but could hear it lapping rhythmically at the peninsula. Why was I, who'd rambled the banks of the Stocking, so skittish about walking a course removed from the power and danger of the river? "Come," she invited as grasses and trees retreated with our advance toward the end of the peninsula and the surround of a gleaming waterway.

There was only one tree left at land's end, a tall white birch, like a gift to Uncle from the abiding magnanimity of River. My grandmother stood small in the tree's shadow. "Come," she said. When I joined her, the birch leaves still dripped rain from the earlier storm and some raindrops bore the gold of the sun's zenith. From each broad sleeve of her dress, she pulled a blanket of the identical material and design that emblazoned her kitchen windows. But these were zigzags of an even brighter green, yellow, beige and red. A bolder fire. She spread one of the blankets on a large, flat stone by the tree trunk; the other, at her feet. She sat on the stone.

"Sit," she said in a near whisper, gesturing me to take my place opposite her. When I sat down, she asked, "Does my ordering you around bother you?"

"No," I answered truthfully.

"It will soon be over," she confided. "But first, we must conclude what River Whale began under Cannery Bridge."

"You know about that?"

"Yes."

"How…"

"No matter," she interrupted. "I have loved you since the day you were born; and so, it was of no small concern to me that you should attempt to end the life I held in my arms only hours after Grandmother set you free." She leaned forward, drawing my eyes into her piercing. "Tom," she intoned solemnly, "when do you think you first saw River Whale?"

"The day I tried to kill myself under the bridge? In the clouds above the railroad track? That's the only time I remember."

"Oh no, grandson. No. In answer to your mother's prayers, he'd been following you long before that." When it finally dawned on me that my grandmother had known all along the depth of my degradation, I felt extremely vulnerable in this most exposed of places.

"Dear grandson," she began in an unexpectedly severe tone, "this is absolutely not the time for self-pity. Tell me what you observe of the River."

"It's too quiet, grandmother. How can it be so quiet?"

"That is when it is at its most powerful. That is when you must come to it...when it will deliver up to you Whale's vision of reconciliation. But you must come to it as does your Uncle."

"What do you mean?"

"Just as he does when he entrusts his vulnerability to the River and its vision of how he may best serve the interests of the People. When you come to the quiet of the River, mindful of your shame but grateful as well for your healing, you will receive its reconciling vision for the good of your People. Be assured of that, dearest grandson." The day's slow demise gradually turned the river from gold to copper. "But you haven't answered my question yet."

"I forget. What was it?"

"The first time you saw River Whale."

"Not the night of Cannery Bridge?"

"No. Much earlier." I tried to recall but could not. "It was a dream...when you were only nine years old." Reconciled to the probability that she knew more about that time than I could remember, I searched my memory for a remnant of the dream.

"I remember one night when I woke up from a dream, crying. I must have been about nine then. Mémère came upstairs to my room and tried to comfort me but I couldn't stop crying. I got so weak from shaking, I couldn't shake anymore. How could I have forgotten that?"

"That's it, Tom," she said with a solemn fervor. "Can you remember what you were crying about?" I looked for the answer in the shimmering copper of the river.

"The locomotive," I cried. "I can see it."

"You are seeing-through to your dream. What else?"

"I'm the engineer and I can see we're running out of track..." I'd begun to hyperventilate and then panic at not being able to catch my breath.

"You're okay, Tom. Trust your vision and it will do you no harm." As soon as I was able to let in my grandmother's reassurance, my eyes were drawn to the shells she wore around her neck.

They were magnified a hundred times their size and lay at the bottom of the River, bellows of a deeper breath and oracles of a childhood memory.

"The engine jumps the track and we fly together into a bottomless black hole. Down. Down. Faster and faster. Then, suddenly...something breaks my fall. Catches me!"

"You know who?"

"River Whale?"

"Of course!" By the power of seeing-through, I watched the great mammal gurgle up through the murk of the bottomless black hole and settle under my listless nine-year-old body with a loud harmless thump.

"Good, grandson. Now listen carefully to what he says. Can you hear him?"

"Yes. He's telling me his name."

"What does he call himself?"

"Blubber Face!" I laughed with the long and sweet hilarity of willow. "I can't believe it. Blubber Face!"

"Now you recall the name?"

"Oh, yes. It made me laugh...I forgot."

"River Whale called himself 'Blubber Face' and made you laugh in the face of Chasm when you were only nine years old. Don't you forget again."

"I won't," I promised.

"By the way, grandson, whatever happened to the locomotive?"

"It disappeared."

"Are you sure?" Swimming in the dapple of tremulous copper and birch leaf, my grandmother scrutinized my face for some sign of recognition.

"It turned into River Whale," I whispered with reverential gratitude. "He was with me all the time." My grandmother smiled one of her rare but radiant smiles.

"Yes, River Whale was with you then. That was the beginning of your seeing-through."

"So, how did I lose it?"

"By the maw of the Great False Face, you entered into and were overcome by your grandfather's shame and began to cultivate your own. But tonight you leave Kayanerenhkunis, having found your way through the eye of humility to bridge-making. And you must not forget, when you leave here, that Kayanerenhkunis is not only a beloved homeland on a great River but first the Woman, She Who Makes Peace."

"Grandmother?"

"Yes, Grandmother of us all. Do not forget, grandson, for it is She who blesses your bridge-making today with the water that brings you River Whale and the arrow of your vision. The Dark Woman, as you recall, named the arrow of your vision 'Straightaway,' 'Ladder,' 'Rod' and 'Backbone of Whale.' These are your familiars. Listen to them always for they speak the language by which River Whale travels to your heart with the medicine of reconciliation." The imperviousness of copper dissolved in the flames that leaped at my grandmother's back through black birch leaves. The River was no less quiet for its dance of fire.

"Grandmother, is the Great False Face and Uprooting one and the same?" I asked, moved by an irrepressible impulse.

"The Power is known by many names." Her tone told me this was her definitive answer and not to push any further. "Our time together is growing short, Thomas. You must be out of Kayanerenhkunis before dark. That is essential. Not only that, but you must drive home to Ingram tonight."

"Why?"

"Tonight."

"But…"

"Tonight." Though my grandmother's voice remained calm, it vibrated with an undercurrent of urgency that had begun upon our leaving her house and intensified considerably since our arrival on Uncle's Broken Arm. "Tonight."

"How can…?"

"You get back in your car and drive. As simple as that. In the first place, dearest grandson, you don't belong here. Even though you were born to us, this is not your world; it holds no prospect for you. Whatever you need of Kayanerenhkunis, you carry with you. Close to your heart as I hold you close to mine." Though the orange-red of the River's fire gleamed behind her, it danced in her eyes. Despair seething in Pépère's pipe, I feared. The pulsation of orange-red embers from the dark memory of a living room not for the living. I trembled.

"No," my grandmother said gently. "This is Kayanerenh-kunis. Remember, as you watch the fire dance on the River of your first and second births, that it is ever the new fire, the same which, by the power of your seeing-through, penetrated the poison of your grandfather's shame and transformed it into the living water of his peace. Learn that Grandmother's gifts are neither frivolous nor short-lived, grandson."

"What about my mother?"

"What about your mother?"

"Where is she?"

"How does that concern you? All you're required to know is that she is well and that she neither needs nor desires to see you at the present time. Let her be. Be assured only that she bears you ever in her heart. When she is ready to see you, she will find you. Have no fear." Though I received these revelations with composure, I wondered with a twinge in my heart why my mother, Lora, hadn't kept me with her in Kayanerenhkunis. "For the same reason," the old woman answered my misgiving in a voice even quieter than that of the River, "that your father threw himself down to his death in the Stocking."

"What are you saying?" I erupted, not at all able or willing to grasp the connection.

"They were both convinced," she explained in a most soothing voice, "that they were utterly alone. There is nothing more I can add to that, Thomas. You must not look back but ahead. What you need to know is that your mother and father loved you and were not without courage, despite what others might think."

When she paused, she'd become indistinguishable from the flux of molten copper. "Your mother," she continued, "displayed a measure of her courage within what is known in these parts as the 'Indian Movement,' but that's surely not for me to tell; she will share that with you when and if she's ready. As for your father, who can imagine the courage it took to fight his private hellish war with your grandfather? You know something of that, don't you? Now you must find your own. Go home to your love and to your life."

As shadow seized Uncle's Broken Arm, my grandmother disappeared altogether. With her dissolved the trunk and panoply of the white birch tree. A song in the gentle language of Potter Place issued like the trill of water over pebbles from the hidden source of all my grandmother's words, her harshest as well as her kindliest. It was the song I'd heard long ago with the heart of a child who could not sleep, lullaby of Mary, the Mother of God, who crooned to the secret longing of a motherless child. I rose from my blanket and walked toward the stone where I last saw my grandmother sitting. With tentative footsteps I probed the ground under me until the stone, seemingly impatient with my timidity, lunged forward and brought me headlong down. The song faded. My grandmother reappeared, standing over me, radiant in the beauty of her youth, her clasped hands extended high above my head.

"Stand," she said, moving backward two or three steps. When I came to my feet, she solemnly opened her hands to reveal a miniature sun as orange-red as the great furnace behind her. No sooner had she released the fiery orb than it flew to my chest as an eagle spirits prey to the voracity of the nest. Fever raged through my body until I was overcome.

When I awoke, she gave me her hand and helped me to my feet. She was my old grandmother again.

"That was communion for your disbelief," she simply said. "Come. We have little time left." She walked swiftly westward back toward the crook in Uncle's Broken Arm but at a pace clearly designed to keep me in tow and safe from twilight's charm. "Shhh." She gestured me with uncharacteristic animation to approach slowly and quietly. When I came abreast of her, she took me by the hand. "Wait," she whispered. From the nearby western shore of the peninsula came a crackle of twig, slashings of sedge and the rattle of cattail. Grandmother squeezed my hand and bade me with forefinger to her lips to be exceptionally still. An invisible crash upon the land. Thud upon thud, upon another. Then, an uncanny silence. A shudder. Strafings of water into grass.

The acuteness of my hearing I attributed to the fiery communion my grandmother had made from River's deepest flame. I could make out even the silences of approach along the bank until at last the red doe appeared. I saw her dark brown eyes first. Letting go of my hand, my grandmother advanced to greet her. No words were spoken between them, only profound acknowledgment. When the doe looked past my grandmother at me, I felt her warm breath tickle my face, and I trembled from head to foot. She then turned and slid down the bank into the river, leaving me with the urgent conviction that I must return immediately to Anna. It was the last I saw of her.

"Where's the bridge?" I called out to my grandmother, who'd already cleared the blackberry bushes and was well on her way to the rocky clearing high above the river.

"What bridge?" she shouted back, not bothering to turn around, and forging ahead toward the pines on the hill.

"What about the ravine?"

"What ravine?" She laughed her delight at a breathtakingly high pitch. By the entrance to the woods, she turned to speak. "Maw creates chasms where there are none," she explained with deliberate enunciation. "Vision finds danger where none is apparent. Remember, grandson." Her lilting laughter echoed across the clearing and along the river bank while she vanished in the wood, leaving me to find my way back to her house.

Certain of the path by which I'd slid downhill into the clea

ing, I turned for one last look at the St. Lawrence River and Uncle's Broken Arm. From the vantage of cliff, I saw the crimson river as the immense cup of Cana delivering to the world the finest wine of celebration. I saw my Pépère hold up to the brilliant outpouring not only his crystal goblet of redemption but his heartfelt congratulations to Lora, my mother, and to his son, David. As I peered one last time into the dusky water by the peninsula, I shuddered, as had the doe, with concern for Anna. I ran through the clearing and uphill through the pines to my grandmother's house.

I found the kitchen pitch dark except for the flickering light of two large candles on either side of the old woman working by the sink.

"Sit," she said. "I'm fixing you some lunch for your trip home. Here, have some coffee," she added, handing me a large earthenware cup from which filaments of steam curled about the flame of the first candle.

"Thank you," I said, careful to take the cup by the handle. Before I sat down, I noticed the carpet of circles. In the candlelight, chunks of dark bread and white cheese, redness of apple and half moon of banana seemed to float into the brown paper bag on the counter. As soon as my grandmother had finished folding the bag shut, she joined me.

"What? You haven't finished your coffee yet? Come. Set the cup down. We have no time for dawdling." No sooner had I placed the cup on the floor behind my chair than she took me by both hands and pulled me up. "Stand," she ordered in a subdued voice. "You're not going to let me do all the work, are you?" She laughed. "Come here and stand in the middle of the white circle." She guided me by the shoulders. "Exactly in the middle." My feet just fit. In fact, it was a perfect fit from heel to toe.

"Is this okay?" I asked.

"Just fine," she answered. "White in the center of the square of four. Red. Yellow. Blue. Green. East. West. North. South." She ·tood back and reached once more with her right hand into the left sleeve of her dark purple dress. With one swift motion, she retrieved a small black leather pouch that she lifted carefully and reverently to the level of my eyes. "Do you see?"

"Yes."

"Do you know what this is?"

"No."

"This is your medicine. The medicine of He Who Waits by a Bridge." The solemnity with which my grandmother spoke my name evoked a sense of awe and responsibility in keeping with the ceremonial revelations on Uncle's Broken Arm. "The black bag is a memento of your encounter with the Great False Face by whose left eye you must be careful always to proceed to vision. Look at the wall. Behind me. At the wall." She seemed annoyed by my uncertainty. "Do you see?"

"It's not here. The mask isn't there anymore."

"That's because it's with you...for your contemplation when you are faced with the need for healing vision. It is the container. What does it contain, grandson?"

"I don't know."

"First, it is Canicula, the brightness of Sirius, the Dog Star, the harbinger of Whale. Then, it is the white stone of Potter Place, eloquent commemoration of the four requisites of vision—Straightaway, Ladder, Rod and Backbone of Whale. Lastly, it is the heart of Stone, your trust, the reliquary of River Whale's ashes from which Grandmother brings forth the light of your vision and the water of Her healing. That is the living injunction you will carry around your neck the remainder of your days."

"Always?"

"Yes. Now bend so I can reach." When I bowed my head, she placed the pouch around my neck by means of a black thong. "That stays where I put it, do you understand?" I nodded. "You never take it off," she added with an exaggerated scowl. In response to my quizzical lift of eyebrow, she smiled jubilantly. "Don't worry, dear. It's made to last."

As soon as I straightened up and the medicine bag settled under my shirt, each of the five circles in the carpet glowed till the kitchen was awash with rainbow and I was lifted momentarily from the floor by a blinding explosion of white light underneath me. "Down to earth, child!" my grandmother cried out in a shrill unearthly voice. Darkness returned, breached only by the flicker of the candles. I stood solidly on the floor. "Hurry," she shouted as she slapped the brown paper bag into my hands and rushed out the kitchen door. I hastened to follow.

We passed the cross in silence—it seemed to soar in the fading crimson of the sunset. I saw Pépère sit tall by the window in the nursing home, upright timber of his Christ's cross to withstand the tempest of his shame. I saw grandfather Jake walk the span of an eagle's wings into the unknown of a cloud. While my grandmother and I hurried through the pine grove, I heard the wind rise, howling through the metal grill of the cross, and subside. We kicked together through wet grasses toward the museum. Though the great Eagle of the totem had flown to night, I felt the piercing of its eye, beak and claw where the medicine bag lay against my chest.

"Your watch is on the seat," she said as I stepped into the car. "Start the car." Taking my left hand in both of hers she said, "You're not ever to come back. Do you hear?"

"Yes."

"No need for long journeys, for pilgrimages anymore. From now on, dance. You can dance anywhere you like; on the banks of Stocking River, in your solitude, in Anna's new car." She smiled. "When you dance, you rouse the River Whale. When you dance you have your Grandmother's ear. When you dance, your People dance with you and pray for your vision. You have no need to dance in the longhouse for River and Whale to come to you. Dance for your People. Dance for peace, grandson. Now go to your love."

She leaned in the car and kissed me on the cheek. With her left hand, she pressed lightly against the medicine bag and once again I felt Eagle strike deeply into my chest. "Goodbye, my dear." When she stepped back, I knew she was waving her last goodbye. I watched her become absorbed by a darkness darker than night. I clung to the hope I'd not left too late.

16

Complicities

Near seven in the morning I walked, unshaven and bleary-eyed, up to the second-floor nurses' station at St. Philomena's. Throughout the night, a growing premonition dictated that I should drive directly to the hospital. Puzzled by my calmness, I looked for Anna.

"Jo," I called out as I recognized her best friend. "Where is she?"

"Tom, am I glad to see you," the petite blonde shouted as she came around the desk.

"What happened? Did anything happen to Anna?"

"Slow down, Tom. Everything's okay now." She grabbed both of my hands in an effort to reassure me.

"Are you sure? What happened?"

"I'll tell you," she said, pulling me aside into a little alcove out of the way. We sat down in front of a bay window through which the pale light of the new day filtered in. "She's out of danger, Tom. She's sleeping now, but was asking for you before she fell asleep."

"Jo, what happened ?"

"She almost lost the baby, Tom."

"Baby?"

"A near miscarriage."

"My God!" A dread, like none I'd experienced during the critical moments of my journey to Kayanerenhkunis, struck my heart like a thousand darts hurled by the Great False Face in the frenzy of a fearsome dance.

"She's all right, Tom. I promise. She's fine. And...so is the child."

"Tell me, Jo. What happened?"

"When she came in around seven last night, we couldn't stop the bleeding. As soon as we got her into the E.R., the lights went out. When they came back on, the doc said the bleeding had stopped. 'A miracle,' was all he said. It was a miracle, Tom. It really was."

"I believe it," I said dispassionately. I only questioned the time when the miracle occurred. I suspected that the healing had taken place when the eyes of the doe met mine by water's edge on Uncle's Broken Arm. "Can I see her, Jo?"

"You can go in and take a peek. Not for very long. She needs her rest. Let me just check to see if they've got everything straightened out." She was rattling edgily on. "Just wait here a sec. I'll be right back."

"Come on," she urged, waving as she rushed by and disappearing around a corner.

I followed her into a room halfway down an interminably long hospital wing. It was a room similar to my grandfather Têtreault's; and like his bed, Anna's was by the window. Still drawn against the early morning sun, the blinds made it impossible for me to make out from the doorway the face I longed to see. What I detected was the stillness of Anna's body as it lay beneath a single sheet. It was clearly not Anna's usual stillness, which always generated excitement and anticipation. The sheet, like the skin of an inflated balloon, seemed an empty promise. Fearing death had not yet relinquished its hold on the life that meant more to me than my own, I felt the airy maw of the Great False Face suck the breath out of me in anticipation of devouring an untried and tender vision.

As I struggled to hold back my tears against that emotionality which the Dark Woman warned would interfere with seeing-through, I reached instinctively for the black bag that hung from my neck. Suddenly I was transported from a nondescript hospital room in a small fishing village to a timeless place unique in all the universe where ordinary trust is transformed by Grandmother into extraordinary power, where poisons provoke healing and death engenders life. I saw myself standing by Jo with a baby in my arms. I saw Anna lean over me while I lay under Cannery Bridge. I heard a strong voice, my own, proclaim, "As love draws vision from the brittle carcass of Dragonfly, so..."

"Look," Jo said, tugging at my arm. "She's moving." I saw the shroud stir and saw-though to the likeness of Father Têtreault rising, luminous, from my Pépère's ashes.

"You go first," I urged Jo, wanting to compose myself before I approached Anna. While Jo made her way around the bed, I noticed nourishment trickle down the tube into Anna's arm and was overwhelmed by the thought of how little stood between a life and its extinction.

"Honey," Jo called. I walked slowly to the foot of Anna's bed. Distressed by the pallor of her complexion, which looked more alabaster than flesh, I watched for some sign of life while Jo held her hand and tried once more to wake her.

"Anna," Jo continued. Slowly Anna's eyes opened. When she turned, I looked for the smile with which I expected her to greet her friend but saw none. "Someone here to see you."

"Tom?" Anna called out at a pitch her voice could not sustain. While she repeated my name in a whisper, I came to her side.

"I'll see you later," Jo said, kissing Anna's forehead and moving back to let me pass. "Not long, Tom," Jo whispered. "She needs her rest." I nodded. She patted my shoulder and left the room.

"Hi, Anna," I said as I leaned over to kiss her cheek.

"Oh, you can do better than that," she said weakly, sliding her hand over for me to take. I kissed her lightly on the lips.

"Better," she quipped, forcing a smile. "How are you?"

"What about you?"

"I can see that you're well," she said, ignoring my question."

"You…"

"We're fine," she smiled more freely, moving her hand over the sheet to her stomach and letting it lie there. Her cheeks flushed momentarily. "We're doing fine."

"You and the baby?"

"Who else?" she replied in as loud a voice as she could muster. "Our baby, yours and mine," she added, holding my eyes fast with the earnestness of hers and squeezing my hand as hard as she could. "I've got something else to tell you, my darling, but it'll have to wait. I'm pretty tired."

"You can tell me later, Anna."

"Tomorrow, Tom. Come back tomorrow morning. We'll be much better then." Her hand moved slightly over her stomach. "You'll see. Now, go home and get some sleep." Before I'd kissed her goodbye, her eyes closed, the hand I held went limp and the stillness returned. But when I left, it was with the reassurance that the stillness that now gripped Anna and our baby was one of healing and renewal.

Having slept through that day and night, I awoke the next morning while it was still dark. Awaiting sunrise, I remembered the sleepless hours I'd spent on the night of the new moon. I recognized the unprecedented clarity of vision I experienced that night as the initial but critical consolidation of the elements of seeing-through. It was the beginning of the fulfillment of the promise made by River Whale to a terrified nine-year-old fifteen years ago.

Before I saw the first brilliant point of red sun tincture

the horizon, I remembered the crimson flare from the inlet on the night of the new moon. I remembered with exquisite clarity how it had transformed first into the seething embers of a meerschaum bowl and then into the constant glow of a votive lamp. Today, before the epiphany of the sun, I contemplated yet another and the last of its transformations: the orange-red conflagration on the River of the Fourth. This is what the red flame on a distant buoy had become. The Dragon Fire.

Fire in the eye of Eagle.

Fire in the eye of Whale.

Rainbow focus.

Fire of obdurate and enduring transformations.

Grandmother's Gift.

"I must not forget the Dragon," I remembered telling myself over and over again after the night of the new moon. "Face him every day...every day of your life," the Dark Woman had said. She'd called Dragon the fearless ancestor of Whale. Dragon Fire was the essence of vision. It was the potentiality in each of us to remember the first light dawning from the original darkness. It embodied the paradox of the dark and the light. It threatened the visionary with life's most pernicious intoxications—the excessive light of arrogance and the excessive darkness of fear. There could be no vision or reconciliation without Dragon; no antidote of forgiveness to be drawn from the heart of shame. To be bridge-maker, I must face Dragon every day till the end of my days. I breathed deeply of the dawn and of Anna's promise that the shining of the new day would find her and our baby well.

"Tom," Anna called as I entered her room. She was sitting at the foot of the bed, facing the door.

"Hi," I answered with the enthusiasm of seeing her up. She remained sitting but extended her arms toward me as I walked across the room. The blinds were raised and she appeared radiant in a white cotton bathrobe. Color had returned to her cheeks. "You look wonderful," I said as I leaned over to kiss her.

"You look pretty good too. Yesterday you were just a blur. I'm so happy to see you." She was crying.

"You look wonderful," I said, struggling to hold my tears back. "These are for you." I showed her a small vase of white daisies.

"Oh, put those down!" She pulled me down by the neck and kissed me. I began to cry convulsively. "It's okay to cry, Tom. It's okay." We held each other until our tears subsided. "You still have those flowers?" She was laughing.

"Yeah."

"You can put them down now...over there on the table." I put the daisies on the night stand by the window. "Sit by me," she directed. I smiled broadly, thinking of how many orders I'd received in the last two days from women whose instructions had not only deepened my perspective on life but actually saved it.

"What are you smiling at?" Anna asked.

"Oh, you just reminded me of someone," I answered, settling down on the bed beside her.

"Were you surprised?"

"About the baby?"

"Yes."

"Disappointed?"

"Oh no, Anna. No." I put my arm around her, pulled her close and kissed her gently on the cheek. Her face was still hot and wet from crying. "No, I'm happy about that."

"I'm glad. So am I."

"But how did you get hurt?"

"Saturday I worked a double shift, three to eleven and eleven to seven. Sunday I slept till about one in the afternoon. After supper, when I was reaching up in the cabinet to put the dishes away, I got so tired I fell to the floor. Then, the bleeding started."

"My God!"

"I yanked the phone down from the counter and made the call. The EMT's got there before I passed out."

"I don't know what I'd ever have done without you, Anna." The tears started again and so did the struggle for control over my emotions. Just when I'd begun to feel, I was faced with the difficult choice between seeing-through and experiencing a full range of human emotion. Unwilling to return to the numbness I'd known before, I was determined to work out the compromises necessary to cultivate and ensure both.

"Remember me saying I had something important to tell you?"

"I remember."

"Jo said the lights in the E.R. went out while I was on the table. For me, they were out long before that."

Anna pulled away a little so she could look into my eyes. When she'd turned sideways toward me, she took my hands in hers. "When it went dark, I felt myself moving, carried along without any effort of my own. I was floating in comfortably warm water. You can't believe how soothing it felt...and I wasn't a bit afraid. I just lay there in the dark, letting myself be pulled along and soothed by the water. Then, a beautiful woman with brownish skin and silver-gray hair appeared to me, walking knee-deep in the water I somehow knew was well over our heads. She guided my paralyzed body with the gentle pressure of her hand under the small of my back. She kept saying to me in the kindest voice I've ever heard, "Anna, don't worry, you'll be home soon. Enjoy the ride."

"My grandmother."

"What?"

"Was she old?"

"It was hard to tell. She looked somehow old but then again, she appeared young, strong and very agile."

"That was my grandmother, Anna. She was the one who was helping you. It had to be her." With the sun warm on our backs and a subtle breeze teasing at us from the open window, Anna and I sat holding hands in that place where thresholds of promise appear as suns set, where planets arise with the extinction of stars, and where frail life takes hold against incalculable odds.

"What was she wearing?" I asked.

"A long, dark purple dress with wide, sweeping sleeves."

"Anything else?"

"Oh yes. A beautiful necklace made of seashells."

"Can you describe it?"

"There were four strands, each of a strikingly different color—white, pink, lavender and black. I couldn't take my eyes off them."

"Anna, that was my mother's foster mother helping you. I'm sure of it."

"How?"

"I don't know, but that was her. That's how she was dressed that afternoon. Sunday. There's so much I can't explain, so much I don't understand myself. All I know is somehow she got to you when you needed her. Tell me the rest." When we'd shared the first pieces of the puzzle, a great calm passed through Anna's hands into my body as though her experience was freeing me up from the need to know how the pieces fit. The pressing need to understand, I realized only too keenly, was mine. Somehow complicit in my overall and continuing education, Anna seemed, as had my grandmother, to be playing the game and helping me see without forcing the mystery.

"She guided me to shore, lifted me out of the water and carried me in her arms to this big birch tree where she carefully positioned my back against the trunk. 'Stay here,' she told me. 'Don't you dare move a single muscle away from this tree.' Then, she gave me one of the most beautiful smiles I'd ever seen."

"Oh, she saves those for special occasions," I said, laughing.

"What?"

"You've got to know my grandmother."

"I do."

"Not Mémère Têtreault," I countered, still playing the game in earnest.

"I know." And Anna laughed.

"What happened then?" I squeezed her hand slightly in deference to her experience and participation in a mystery that still eluded me, and perhaps always would.

"While I kept as still as I could, with my back pressed up against the tree, these red-orange flames burst out of nowhere…I felt an unbearable heat wash again and again up into my groin until I passed out. When I came to, the air was so crisp and clean. The raindrops dripping from the big birch tree were bright with the color of amethyst. I felt no pain or fatigue and knew that the baby and I would be well."

"I was there, Anna," I blurted out, unable to contain my excitement. "I was there when it happened. We were on Uncle's Broken Arm…together."

"Where?"

"That's the name of a tiny peninsula that sticks out into the St. Lawrence River. My grandmother and I were sitting under that same birch tree when suddenly her face darkened so that I could hardly see her anymore. That must have been when she went out after you. I didn't see you when she brought you back," I said wistfully. "I wonder why she didn't let us see each other. She just kept telling me I had to go home as soon as possible. That's all she'd say." Anna's blue eyes shone with the sapphire of a deeper recognition.

"She was praying, Tom."

"She probably had her hands full, praying for the three of us."

"Then, it became very, very quiet…so quiet I could hear the raindrops roll off the leaves and hit the ground in little explosions. Not long after that…she came."

"Who?"

"The doe. I could hear her coming out of the river, splashing around...shaking the water off as she came ashore. When she saw me, she didn't run away...just stood still for a minute, then started walking toward me...stood as close to me as you are now and stared into my eyes for the longest time."

"My mother. I saw her too," I said so softly I didn't think Anna heard me.

"I know." I was left again feeling that she'd been made aware of things that I could not learn on my own but must be taught by the women who loved me. There was a conspiracy afoot, I thought, to teach me lessons of bridge-making that do not come naturally to men.

"Thanks, Anna," I said. She didn't ask why, knowing precisely what I meant.

"She talked to me, you know."

"I'm not surprised, but how?"

"Not with words or sounds. Just with her eyes."

"What did she say?"

"She told me the baby and I would be okay, that we were going to have a little girl, that her hair would be fire-red, that you would be a good father...and a couple of other things you really don't need to know right now."

"A little girl? She told you that?"

"Yes."

"Amazing!"

"It is, isn't it?" Anna, svelte in her white robe and the sheen of the new sun, was returning quickly to her animal nature, more cat than deer, more like my Mohawk grandmother than anyone else I knew.

"You believe it all, don't you?" I asked.

"Don't you?"

"I know I should but..." Anna took my face between her hands and held it up to scrutiny with a strength from which, with my greatest effort, I couldn't break free.

"You will," she said, then kissed me with the ardor of her love for me from which I knew my frail trust would take its proper nourishment. She didn't laugh when I thought she would.

"No laughing matter," she said without a hint of a smile.

"You know what happened to me, don't you?"

"Not all of it, my darling. You'll have to fill me in…but not today. I'm getting tired. You go home. We need our rest," she said.

"See you this afternoon," I said as I got to my feet.

"No, you won't," Anna objected firmly. "I'm going to walk some more this afternoon and then I'm going to rest. You're taking me home tomorrow and I want to be ready. First thing in the morning, okay?"

"Sure."

"First thing. And if you think you saw some improvement in me today, just wait till tomorrow. By the way," she said, holding me back by my belt buckle, "Did you talk to Mémère yet?"

"Yes, yesterday before I went to bed. She was worried about you. I'll talk to you about it when I see you tomorrow. Get your rest now."

"I love you," she called out before I went out the door. "Thanks for my beautiful white daisies."

The next morning I was in Anna's hospital room at nine o'clock, the time she'd appointed. When I knocked at the door, I startled Anna and Jo sitting on the edge of the bed, looking through the window at the rain.

"Oh, we lost track of time," Anna said, turning toward me.

"I know how that can happen," I answered, recalling how my perception of time had been manipulated by forces beyond my control during my pilgrimage to Kayanerenhkunis.

"But you're right on time. It's nine on the button," she enthused as she jumped up from the bed.

"You look great," I said, remarking how the blush was back on her cheeks and how fit she looked in her jeans and rose organdy blouse.

"I told you I'd be ready to go. I feel fine."

"That was nice," Jo said as she stood up, "just sitting together and watching the rain."

"When we were kids," Anna said, addressing me, "we loved sitting in the window when it rained."

"Or playing outside," Jo added, "stomping through every puddle we could find. You'll call me tomorrow?"

"Of course. Here," she said, handing her the daisies and giving her a gentle pinch on the cheek. "Would you take these down to the car for me?"

Jo stood in the rain, watching us drive off.

"She tried not to let it show, but she was really worried about you," I said.

"I know."

Anna's small red Toyota became a cocoon against the driving rain. A place where the three of us could be contained by the mystery of Grandmother's turning the poison of our frailties into the medicine of healing one another. A place with a view through the dark day to a bright field of cornflowers and goldenrod. We spent most of the day in bed, holding each other and listening to the rain. Our conversation turned inevitably to my foster grandmother. Though Anna listened intently, I wondered how much she already knew.

"Let's have a look," she said. "She gave you that, didn't she?" Leaning over on her elbow, Anna tugged at the black leather thong around my neck till the bag emerged from under my tee shirt. "You know what that is?" she asked, taking the pouch into her hand.

"Yes. It's the medicine my grandmother gave me before I left Kayanerenhkunis. She said it would bring me the power of the River Whale of my People whenever I needed it."

"For Reconciliation. No?"

"Yes," I answered, not troubled by the depths reflected in her eyes.

"I trust her," Anna said softly, slipping the bag under my shirt and lying back on the bed. She kept her eyes closed while she held my hand at her side. "I had a dream last night, Tom."

"What about?" I asked, suddenly reminded that my mother's name was She Who Dreams by a River.

"It was about you and your grandmother. How she came to you on the back of a great black whale, silver-haired, youngish in appearance and as beautiful as she was, guiding me through the water to the white birch tree on the peninsula. She rode the whale onto a stretch of beach along the Stocking River just below your Mémère's house. You were sitting on a big rock overhanging the water, untangling your fish line. All of a sudden, I heard a roar and then a hard whistle across the beach. It seemed as though everything was happening so fast. You fell from the rock and the whale pinned you up against it with his nose."

"His nose?"

"Why not?" She laughed. "Your grandmother hopped off the whale and watched you struggle to get loose. 'Having fun?' she asked you, laughing all the while almost as hard as you were struggling."

"Where were you, Anna?"

"I'm not sure but it felt like I was perched high up in the birch tree nearby where I could see and hear everything. 'Hi,' you said to her. "'Most eloquent,' she said. 'But that's all right. You're still learning…and learning fast, I might add,' she said, turning around for a moment to look up at me. 'You do see the rightness of living in your world?' she asked you.

"'Yes,' you said.

"'With your beloved and with your little baby girl?'

"'Yes,' you said.

"'I brought you a friend,' she said, patting the whale, 'just so you'll know him when he comes to you. Show me your medicine bag.' You pulled it from under your shirt and showed it to her. 'Good,' she said, 'you see it's the same color as River Whale's skin. You see that?'

"'Yes,' you said.

"'Okay, you can put it back under your shirt but don't you ever take it off. You hear?'

"'I won't,' you answered. Your grandmother offered you her hand.

"'Take it,' she said. As soon as you did, the whale wiggled backward and set you free. Then, she placed your hand on the whale while she talked to you. 'Just as River Whale brought you the power to release your grandfather to the fields of his youth and to the shallows of his beloved river, so will he bring you the power to release the heart of your Mémère to the peace that has eluded her these many years and that she so richly deserves. Go soon to your Mémère Têtreault. You need her as much as she needs you.'

"The whale began to quiver. Your grandmother leaped on its back like a cat. 'Dance the River Whale,' she said with such emotion I wanted to cry. 'Remember, my grandson,' she continued, 'that to dance the Whale is to let it dance you, to let it enamor you of its vast memory of and its deep love for the People. Remember.' The whale shimmied back over the sand into the water. When they were well out into the river, your grandmother shouted to you, 'To dance the River Whale is to bridge the chasms of the heart, to bridge one human being to another, one generation to the next, the whole People to its eternal origins. Believe me when I tell you your father has done that; remember him for it. Go to your Mémère soon. Goodbye, grandson.' She waved. The whale swung around and sounded. They were gone. You stood for the longest time, watching the river for them to reappear. That's how the dream ended."

The silence of the contemplative cocoon lasted until the eloquence of my grandmother's message became intolerable to me. It was a message I would need to assimilate over time and by bits and pieces.

"Do you want to see Mémère by yourself?" Anna asked as she ran her fingers slowly through my hair.

"I'd like you to come with me."

"You know I will. I'm getting stronger by the minute. Sunday okay?"

"Sure. I'll call her every day in the meantime to talk to her and let her know how you're doing. She loves you, you know."

"I love her too." As we cuddled in our cocoon made comforting by the steady beat of rain on the roof, I savored the rightness of being here with Anna and our baby girl of the fire-red hair.

17

Totem's Circle Dance

Waiting with Anna on Mémère's front porch, I couldn't keep my feet in place. The aroma of the red and white roses in the front yard, made unusually pungent by the strong breezes blowing from Stocking River, made me nauseous. Overcome by the absurd notion that the Great False Face had sucked me into the vortex of the roses' decay, I was suddenly confronted by the enormous changes undergone not only by me but by Anna and my entire family since we last stood here.

"Why don't you ring the bell?" Anna prodded. I pushed the button.

"Mon Thomas," my grandmother Têtreault shouted from the kitchen the instant the bell sounded. "Mon Thomas, Anna." She ran to the door with dish towel in hand, flicked the hook up and pushed the screen door open. "Entrez, mes chers, entrez tous les deux. Comme je suis heureuse de vous voir. It's so good to see you." With the excitement of seeing us, she'd lapsed into her native French but caught herself quickly. "My dear," she said as she took Anna by the hand, "I heard how sick you were. My, my," she added, wrinkling her brow and shaking her head. "How are you feeling now?"

"I'm fine, Mémère, just fine."

"And the baby?"

"Just fine too."

"I'm so happy everything turned out okay. Ma pauvre petite." She gestured for Anna to bow down so she could give her a kiss. "I'm going to be a great-grandmother?" she asked, looking up at me.

"Yes, Mémère," I said as I walked toward her. "What do you think about that?"

"C'est merveilleux! It's wonderful," she corrected herself. As I bent down to kiss my little Mémère, almost picking her up from the floor with the joy of seeing her, I couldn't help wonder how Pépère would have reacted to the news, had he still been alive. Given the changes I knew he too had undergone, I hoped he would be happy for us. Alerted to the screen door being ajar, my grandmother rushed past Anna and me, swinging her dish towel at the invisible fly that might venture in.

"How I hate the flies, Anna," she muttered good-naturedly while securing the door. "Come now," she said as she ushered us into the kitchen. "We don't want the dinner to get cold."

We all knew where to sit; Anna at the left of the table, in my old place by the window; I, in my grandfather's by his window, across from Anna; and Mémère, in her usual place, facing north and the river. With Mémère's informal invitation for us to be seated, a new ritual was begun, a conviviality never before shared at this table. My eyes returned again and again to the wall space between the two windows and their lace curtains embroidered with pink and red roses, because it resembled in location and orientation that from which the mask of the Great False Face hung in my foster grandmother's kitchen.

I was struck by the realization that transformations of a deep and essential kind had been effected not only in my perception of things, but also in the structure of the reality of my childhood home since I'd been away. Not the least of these transformations was the confidence I saw manifest itself in the ease of my grandmother's bearing and the forthrightness of her interaction with Anna and me. She'd always been quick and sure-handed, but a novel fluidity replaced that subtle hitch in her movements that reflected her fear of doing or saying something unacceptable to my grandfather. I understood that the unrest that dogged today's visit demonstrated my insidious involvement in the old structure, and my deep-seated doubt regarding its capacity to change.

It was almost one o'clock when we finished eating and talking about my journey to Kayanerenhkunis. Though my grandmother was disappointed that I'd not found my mother, she was pleased that I'd seen, even for a brief time, my place of birth and to know that her David had been happy there. I said nothing of danger, of strange manifestations or extraordinary events. Nothing about colloquies with a Dark Woman. My grandfather wasn't mentioned once during dinner. I feared I'd be the one to introduce the difficult topic of his death.

"Thomas, ton Pépère est mort paisiblement dans mes bras," my grandmother said out of the blue with a quiet confident voice. She placed her hand gently on Anna's arm and translated for her. "Thomas's grandfather died so peacefully in my arms." Anna and I received the news in a silence like none I'd ever known in this house. It was the silence of Cocoon where thoughts of stars are warmed by the light of children's eyes as they watch them dance the skies. I thought about our daughter of the fire-red hair and about the stars that would pierce her skies and fill her dreams. I saw-through to the crown of stars that shone like white diamonds around my tiny Mémère's head.

"Mémère," I ventured with the confidence she inspired, "when did Pépère die? Exactly? What time was it?"

"He died shortly after midnight a week ago today. August fifteen. La fête de l'Assomption de Marie." Tears, brimming her eyes, sparkled with the radiance of the diamonds that encircled her head. Did she know that my grandfather had died during my ordeal in the clearing precisely when I seized the brilliant emblem of forgiveness to bridge the chasm of his shame? I wasn't surprised. What I hadn't known and my grandmother confirmed for me was the exact time of my grandfather's death. I began to cry too at the news that my Pépère died in peace a week ago today in the early morning hours of Sunday, August fifteenth, the day Anna and our baby daughter were saved by the healing power of the River of the Fourth.

"I'm glad, Mémère. I'm very glad to hear that."

"I know how difficult it must have been for you to forgive him. He could be such a hard and stubborn man. But I think you would have been pleased to see his poor body relax and his face smile just a little when he looked at your Papa's picture. He was holding it in his hand. Il était radieux, mon cher. He died like that. You would have been pleased."

"Mémère, do you know what I'm thinking about right now? The time he pulled me out of the river. Do you remember that day?"

"Mais oui. Of course."

"I could've drowned. But he wouldn't let me go. He kept talking to me and trying to get me to reach out to him from the rock...till I finally did. He saved my life."

"He loved you, mon Thomas."

"I know he loved my father too."

"Yes." In a sudden surge of wind, the diaphanous white curtains billowed the radiance of the sun and tossed pink and red flowers madly about. But there was no radiance to compare with the crown of stars my Mémère was wearing. It was a crown that trembled in and out of my vision for reasons I was sure only my foster grandmother or the Dark Woman could explain. Or was it that my Mémère had always been so uncomfortable wearing any kind of glory that even the stars themselves were troubled by the embarrassment they might cause her? I smiled at my grandmother and kissed her on the forehead.

"Mémère, did Pépère ever study to be a priest?"

"Yes, Thomas, but how did you know that?" She narrowed her eyes and leveled them at mine.

"It doesn't matter," I answered.

"Oh yes, it matters. How did you find out? Did anyone in the family tell you?" She was searching my eyes for the answer.

"No. No one in the family."

"Who then?" She was relentless, and her uncharacteristic determination made the stars in her crown brighter.

"It just came to me while I was away...like a dream."

"Bon," she said. She was visibly relieved. "That means only your Pépère could have told you."

"In the dream?"

"Yes. Before he left us, he told me that he wanted to tell you, because he believed that his silence, his refusal to tell David, had led to his death. Only minutes before your Pépère died, he prayed to your Papa to help him find a way to let you know." Immediately I remembered the two great snakes with their coils of silver, heads of gold and eyes of blue sapphire. They'd told the truth.

"He was dismissed by his superiors the day before his ordination." He was to be ordained at ten o'clock the next morning. At eight o'clock the night before, he was called into his spiritual director's room and told he would not be ordained."

"Why?" I asked.

"He was told that the council of priests at the seminary was not required to give him an explanation...but his director told him anyway. They said he was not teachable, that, having too much a mind of his own, he would have trouble obeying his superiors."

"That's it?"

"Oui, Thomas."

"Where was this place anyway?"

"Not very far from Montreal." I recalled how, from the cliff above Uncle's Broken Arm, I'd watched the sun set jubilantly over the St. Lawrence River's north shore. But now I saw that sky, a dark cup prepared to receive the blood red wafer of sun as it hovered whole over the spangled city of Montreal. I wondered whereabouts on that sprawling shore my Pépère Têtreault had received his devastating rejection. What an unholy communion of his own bitter blood had he been made to swallow that night long ago when the sun set over the St. Lawrence and his agony of shame. "L'amertume" was what the two great Snakes insinuated my grandfather had drunk that night. Bitterness became the poison that eventually consumed him. During the years, my grandmother had stood helplessly by while the rankling shame turned to despair.

"Mémère, did Pépère have a brother?" I asked, avoiding my grandmother's eyes.

"Non, mon cher. Two sisters. Both gone now."

"Are you sure?" I persisted, finally looking at her. Resisting the thought that Father Têtreault at the shrine in Enfield had only been a figment of my imagination, I pursued the notion that he was somehow related to my grandfather. "No mention ever of a cousin, some relative who was a priest?"

"Non, Thomas. Why do you ask?"

"Nothing important, Mémère. I just wondered." I wanted to believe Father Têtreault was my grandfather's flesh-and-blood twin. Perhaps he knew more about my grandfather's dismissal and could shed some light on what I thought a cruel implausibility. Perhaps I could find the old priest again and he would tell me what really happened. Even after all that had transpired during my pilgrimage to Kayanerenhkunis, I didn't want to concede that he too was simply a part of the conspiracy Grandmother had contrived to bring me back not only to my senses, but to the deeper call of my destiny. I found myself wanting explanations.

"Mon pauvre," my grandmother began with a deliberateness which bespoke her new self-possession, "there are things in this world we are not meant to understand." The pink and red roses of the window curtains, bouncing on gusts from the river, shook themselves loose from their diaphanous ground to dance circles around our heads. While I became flustered by the dizzying twirl of the roses, my grandmother and Anna remained composed. I thought I heard a wispy voice declare: *Such a slow learner...*

"Why didn't he just tell them all where to go and use what education they gave him to make a good life for himself?" Remembering the long days Pépère put in as a custodian at the courthouse, I felt resentment boil up in me and the compelling need to fight the battle that, whether by necessity or choice, he had not fought.

"Thomas," Mémère said, "I know it must be very hard for you to understand how he felt. It was so different then. The priesthood was everything. To have a priest in the family was the most wonderful thing that could happen."

"Sorry, Mémère. I can't see it. To let himself go like he did?"

"Did you know that your Pépère's father died when Omer was just a little boy?"

"No."

"His Maman had to bring her three children up by herself, working on her uncle's farm, cleaning house for other families...no time at all for herself."

"You never told me any of this." I was feeling more confused than resentful.

"There is so much we didn't tell you because your Pépère was afraid you would find everything out. He wouldn't have been able to take that."

"So what? That wouldn't have made any difference to me."

"But it would have made all the difference in the world to him. I think he believed he owed it to his mother to become a priest. Like most French Canadians, she felt, I'm pretty sure, that to have her son become a priest was a sign from God that she was doing a good job of bringing up her children."

"Did she push him to be a priest?"

"I don't know. Your Pépère never..." Before my grand-mother could complete her sentence, intense heat washed down on us from the wall space between the windows. When I looked up, I saw the red mask of the Great False Face slowly materialize with its blood-red face, saffron yellow eyes, black spaghetti hair and circle maw of the deepest purple hue. From the pupil of each eye an incandescent point of light burst forth, first the one, then the other, growing inordinately in length, circumference and lumi-nosity until the two great Snakes of the New Hampshire clearing loomed up, glowering and lunging at each other like maniacal Jack-in-the-Boxes. The exercise seemed to go on forever until the antagonists, overcome by futility, leaned against one another from sheer exhaustion and for mutual support. Slowly intertwining, they slithered as one down along the crook of the grotesque nose and retreated into the purple maw.

"Your Pépère thought he was a failure, Thomas. I know he believed it with all his heart. The shame was like a poison in his heart. It killed him. He didn't mean to, but he killed David with the poison too."

"What do you mean, Mémère?"

"He tried to make your Papa become a priest. He wanted his son to succeed where he had failed." My grandmother's stead-fast gaze was trying to penetrate to my heart with the truth as honestly and passionately as she'd come to know it.

"What?" I asked, thinking I'd heard wrong.

"He tried to force him to study for the priesthood. He knew it was wrong, but he couldn't help himself. He thought if David became a priest, it would make up for his own failings. Your father told him he would have none of it, that he wanted to decide for himself what he would do with his life. They fought, then they stopped talking to each other. That's when your Pépère's long silences and terrible headaches began." I looked over at Anna and was relieved to see her face calm and full of color, despite the revelations that must have affected her as much as they did me. She answered my concern with a smile.

"Finally," my grandmother resumed, "the poison would take his only son from him. L'amertume," she whispered, shaking her head. She paused as she was finding it almost impossible to get her words out. Her eyes glistened again. "He would not hear of your Papa marrying your mother."

"Because she was an Indian?" I asked in a strong voice. That was one of the objections my grandfather had raised in opposition to my mother.

"Oh non, mon cher. Only because she was a woman. He would say anything if he thought it would change your Papa's mind. He was too stubborn and blind to see that all his name-calling just made things worse. But he wasn't prejudiced. No. He hated only himself. Do you know what I think, Thomas?"

"What, Mémère?"

"I believe your Pépère was asked to leave the seminary because the priests mistook his curiosity for stubbornness. You know how he was always studying things to see how they worked...to fix them when they were broken. That is why they liked him so much at the court. He was always trying to get to the bottom of things, sometimes going too deep to suit me. Maybe he was too curious for his own good...but he only got stubborn later. I believe with all my heart that the only person he ever hated was himself...Omer Têtreault. I am sure of that." Mémère's tears ran freely down her face. I rose from the table and walked over to the kitchen sink.

"Anyone for a glass of water?" I called out into Pépère's vegetable garden.

"Non, pas moi," Mémère answered.

"Me either," Anna said.

"When your Papa came to show his new wife and baby

boy, your grandfather was no longer here." I had my back turned
to my grandmother but I could feel her staring through me. Her
words struck forcefully between my shoulder blades to my heart
with an uncanny precision. "He was already dead. I make no
excuses for him. I make no excuses for me. We both did wrong.
But I know in my heart that your Pépère, the man I knew when
we were married, died from his own poison a long time ago. He
came back to us for a while when you were a boy because he
loved you so. But he never stopped blaming himself for your
father's death and finally it got the best of him. He told me over
and over that he deserved his cancer. He wished on himself the
worst possible death for what he did to your Papa, your Maman
and you. He told me so again last Saturday...the day before he
died." I remembered the broken man as I'd last seen him in the
nursing home, clinging to life by a thread.

"But he died in peace, Mémère," I said, observing how
green and full Pépère's garden was and how tenderly my grandmother had looked after it. As the wind from the river continued
by turn to flap and fill the curtains, it bore the smell of ripening
tomato into the kitchen. I recalled how sometimes in the early
evening my tall and handsome Pépère, of those days when we
were fishing buddies on Stocking River, used to pluck two of the
biggest and reddest tomatoes from the vine for us to eat right in
the garden. The tang of tomato followed me back to the table
where I stood for a moment over my tiny grandmother.

"Mémère, did you ever see my mother after Papa died?" I
asked much more loudly than I meant to.

"No," she replied, staring at the wall where the Great False
Face had made his startling appearance. "I thought maybe I saw
her at the funeral in the back of the church. I'm not sure. I don't
know..."

When I sat back down in Pépère's chair, my tears flowed
not solely from the communion of bitterness my grandmother and
I had shared, but from the heartfelt conviction that my grandfather

and mother had joined us at the table; he, simply with his offer of remorse and she, as simply with her forgiveness. Staring through Pépère's window at the towering oak from which he tried to hang himself, emblem of what the Great Snakes called our family's "amertume," I saw it as the prism from which the Rainbow Bridge would flow, and forever unite the doe splashing orange-red fire in the River of the Fourth with the man rising from his sleep to sow diamonds from dreams on the darkest pools of the Stocking's dawn. Never again would that tree cast a shadow of shame.

The willow. It filled the horizon when Anna and I stood atop the first of the two hills in St. Anne's Cemetery. As we gained the top of the second hill, the demarcation of the stone wall came into view. The mystery of the river, I felt as never before, lived just beyond that.

"It's so beautiful up here," Anna said as we walked through the yellow leaves under the willow.

"There are a lot more dead leaves since the last time I was here," I said. "How come so many?"

"Fall's just around the corner? Maybe because it's dry up here. I don't know." She knelt on the ground and picked up a handful of the slender leaves. As she stood up, she let them slide through her fingers and flutter back to their anonymity among the rest.

"Maybe it's dying," I said.

"It's not," she reassured me as we walked toward my father's and grandfather's gravestones. I followed and stood slightly behind her as she read aloud my father's epitaph: "'David Têtreault, son of Omer and Véra, father of Thomas; born 9-6-1928; deceased 4-12-1952.'" I shuffled through the leaves to my grandfather's stone where I traced his newly inscribed name with my finger. "Omer Têtreault," his epitaph read, "Epoux de Véra Pomerleau, père de David, grandpère de Thomas, né 6-25-1898, décédé 8-15-1976."

"I didn't think they'd have his stone engraved yet," I said turning to Anna.

"Your Mémère saw to everything, didn't she?"

"I should've been here with her."

"No, you shouldn't have...and she knew that better than anyone." Anna took my hand and led me to the stone wall. We stood silently, looking down through the trees at Stocking River shimmering in the late afternoon sun. When we turned around to sit on the wall, I was struck by the perfection of the gold circle of leaves under the willow.

"As bright as the river, isn't it?" Anna offered, reading my thought.

"Anna, did you see anything out of the ordinary when we were at Mémère's?"

"You mean on the wall?" she responded without hesitation.

"What did you see?"

"The mask."

"What else?"

"Want me to tell you everything?"

"Everything."

"Well, I saw this long, bright green tongue hanging from its huge purple mouth..."

"The Snakes," I interrupted excitedly.

"It just hung there for the longest time. Then, it curled itself up and floated down to the ground like that." Anna pointed to a flotilla of yellowish-green willow leaves gliding earthward after a sudden gust had shaken them loose. "It took root and started to grow into a bright green stalk...taller and taller until it reached the level of the mask's eyes. Then, it began to shed its husk, peeling back one giant leaf after another...like a flower...opening slowly. I couldn't believe my eyes. It was the most unbelievably beautiful totem pole you ever saw."

"I didn't see anything like that."

"Although I knew the animals were made of wood, they seemed so real...like they were alive."

"Anna, do you know if Mémère saw it too?"

"Yes."

"Everything you saw?"

"She did."

"I'm glad." Anna smiled.

"First," she went on, "there was an enormous turtle at the bottom, then a bear, a wolf, a whale and finally, at the top, an eagle. Then, it disappeared. No totem pole. No mask. Nothing."

"That's it?"

"Then, they came."

"Who?" I felt the rays of the late afternoon sun bury themselves in the hollow of my back and marveled again at the perfection of the golden circle under the willow that encompassed the two gravestones and raised them up in its splendor to the promise of resurrection.

"First, it was the two men coming from one end of a golden field; then the woman and child, from the other end."

"My grandmother?"

"Yes," Anna affirmed from a knowledge I dared not question. "The woman who walked beside me in the water and carried me to the birch tree where I was healed and our daughter was saved."

"The child?"

"I saw our little girl let go of the woman's hand and run through the field, her hair blowing like the flames of a red sun. She was calling out at the top of her voice, 'Grandpa, Pépère! Pépère, Grandpa!' As soon as she reached them, she grabbed their hands and said, 'Come with me, my Grandpa and my Pépère. Let's go to the dance.' Holding each tightly by the hand, she led them, running downhill, to the dance."

"What dance?" I asked, puzzled. Before Anna could respond, the willow tree began its answer by transforming itself successively into white birch, oak, and finally into the totem pole that Anna had seen in Mémère's kitchen.

This is the dance, a familiar voice intoned.

"It's you," I shouted, overjoyed. There was no mistaking the voice. It was my godmother's. The Dark Woman.

"Do you hear that, Anna?"

"No," Anna answered absent-mindedly, completely taken by the numinous beauty of the totem pole.

"It's you. I thought you said I'd never hear from you again."

Never as on your pilgrimage of initiation. Only rarely. But I come now to show you the dance. Do you recognize the totem pole?

"Yes. It's from the museum in Kayanerenhkunis."

It is the Whale Way, godson. River Whale, who mediates between you and the People, knows this way well. When you need to go to the source, call him by dancing the Totem's Circle Dance.

"What's happening?" Anna shouted as the earth began to move mightily from its center. Turtle, Wolf and Bear quaked. Quivering with Grandmother's will to life, Whale leaped left with the stealth of willow as Eagle soared right with the litheness of birch to draw a great circle in the middle of the fallen leaves. At first, the whole gave the appearance of the climactic moment of the Mass when the body of Jesus, as wafer of bread, is held above the cup of his blood, the sign of his rising. Then, the wafer, full of the dynamic strength of ancient oak, began slowly to tip, as though it were on a hydraulic hinge, till it came to rest on the holy ground within the circle of leaves.

It was the circle skin of a drum. It was an imperishable floor for dancing.

"Look," I called to Anna. "They're coming!" They'd reached the top of the first cemetery hill.

"Oh!" Anna cried. We rose to our feet and walked a few steps toward the willow. "She's wonderful!" The little girl was running up the hill first, her orange-red hair streaming, her grandfather and great-grandfather in tow. The People, having come from across the continents and the ages, followed—young, old, all of a mind for celebration. When the last of the People had gathered in the circle, they made a place in portentous silence for the little girl and her two escorts at the center. Then, the earth shook mightily as the People beat the sacred drum to the rhythm of a child teaching her Grandpa and Pépère how to dance.

DESPERATE CHOICES

Panic-stricken, out of breath,
He cried out in the night.
What can I do, who can I trust,
To understand my plight?

Faced with my weakness,
Confronted with my shame,
There's no sense in excuses,
There's no one else to blame!
I've lost my faith in myself;
I've given away my youth.
Is it too late to change?
I need to know the truth!

Desperate choices filled the dark,
Doubt haunted the alley way,
Demons of fear stood ready
To count this soul as their prey.

A bottle went crashing, against the
    brick wall,
A light dispelled the gloom,
Amidst the smell of alcohol,
One human being—defiantly
    refused his tomb.

Ancient ancestors stood at his side,
Although he could not see,
Their silent forms pointed the way,
Great Mystery heard his plea.

Gentle arms reached out to him,
Allowing wracking sobs to subside.
Words of comfort opened his heart,
Healing the hopeless image inside.

That night passed, many years ago,
And his will to live remains.
That man stands tall, for all to see,
With his warrior spirit reclaimed.

                    —*Jamie Sams*

ABOUT THE AUTHOR

Ron Mercier lives in the Berkshires of Western Massachusetts. In *Dance the River Whale*, he draws inspiration from his French Canadian heritage, New England background, and the Native American spirituality of the northeast region. Born and raised in Worcester, he pursued his liberal arts education and training for religious life at houses of study in Maine, New Hampshire and Massachusetts. Ordained to the Catholic priesthood, he later married, helped raise three sons, taught high school and college English, and practised psychotherapy, primarily as a geriatric specialist.

His interest in the fundamental symbols that serve to bring divergent cultures and spiritualities together for mutual understanding and community building continues to drive his exploration and inspire his writing.

ORDER FORM

CALL TOLL FREE 1 (877) 499.2255 & ORDER NOW!

Company name: _____

Name:_____

Address: _____

Apt No: _____

City: _____

State: _____ Zip: _____

Telephone: (_____) _____

Please send _____ copies of *Dance the River Whale*

    @ \$13.95 each (\$16.95 Canada)   \$ _____

Sales tax: Add 5% for books shipped to

    Massachusetts addresses   \$ _____

Shipping & handling: \$3.50 for first book

and \$1.50 for each additional book   \$ _____

          TOTAL   \$ _____

Payment by: ❏ Check (to Deerbridge Books)   ❏ VISA

       ❏ MasterCard   ❏ AMEX

Card number: _____

Name on card: _____

Expiration date: _____ /_____

Fax orders: (413) 442.5025

Telephone orders: **Toll free 1 (877) 499.2255**

          (have your credit card number ready)

On-line orders: Orders@DeerbridgeBooks.com

Postal orders: Deerbridge Books, P.O. Box 2266,

          Pittsfield, MA 01202